Barnaby Walter was born and raised in Essex. After spending his childhood and teenage years reading compulsively, he worked in bookshops then went to the University of Southampton to study Film and English followed by an MA in Film & Cultural Management. He is an alumnus of the Faber Academy and formerly worked in social media coordination for Waterstones in London.

x.com/barnabywalter
facebook.com/BPWalterAuthor
instagram.com/bpwalterauthor

B P Walter Thrillers

A Version of the Truth

Hold Your Breath

The Dinner Guest

The Woman on the Pier

The Locked Attic

Notes on a Murder

The Garden Party

SCUTTLE

BARNABY WALTER

One More Chapter
a division of HarperCollins*Publishers*
1 London Bridge Street
London SE1 9GF
www.harpercollins.co.uk
HarperCollins*Publishers*
Macken House, 39/40 Mayor Street Upper,
Dublin 1, D01 C9W8, Ireland

This paperback edition 2024
First published in Great Britain by
HarperCollins*Publishers* 2024

A catalogue record of this book
is available from the British Library
ISBN: 978-0-00-865780-2

Printed and bound in the UK using 100% Renewable Electricity
by CPI Group (UK) Ltd

For Rebecca (with my eternal apologies for the spider-based horror content)

I'm saying, I'm an insect who dreamt he was a man and loved it.
But now the dream is over and the insect is awake.
I'm saying… I'll hurt you if you stay.
— *The Fly (1986)*, screenplay by Charles Edward Pogue and David Cronenberg

I heard one cry in the night, and I heard one laugh afterwards.
If I cannot forget that, I shall not be able to sleep again.
— *Ghost Stories of an Antiquary*, M.R. James

Prologue

I dragged the body through the darkness. Kept it close.
Leaves. Blood. Screams.

It's screaming it's screaming it's waking wrap it tight wrap it tight bind it tight

It mustn't escape mustn't escape

Must bind it

Wrap it

Bind it tight

Part of my mind could make out the shouts. The shrieks in the night. Getting nearer. But my thoughts were far from clear. There was a quaking in that side of me, an energy pushing me on. Pushing me to do terrible things. Things that would otherwise sicken me.

It's moving it's moving mustn't escape it mustn't escape

Tie it up

Tie it up

Bite it

Bite

Bite

I registered another shout without understanding what it meant. It was like I both heard and felt it, like the sounds were vibrations I could pick up on, decode, without having to hear the words. I couldn't think about things clearly, even though I tried. Tried to hold on to the thoughts I knew belonged to me, to the proper me, the part of me that knew what I was doing…

Feed

Feed

Feed

Feed

Part I

AWAKENING

Chapter One

THE BOY

25 October 2024

I woke up breathing hard, my heart pounding, the duvet on the floor. I was cold and hot at the same time, my arms and legs twisted around a bundle I was clutching on to. My pillows. Both of them, twisted and clumped into one mass. I pulled them apart, punching them back into a more pillow-like shape, and returned them to their normal spot and lay back. I'd had a dream—a nightmare—but I couldn't remember what it was about. The feeling, however, was still there, lingering in my mind like a dull ache, as if from a wound that hadn't quite healed.

A horrible sound cut through the darkness of my room. Screeching, mechanical. Violent, almost. I sat up, swung my legs out of bed and stood, listening. It was coming from the garden. I went over to the windowsill and looked out, blinking in the grey morning light. It was that prick from next door—Eddie the quad-biker. He was strimming his lawn at 6.40 on a cold October morning. That was the kind of guy Eddie was. Didn't give a fuck about anyone else. Just did his thing. There were only two other houses on our little country road and we were unlucky enough to be saddled with him as a neighbour.

I pulled the curtains open. My floor-to-ceiling bedroom window was cut in two, with a rim that allowed you to open the top half outwards. On this small ledge I could see something moving. A small money-spider, running across it. I wasn't sure why, but I decided it should be freed, so I opened the window to let it out. That was when Eddie looked up from over the fence.

'Ah sorry to wake you, mate?' he called up, grinning, as if he was pleased someone had noticed how productive he was being at that time of the morning.

I frowned down at him and nudged the money spider out of the window. It didn't seem to want to leave my hand, so I gave it a firmer push and it made its way down the outside of the glass.

'You awake, Hudson?' My dad's voice sounded from the corridor outside my room.

'Yeah,' I replied.

He opened the door and looked in.

'Bloody Eddie with his strimmer,' he said, nodding at the garden. 'He woke me, too.'

I shrugged and sat down on the edge of my bed. Looked at my feet. Brushed aside an abandoned paperclip on the floor with one of my toes. I was pissed off. I hadn't forgotten the argument we'd had the night before. An argument that started with a heated discussion about plans with my friends on Halloween and ended up with a row about how suffocating Dad could be. He'd reminded me that at least he was here, and not living in America like Mum, but if I thought she'd be a better parent perhaps I should talk to her more, rather than avoiding her calls. He had a point, and that was what had hurt. I *had* been avoiding talking to her. I just didn't get the point. If she was going to live her life so far away from us, why should I bother making the effort?

I wasn't in the mood to go through it all again now, with a school day stretching out ahead of me, so I just stayed silent. Eventually, Dad asked, 'Why's your duvet on the floor?'

I shrugged again, letting out a sigh. 'Fell off in the night.'

He was silent for a few seconds, then he said, 'Well, get dressed. I'll make us breakfast.'

I spent a minute or two staring out of the window, finding it hard to motivate myself to move. From my seated position, I could no longer see Eddie, but instead had a far-reaching view across the fields that our houses backed on to —fields that ended with a few more houses and some trees. The trees that formed Barret forest, swaying in the distance.

Eventually, I forced myself to get up. I showered quickly then pulled on my school uniform, not bothering to do up my top button or fasten my tie. In the kitchen, I slumped down on one of the chairs at the kitchen table, dropping the bag containing my sports kit carelessly on the floor, and took a slice of toast off the plate in front of me.

'Morning,' Mattias said, looking up from his iPad.

I grunted in response, knowing it would annoy Dad. Perhaps he was keen to avoid another shouting match, but he chose to say nothing, but I saw him and Mattias share a look. Since their wedding a few years ago, I had waited for Dad and Mattias to drift apart, for me to be proved right that Dad marrying a much younger man—someone closer to my age than his—was simply an early midlife crisis. But they hadn't drifted apart. Things had stayed the same and I'd had to face up to fact we were stuck with him.

'Have some fried eggs,' Dad said, tipping two onto my plate without waiting for an answer. There was something about the way they collapsed in on each other, a drip of grease sliding off the top one, that killed any hunger I might have had.

'Kenny will be here in a minute,' I replied.

I saw Dad's smile morph into something stiffer, less relaxed. He wasn't a fan of Kenny. Considered him a bad influence. Probably right, but I wasn't about to stop hanging out with him because of it.

'Is the party in the woods on Halloween Kenny's idea?' Mattias asked, setting aside his tablet and helping himself to eggs from the pan.

I noticed Dad's head jerk up. He gave Mattias a short, sharp shake of the head and glared at him. It was obvious what he meant: *Let's not bring all that up again.*

'Yes,' I said, simply.

Mattias clearly thought he needed to prove he was on my dad's side, 'I think your father's right to be concerned—the woods at night can be a dangerous place, especially Barret forest. You know you get barely any phone signal in there it's so thick with trees. It's normal for parents to worry.'

It was my turn to frown at him. 'Well, it's lucky you're not a parent, then, isn't it?' I said it bluntly, deliberately to wound, and I saw the hurt in Mattias's eyes. I felt bad afterwards, but the fact he was always trying to be friendly rubbed me up the wrong way.

'Don't talk to your stepfather that way,' Dad said. 'And don't start with that tone this early in the day.'

'I'm not *starting* with a *tone*,' I snapped back. 'If parental concern was so fucking important, maybe you could bring that up with Mum when she next tries to get in touch. Maybe then she'll realise choosing pills and alcohol over me wasn't such a great move.'

'That's unfair,' Dad said. 'Your mother has … *had* her difficulties.'

'I know, old news, Dad.'

'And like I said last night, I appreciate it's been difficult for you. I think we should see her wish to be in contact more often as … well, as a positive sign.'

I got up and left the table, picking up another slice of toast as I went.

'Hudson, please sit back down,' I heard Dad say, trying to sound reasonable, but I didn't reply. Tugging on my school blazer from the hook in the hallway, I grabbed my rucksack and opened the door. Kenny stood there, his hand raised, about to press the doorbell.

'Perfect timing,' Kenny said, smiling. Dad didn't like

Kenny's smile—he said it looked as if he was always smirking. It was one of the many things Dad would criticise Kenny about. I suppose he may have had a point, but since I wasn't one for smiling much at all, it was probably best if I didn't judge.

'Hudson,' a voice called from down the hallway. I turned and saw Mattias walking towards me, clutching something. 'Here, you forgot this,' he said, holding out the sports bag.

'Oh ... er ... yeah, thanks,' I said, taking it from him. It made me feel bad for getting cross with him earlier. He was nice, even if I found him annoying sometimes. But I knew I'd have found whoever my dad had chosen as a partner annoying.

I said goodbye, offering him a small nod, hoping he'd take it as an apology. As soon as the door had closed, Kenny shook his head and said, 'I still think it's weird every time I see him—your dad being with a guy so young.'

This was something Kenny often said, and I thought it might have something to do with the fact his own father had had an affair with his much younger secretary—the 'typical tacky cliché', in Kenny's words—but in the end had decided to stay with his 'age-appropriate wife and make it work'. I wondered if Kenny's comments about my stepfather's age were because my dad had found love with a much younger partner not through an affair, but rather a relationship that had led to marriage.

I offered one of my usual responses. 'There's only eighteen years between them,' I said. 'It's not as much as some couples.' In truth, there was closer to nineteen years when all the months were taken into account. My dad was forty-one and Mattias had only recently turned twenty-three.

'You and him are practically the same age,' Kenny said as we turned the corner onto the main road that led up to North Woodingham Secondary school, or as we liked to refer to it, 'The Prison'.

'Yeah, I know,' I said, tired of the subject now.

'I mean,' Kenny used his fingers to work out the sum, 'he must have been, what, six or seven when you were born? And now he's, like, your second dad? Madness.'

I stayed silent for a while. When Kenny had first voiced something like this, I'd wondered if there was an element of homophobia behind it and whether he would have commented on it had Mattias been a woman. But since becoming friends when I joined the school a couple of years ago, he'd never said anything obviously anti-gay, or at least not in my earshot, so I ended up pushing this aside. One of my dad's pet hates was what he called 'imagined discrimination', and he said it was usually best 'not to presume the worst in someone'. He felt that attitudes we often rush to condemn as rooted in hatred are often actually more innocuous and sometimes come from a totally different place. 'An emotional response is a valid response,' he once said, 'but it doesn't mean it's the *correct* response. Just because you *feel* something, doesn't make it real. Becoming emotional clouds the brain. Always remember that getting angry and upset can lead to rash behaviour, and rash behaviour can lead to the wrong choices or conclusions.'

Kenny eventually moved the topic of conversation on to

the Halloween party. He was the mastermind behind it and had spoken of little else since. 'It's going to be wild, mate. *Wild*. Loads of girls coming. Including Kirsten. Your *special, beautiful Kirsten*.' He said these last two words in an exaggerated Irish accent, presumably in reference to the light Belfast edge Kirsten spoke with. He nudged my shoulder when he said the name, his meaning clear. Kenny thought I fancied Kirsten, and if I was honest with myself, he was kind of correct, although I'd never said it outright. I wouldn't trust him not to go and tell Kirsten, or anyone else he came across, for that matter.

'Just fucking talk to her. You never do, just moan at me about how you like her flowery perfume. You need to lose this whole virginity thing at some point.' He flapped his hand, as if the whole concept of being a virgin was a silly new fad he didn't believe in.

'Trust me, I want to, I just…' I trailed off, unable to finish the sentence properly, embarrassed to say that I found talking to girls terrifying. When it came down to actually *doing it* I'd be right there, ready. It was just the bit that came before it: the awkward chat, the trying to ask them out on a date or letting them know you'd like to spend time with them at a party—all of it was a massive mountain of stress I had no hope of climbing.

'Last time we went to the woods, Charlene gave me a hand job behind a tree,' Kenny said, proudly, as if it were his life's achievement.

'I know. I was there.' I set my mouth in a grim line, remembering the heart-rate quickening mixture of embarrassment, fascination and white-hot envy when I'd seen Charlene unzip Kenny's jeans and push her hand inside as she kissed him.

'Fucking classic.' He grinned. 'I'm sure she'd do you, too. I'll ask her.'

'No, don't,' I said straight away, mortified by the idea.

'Fine, just come to the forest. It wasn't a problem last time so I don't get why—'

'Because that was on a Sunday afternoon in summer. Now it's … dark—there's practically no light—and it's much colder.'

This made me sound like a child, and I was well aware we were in the middle of a surprisingly mild autumn.

'I'll have to see,' I added vaguely. 'My dad wasn't particularly pleased when I brought the idea up.'

Kenny shook his head, his mouth in a grimace. 'Your mistake is to always ask for permission. Your dads need to get to grips with the idea that little Hudson is now big Hudson. You're going to be eighteen in, like…'

'Just under two years.'

'Well … two years can fly by. After school just go home and tell them you're going. Or better still, don't bring it up at all and just sneak out.'

I'd thought about this already. I *could* sneak out. I'd never done it before, but something about the thought made me feel reckless and excited.

'Come on, just do it,' Kenny said, 'Halloween night in the woods. It's going to be epic. I can feel it.'

Chapter Two

THE FATHER

25 October 2024

'I'm not sure about that Kenny kid,' Mattias said to me as he came back into the kitchen.

'You and me both,' I replied, starting to clear away the breakfast things from the table. 'Listen, I'm sorry … well, I'm sorry for last night and the whole row about Hudson talking to his mother more. He normally shrugs and grunts if I suggest he talks to her and I didn't realise he was going to get as angry as that. And I'm sorry for how he spoke to you this morning.'

'You don't have to apologise. Families are tough, I get it. It's OK.'

'I think you're right about Kenny, though,' I said. 'I get the feeling Hudson's only friends with him because he was the first kid to talk to him properly when we moved here. And now he's fallen in with that crowd. I think he's eternally scared of standing up to Kenny in case he casts him out—you know what teenagers are like. Still, it's not a healthy foundation for a friendship.'

Mattias put his arms around my shoulders and kissed me. My hands were full of plates containing crusts of toast, otherwise I'd have returned the embrace.

'Why don't you put those things down? Have another coffee. Relax.'

I smiled but shook my head, conscious I should start getting ready for work. 'I'm sorry, I wish I could, but I should get started on my work.' I felt bad brushing him off, and even though Mattias had assured me it was all OK, something he'd said about families snagged with me. I was conscious he didn't have one.

He'd grown up in a children's home, had a bunch of foster parents, and the final lot he ended up with sent him off to boarding school, so he never got to experience much of a traditional 'home life'. Then again, if I thought back to my own upbringing, I'm not sure anyone could have described mine as traditional. Turbulent, perhaps, would be a better word.

Mattias headed out to his studio in nearby Newcastle and I settled myself down in my office to get started on work for the day. I was on a study sabbatical from my university-lecturer role, trying to complete a paper for a film theory anthology.

As I logged on to the computer, I saw a notification in the corner of my desktop on the icon linked to my personal email account. I somehow knew it would be her as soon as I clicked on it.

Did you talk to Hudson?

I considered replying with something blunt, feeling a rising surge of anger at how her request to speak to her son on Zoom had caused an all-out row. Somehow, Hudson's request to spend Halloween in the forest with his friends had gotten tangled up in the discussion, about how overprotective I am with him, worried that he'll end up having a breakdown like his mother, how I stopped him enjoying a normal life because I wanted to be 'the good parent'. How I always had to prove something. Prove that I wasn't like the mother who had abandoned him. Although, that last bit wasn't entirely true; I'd taken him away from her. Rescued him from her, or at least that's what I told myself. I'd brought him to England and given him a stable life away from everything that had happened on her ranch in the US.

When he openly criticised his mother, I tried my best to defend my actions whilst remaining respectfully diplomatic. I told him it was more complicated than a case of good-parent, bad-parent. That there was a lot about the situation that he was too young to understand.

In the end I had typed back to Adelaide.

I'm sorry, but I don't think it's the right time for him. I think he's stressed with school. Maybe at Christmas.

An hour later her response had come through.

Fine.

I felt a stab of both annoyance and sadness when I looked at that one word. There was a time when Adelaide and I composed long emails to each other, back in the early days of our relationship, pouring our youthful angst into essay-length pieces meant for each other's eyes only. She was the best friend anyone could wish for. I had tried to be the same for her.

It still amazed me how a drunken mistake one night could change everything. How a platonic friendship could alter so much in the space of such a short time. A night that had changed the course of my life. It had led to me becoming a father. And for her, it had paved a dark path towards depression, anxiety and addiction.

How different it should have been. We'd been so optimistic, choosing to leave the UK for her native US. I'd managed to secure a part-time research job at a university and we'd agreed to move into her late father's ranch in Texas. We were adamant we had it sorted. A few months after our arrival, she gave birth to Hudson. We tried our best. But then her demons arrived. And no amount of substance, however much she put into her body, would ever be enough to keep them at bay.

I ended up losing a lot of the day to rumination. Eventually I shut down the computer and pottered around the house, picking up discarded socks in Hudson's room, putting on a load of laundry, all the while wondering if, maybe, my overprotective nature would backfire. Maybe Hudson would go off the rails. And then where would I be? I stabbed at the settings buttons on the washing machine and sat down as the calming sound of the spinning drum filled the kitchen. My thoughts drifted to Mattias, how it always fell to me to sort out Hudson's rudeness towards him. Make sure Mattias was OK, didn't take it to heart, even though I knew it must be hard on him. I never could quite shake-off the feeling that I'd become the inadvertent father-figure for two boys, rather than one. That my own husband's orphan status had perhaps played a part in him falling for me. Perhaps, deep down, he wanted a parent to guide, comfort and reassure. And I'd stepped into that role, happy to help.

Ten minutes later, I'd decided. When Hudson came home, I'd tell him he was allowed to go to Kenny's party in the woods. This wasn't a horror movie, or a true-crime documentary. This was real life. And in real life, most things turned out completely fine.

Or so I told myself.

Chapter Three

THE BOY

25 October 2024

The topic of the Halloween party in the woods was inescapable for the rest of the morning. Kenny and two of our other friends, Jack and Alex, spent most of our science lesson discussing who would bring which drinks. At break, we sat in the cold quad area outside the Humanities block, Alex was recycling some local folklore about the forest and the 'tonnes of scary shit' that had gone down in Barret Forest over the years.

'There have been deaths in there. More than usual.'

'What's usual for your average forest?' Kirsten had asked, sitting down on the bench next to me, brushing a few leaves off its wooden surface. I felt my stomach lurch as the outside of her coat brushed against my sleeve, caught the scent of her perfume as the wind rippled her hair. I could feel Kenny grinning at me, so I deliberately avoided his gaze.

'Oh, I'm sure most forests have dark histories, you know,' Alex said. 'No one's doubting that. I'm just saying Barret is worse than most. Rituals. Drownings. Apparently, in the eighties a girl drowned in a stream in there, but some think she was murdered.'

'It was an accident,' Kirsten said. 'I saw a news article about it a little while ago. A group of children had been playing in the woods and one of them got their foot caught in a branch under the water and drowned. It's awful, sure, but not …well…'

'Spooky?' I offered. Kirsten nodded, but Kenny rolled his eyes.

'*Spooky?* How old are you?'

'I think spooky is exactly the word for it,' said Alex. 'Apparently her ghost haunts the woods.'

'Yeah, right, a one-legged girl hobbling around the place,' Kenny laughed. 'I hope she doesn't stumble into our campsite.'

'Nobody said anything about her being one-legged,' Alex said, tutting. 'I don't think her foot or leg came off.'

'And I don't think you should be talking like that about a real case. She was someone's child,' Kirsten said.

Alex waved a dismissive hand. 'It was decades ago, anyway. But I know of some fucked-up shit that's happening now.' He picked his phone off the table, knocking aside a half-eaten apple, but didn't bother to catch it. He tapped on his phone for a few seconds then put it back in the centre in front of us. 'Look, these are tree trunks that fell after a lightning storm. Watch what happens to these guys when they try and touch them.'

I watched, curious, as the shaky, video footage showed what seemed to be three guys pointing at a tree stump. The blackened tree was situated in a forest clearing and looked as though the top was smouldering. The guys were saying something in what sounded like French and then one of them reached out and touched the top of the tree stump. He snatched his hand back quickly, presumably because he'd been burnt, but the reaction that followed was even more extreme: the young man appeared to seize up, his body going rigid, and collapsed onto his side. It didn't appear as though the young man was having a fit, he just lay still, not moving. You could see his two friends shouting 'Felix! Felix!', as the video footage grew even more shaky.

'What is this?' Kirsten asked, sounding disturbed. 'He's not dead, is he?'

'Keep watching,' Alex said, holding up a finger to silence her.

A couple of minutes passed but eventually the guy who'd fallen to the ground appeared to be coming to, blinking and looking about him. He must have been in his early twenties, but in that moment he looked strangely young. He finally seemed to come to his senses and could be heard shouting 'Fuck!' then half-laughing, half shouting, his friends talking to him in French. The group turned and stared at the tree, not quite believing what had just happened to them. As if to test whether it had been real, another young man moved towards the tree trunk, his movements were slower, more reserved but still he reached out and touched the smouldering wood. And the same thing happened to him, his body went rigid and then he crashed to the ground.

Watching the video sent shivers down my spine. It was a feeling I couldn't explain, and for a moment I wanted to snatch the phone out of Alex's hand and pause the video. I couldn't be sure why, but it felt as though there was something extreme happening to those guys, something far more dangerous than watching them simply touch a burnt tree-trunk and fall over.

Kenny was smirking, 'There've been tonnes of those videos,' he said, 'I saw a different one with a group of other people. I reckon they've got to be fake; must be easy to stand straight and just fall over.'

'Ha, I'd like to see you try and stay that still. It doesn't sound like it's happening in our forest,' said Kirsten, 'Where was that? France?'

'Quebec,' said Alex.

'They sounded French,' she said.

'They speak French there,' Alex said. 'But like Kenny said, there have been other things like this happening with tree trunks and lightning strikes. This guy on YouTube has been putting together a series on his channel about it, how sometimes people seem to vanish or have odd injuries if they touch them—the trees hit by lightning. It's been going on for years, usually around Halloween, but there's been more this year.'

Kirsten sighed, 'Well, wherever and whatever it is, I doubt we'll see many lightning strikes. The weather's supposed to be clear. I'm not being put off by some random video that's probably fake. Engineered viral videos, literally created to get people to share them, are a real thing, you know?' She looked at me and said, 'What do you think, Hudson?'

I stared at her, eyes wide, for a few seconds and then said, 'Yeah ... I think ... yeah ... probably ... probably fake.'

The bell rang to tell us break was over.

'Wow, Hud, thanks for that amazing contribution. Really added something to the discussion there,' Kenny said, patting me on the back.

'Get off,' I muttered, shaking away his arm, which just caused him to laugh.

As we were heading to class, Kirsten caught up with me. Once Kenny had walked ahead out of earshot of the loud corridor, Kirsten said quietly 'He puts you down a lot, you know?'

I glanced at her. I wasn't used to her talking to me on my own, especially not in this quiet, almost conspiratorial way. I felt flummoxed by the attention and wasn't sure what to say, so ended up just shrugging. 'Oh, that's ... just Kenny. He doesn't mean anything by it.'

Kirsten nodded thoughtfully. 'I get that he, like, swooped in and took you under his wing when you were new, but you're not new anymore, you're one of us. Just don't let him walk all over you, OK?' She gave my arm a little squeeze, then hurried off out of the doors to our left in the direction of the Humanities block.

If the corridor hadn't been thick with students likely to

trample over me, her touch probably would have frozen me to the spot. I tried to keep a clear head as I pressed on. I had Maths next, then PE, which always overran into lunch time. I thought it was unfair that just because we didn't have a lesson to go straight into, the teachers thought it was fine to stop the lesson when the bell went, which meant we spent most of our break showering and changing and by the time we were out we hardly ever had any time to grab lunch before we had to head to our next class.

Because I'd left the house in a temper that morning I'd forgotten to grab something for lunch, and didn't fancy the stale-looking sandwiches left over in the canteen, so I was hungry and in a bad mood when I sat down in History and realised I'd left my homework on my desk at home. I explained it was an honest mistake, but Mrs Cornish was having none of it. The mass of beaded necklaces she always wore seemed to click with anger as she told me I'd better buck up my ideas or I'd 'walk into a life of disappointment, poverty and inevitable criminality' as soon as I left school. She wasn't one to underplay things. In the end I told her to leave me alone, and apparently said it a little too crossly as she ended up ordering me out of class. 'To the head of year. *Now.*'

I grabbed my bag and left. I didn't go to my head of year but instead went to the nearby boys' toilets down the end of the corridor and sat in one of the cubicles, anger-scrolling through Instagram. I felt like this sometimes: like every piece of rage in all the world was trapped within me. Sometimes a splinter of it would break off and rush to the surface and I'd end up lashing out or saying something blunt, just to hit back, just to spend some of the energy that burned within me. Using my phone to distract me was one of my go-to coping mechanisms. It normally worked; I followed amazing artists and could spent hours watching their time-lapse videos; starting with a blank sheet of paper and within seconds turning it into an amazingly detailed sketch of a wizard or a dragon or something otherworldly.

Just as I was putting away my phone, deciding it was time I headed back, the bathroom door banged open, making me jump. I'd already unlocked the cubicle but hadn't opened the door fully, so stepped back, out of sight, just in case it was someone from my class. From the sound of it, more than one person had entered. I expected it to be a group of older boys bunking off class—they often did this if they were in separate classes; they arranged a time for them to meet here to chat for a bit. I always thought that the coordinated, covert nature of it was the main appeal. But today it wasn't a group of boys; one of the voices was definitely a girl. I heard a stray laugh and then the voice said, 'Kenny, we don't have time for that. Hands off, I want to show you a picture of the villa.'

So Kenny was there. And I didn't need to wonder who the girl was. It was Charlene, his 'on-and-off friend-with-benefits', although I was sure he only said that to make himself sound grown up.

'Wait, woah? Your parents are buying that?' I heard Kenny say.

'Bought,' she said. 'They put the offer in last week. So

that means, next summer, you and me and a few select guests will be living it up in the Portuguese sunshine.'

I felt a throb of anger within me. Why was she showing Kenny her parents' villa in Portugal? Why did everyone rush to impress him, try to keep him on side? I batted away thoughts about how hypocritical it was of me to think this and strained to listen as Kenny started to speak. I then heard another chuckle. 'Come on, let's have a bit of practice.' I heard them enter the cubicle next to mine, then heard a zipper go. 'Practice for what, Portugal? Or the party next week? I know you like it outdoors.' Charlene laughed in response and said, 'Hopefully this time you won't have Hudson trailing around after you like some sad, lost puppy.'

'Ah, he's not that bad, though I admit his pathetic lonely-virgin thing is getting a bit annoying,' Kenny said. 'And it's so obvious he fancies Kirsten.'

'She's out of his league,' Charlene scoffed. 'Now shut up for a bit, OK.'

I sat there, as still as I possibly could, furious at what I'd just heard. *Sad, lost puppy? Pathetic lonely virgin?*

I felt a prickle of anger on the back of my neck. Then again in my arms, shooting from my wrist up into my shoulders, becoming a sudden sharp pain. An idea striking with a hot rush, I reached into my bag, took out a crumpled half-full bottle of water, took off its lid and lobbed it up and over the side of the cubicle wall. Charlene screamed and Kenny shouted 'Fuck!' I legged it. I heard the door banging off the wall as one or both of them tried to give pursuit, but I was already in the corridor by that point.

Frustrated that I'd had to listen to them in the toilets, I made my way to the library for a bit and nestled myself in the far corner near where they kept local newspaper archives. Whilst there, the tears that I'd been fighting to hold back finally spilled over. I scribbled on the front of my homework diary, just to give my hands something to do, somewhere for all my pent-up anger or energy to go.

'What the fuck, mate?' I saw Kenny wandering over to me, a look of amazement on his face. 'Are you fucking *crying*? Just because that old witch told you off?'

'It's not because of that,' I said, hurriedly trying to wipe my face and gather my bags and blazer at the same time. I couldn't help notice his hair was wet, which gave me a flash of satisfaction that my grenade had hit its mark.

'Then what are—'

'Just fuck off, Kenny,' I muttered as I pushed past him and out of the library. He didn't follow.

Chapter Four

THE BOY

25 October 2024

I went home still hating the world and everyone in it. I was sick of school. Sick of Kenny. Sick of the fact everyone was getting on with each other. At this rate, I'd be the only single guy left in the school by Christmas. I wondered if what Kenny had said was true—if I was just a pathetic lonely virgin. Maybe next summer everyone would jet off to Charlene's villa in Portugal and I'd be stuck at home watching YouTube videos in my room. I opened my laptop and I was served up a video that mentioned 'Crazy Tree Stump Electric Shock' but I clicked away from that.

Luckily the house appeared to be empty, as it often was when I got home from school, with Dad out at the university or the library and Mattias in his art studio in Newcastle. I went straight to my room and sat at my desk in front of my laptop. I turned it on and went straight to Kirsten's social-media accounts. Was she really 'out of my league' as Charlene had said? I started to imagine Kirsten kissing me. Imagined what I'd do if I was like Kenny and casually met up with girls in the boys' loos during class. What it would be like being in a confined space with her, undoing her shirt. Putting my hands on her…

Presuming the house was empty had been a mistake, it seemed, as was not bothering to close the door. Mattias came into view and I turned around and then froze still. I hadn't been doing anything, but I was aware of Kirsten's page, pictures of her sunbathing in her bikini on holiday all over my screen. I considered slamming the laptop shut but decided this would make things worse.

'Have you been … erm … in long?' I asked, not sure if I cared enough about what Mattias thought to be embarrassed.

'Not long, mate,' he said, offering me a half-grin. Not for the first time, I felt Mattias was trying to be both pally and wise, like some older brother who could pass on his worldly wisdom to the young kid who didn't know how things worked in the big wide world. It made me want to hit him.

'I wasn't—I was just—'

'I was wondering if you'd like ravioli for dinner?' Mattias said, cutting across me, which was probably kind of him. 'Your dad mentioned we had some and I was going to do something special with it.'

I frowned at him, 'Special?' I repeated back, indicating that I found the use of the word a bit weird, since it wasn't anyone's birthday and nothing had happened to give us an excuse to celebrate. Then I realised this was a let's-avoid-another-argument thing they'd conjured up together. It wouldn't have surprised me if Mattias had used the words 'a healing supper' or some other posh nonsense. Even though my dad had grown up in Chelsea, it was Newcastle-native Mattias who sounded like he'd walked out of *Downton Abbey*. Apparently he'd been sent to a boarding school at a young age that 'ironed out the northern vowels', or so he said. He wasn't even *born* posh—he was at an orphanage until he was a young teenager, then after a handful of foster parents, he was taken in by an elderly couple who bankrolled him through private school. They died just before he met my dad, and even though Mattias said he'd never really been close to them, they still left him all their money. He had been spending his inheritance on art supplies and studio space in the city ever since.

'Yeah, well, just nice I guess,' Mattias said, 'I can't promise it will be akin to Jean-Georges at The Connaught but it should be edible.'

'I have no idea who that is,' I said, shrugging. Mattias's odd references often irritated me and today it was really grating.

After my dismissive reply, Mattias looked a bit hurt and mumbled something about starting cooking in about an hour. Then he paused, half turning at the doorway, as if he'd changed his mind about something and turned back to face me.

'Look, Hud, let's just have it out, right here and now.'

'Have what out?' I asked, getting angry now, not wanting this discussion to continue.

'All the issues you have with me,' Mattias said, a pinkish tinge setting in his pale skin. 'I get you're not a fan of my presence here, but it's been a couple of years now and I don't feel we've got to know each other properly, and you clearly still have a problem with our relationship. I realise it must be weird your dad being with someone a bit younger—'

'*Significantly* younger,' I cut in.

'All right, significantly younger,' he nodded, although the movement of the head looked more like a twitch of annoyance than anything very positive. 'But essentially, what I'm saying is, I'm here to stay. We're here, all three of us, like this, until you go off to university in a couple of years. So we've got to find a way of getting along. I mean, I can't be that bad, can I?'

I moved my gaze to the floor, now embarrassed. I knew I'd been unkind to him, borderline nasty at times with my temper. I just found it hard to control it when something pissed me off, and more often than not, that something was Mattias. It probably wasn't even his fault. I knew there was more to it than just his age and wanting to be 'mates', that my anger was more about the fact that it had been just me and Dad for so long, and now someone else had become part of our lives. Facing up to all this had been a long time coming, and now Mattias was finally verbalising it all. I felt myself growing weirdly panicky, as if my fight-or-flight senses had been activated.

'Can I ask, Hudson, are you embarrassed about your dad

being gay? Is it because I'm a man that it's difficult? I realise it might be harder for you here, in the countryside, than it may have been in London. Do people say homophobic things at school?'

My eyes snapped up at him, '*What?* What are you talking about? Nobody gives a fuck about me having two dads. Actually, no. They do give a fuck, but instead of hating it, they bloody *love* it. It's the opposite of homophobia; it's like a big celebratory obsession. People presume we all go out on Pride marches as a family. They refer to you and Dad as members of whatever "community" they imagine you're part of. One sixth former even asked to interview me as part of some special issue of the school newspaper because I was "diverse adjacent" and a "golden ally" because I had gay parents. I don't even know what "diverse adjacent" is but it sounds fucking ridiculous.' I came to a stop and realised I was out of breath. I was then stunned to see Mattias was smiling.

He walked further into the room and sat down on the bed. 'Wow, that … does all sound a bit much.'

He continued to smile and clearly thought we were going to have some heart-to-heart, now that I'd let all this frustration out. I definitely wasn't about to become his best mate anytime soon, but I did calm down enough to sit on my desk chair, which felt like a bit of an olive branch on my own terms.

'Maybe we can talk to your dad about all this,' Mattias said. 'He hates all that stuff. That "overly-celebratory nonsense" as he calls it. He could possibly talk to the school and—'

'I don't want that,' I said, quickly. 'That would make stuff worse. I just want everyone to calm down. I'm the one that thinks it should be normal and unremarkable. They're the ones telling me it's this big amazing wonderful thing.'

'Well, I'll say this: be pleased you're surrounded by people who mean well and think they're doing the right thing, even if they're sometimes not. Better that than be surrounded by sneering and nastiness. That can be much worse.'

I wondered for a moment if I was getting an insight into his years in the care home, or perhaps his time at school. But before I could ask him, the doorbell rang. Mattias got up. 'I'll get it,' he said. He gave me another understanding smile and left the room.

I heard Kenny's voice almost immediately and then his feet running thunderously up the stairs.

'Hey, what the fuck, mate? You ignoring my messages on purpose? I said I was sorry, OK.'

I frowned at him, my brain not allowing me to be plunged from one emotionally draining conversation into another so quickly.

'What?' I said, reaching for my phone. Kenny had messaged. A lot. I dismissed the notifications, not bothering to read them now he was in my room in person.

'Yeah, so, basically I screwed up. I get that it was you.'

'What was me?'

'The water bottle.'

I looked at him, embarrassed. 'Oh.'

'Yes, *oh*. I saw it in your bag before PE and put two and two together. And I would be within my rights to be mad at you, Hud, if it wasn't that I felt bad, because, well ... I guess you probably heard me and Charlene chatting shit about you. It wasn't right and it wasn't fair and I'm sorry. I don't think you're ... I can't remember...'

'A pathetic lonely virgin.'

'Yeah, that. I mean, no, you're not.'

'Or a sad lost puppy?'

I noticed a twitch of his mouth at this, as if he was trying not to laugh. 'Well, only sometimes.'

I didn't smile, but I gave him a little nod to show him the apology was grudgingly accepted. I was cross with myself, not being able to stay angry at Kenny for too long. I thought of what Kirsten had said, about how I just let him walk all over me, but I knew if we hadn't sorted this out I'd have it hanging over me all night while I tried to fall asleep. 'Fine,' I said.

'Great,' Kenny said beaming and pulling me into one of his strong, backslapping hugs. He then leaned back and looked at me, hands on my shoulders, 'I really am sorry, Hud. I say things in the heat of the moment or get carried away and shit and... Well, you know I really don't mean it, man.'

He sounded sincere, so I nodded again to show he was forgiven. With one last squeeze of my shoulders, he let go and wandered over to the bed and dropped down onto it, lying on his back and not bothering to remove his shoes.

'It's true though, what I said about Kirsten, about how you fancy her. I know that for certain.' He said this whilst staring at the ceiling, grinning.

'What makes you say that?'

'Because a photo of her on a jet ski on holiday is currently on your laptop screen.'

I almost swore out loud and dashed to the computer to close the open browser. I felt my face burning, a rush of heat spreading from my forehead down across my neck and shoulders. The sensation was so strong, I glanced in the mirror to my left, expecting to see my flesh had turned bright red, but I looked normal.

'Calm down, mate,' Kenny said, propping himself up on his elbows. 'So, the woods. It's decided, right? You're coming?'

I was tempted to tell him nothing was decided. That he'd probably have more fun without a 'lost puppy' ruining his fun. But then he added the clincher.

'If you come with us, I'll set you up with Kirsten. I promise you, it'll be a night you'll never forget.'

Chapter Five

THE FATHER

25 October 2024

When I got in from work, I immediately clocked a coat hanging on the banisters that didn't belong to anyone in the house. I went into the kitchen and found Mattias scrolling on his phone. I put my arms around his shoulder.

'Good day?' I asked, inhaling the scent of his aftershave and hair product.

'Reasonable,' he replied, his hands covering mine. 'All the better now you're here.'

I extracted myself to get a glass of water and came to sit at the kitchen table.

'How long has that boy been up there?' I asked, nodding up towards the ceiling. 'I saw his coat when I came in.'

'*That* boy?' Mattias asked, raising his eyebrows. 'Surely it's good Hud has a friend?'

I bit my lip, thinking.

'What? Still not a fan? What is it exactly that you don't like about him? Sure, he's a bit of a lad, but I think he's harmless.'

I took a sip of my water, let my hands run along the table top. 'I don't know ... just a feeling I get. I think there's something about him, something...'

Mattias shrugged. 'Something what?'

'Something ... cruel.'

'*Cruel*? Bit harsh, isn't it?'

I frowned, thinking. 'You ever had a friend where they show you something on their phone—like, a video, of someone falling over or something not very nice happening, but they think it's funny and think you will, too?'

Mattias was frowning now. 'Er ... perhaps...'

'Well, that's Kenny.'

Mattias sighed. 'What evidence do you have for this? Has Kenny ever shown you a video of someone falling over?'

'No,' I said, feeling a bit irritated now. 'It was just an example of the kind of thing I think he probably does. A bit nasty, you know. I know he was welcoming to Hudson when we moved here, but I don't want him to feel stuck with him. I'm not sure he's a good influence.'

'I guess,' Mattias said, getting up from the table. 'Do you want anything? A drink?'

I shook my head, vaguely.

'What are you thinking about?' Mattias asked as he started to get things out of the fridge.

'Hud. The whole, woods thing.'

Mattias didn't reply as he hacked at the loaf. I sometimes found the rough way he cut the bread endearing. Today it annoyed me.

'Let him go,' Mattias said, simply. 'Just ... try to lighten up with him.'

I thought about this for a bit, then said, 'I think it's the guilt I still feel. When I decided to move us out of London and buy this place, it meant him leaving his friends in London. I wonder ... if we'd stayed ... not that I could have afforded that school for much longer, but ... well he might have found a closer group of friends. Nice people. People he'd want to be friends with for life.'

'It's been four years since then,' Mattias said. 'You've no way of knowing what would have happened. You did the best for him at the time. It wasn't your fault.'

'It *was* my fault,' I said, darkly. I didn't want to think about how I'd lost most of our savings, all the money I'd inherited from my mother and the sale of my childhood family home. I'd been foolish, too trusting of an old university friend, agreed to invest way too much into a sustainability project of his. A project that not only didn't work, but had links to very dodgy organisations. After that, I decided to stick to what I knew: academia and being a good father to Hudson. I sold up our London house and went north for a new start. In many ways, it was the best thing I ever did. I wouldn't have met Mattias, otherwise. But it'd come at a price. Hudson had already been moved about as a toddler from the US where he was born to London, and then

I went and uprooted him again at the age of twelve, bringing him to Northumberland.

'Do you know, it's strange to think about it now, but when he was born, I had this feeling he would be closer to his mother and I would be an irrelevance. He would clutch so tightly to her.'

'All children cling tightly to their mothers,' Mattias said.

'I know,' I sighed, 'I just… They seemed to fit together, like puzzle pieces. And then, through the drugs and drink, she started to fall apart, and it all crept up on us—on me—without me realising how serious things were getting. But after that night, the night that made me realise I'd have to take him away from her … everything changed. I became the protector and he clung to me, instead. It's like, even though he was just a toddler, he knew she'd lead him to danger. And he wasn't just scared of her. *She* was scared of him. That's the odd part. The things she'd say … when she was in the grip of a comedown, or withdrawal symptoms during one of her attempts to get clean … it made my skin crawl.'

I stayed silent for a moment, my mind getting lost in the past.

'You're only thinking about all this stuff because you're unsettled about Adelaide trying to get in touch, about Hudson wanting to be more independent,' Mattias said. 'We've talked about it before. I know you have these feelings of guilt and … well … doubt. That's normal, I think. And Hudson's just trying to be a teenager. He's trying to spread his wings, get some new experiences. And if one of those experiences is a spooky night in the woods on Halloween with his mates, let him do it. It will be a damn sight easier than being the dad who's always saying "no" to him. I think all those horror films you watch, coupled with your guilt complex, is making your over-protective imagination run away with you.'

'I'm sure you're right,' I said, smiling at him. But I wasn't sure. I never wanted to be the one responsible for Hudson being at risk or in any danger. He'd had enough of that when he lived with his mother.

Chapter Six

THE BOY

25 October 2024

Before I went to bed last night, Dad told me I was allowed to go to the party in the woods. I hadn't expected him to back down, and I suspected, by the way he sat smiling, that Mattias had something to do with him changing his mind. I suppose I should have been grateful, but I chose not to look at him directly.

'But if there's any heavy drinking or drug taking, I want you to phone me right away, OK?'

I nodded.

'And if you're scared at all— Don't look at me like that, I know you've been there before, but forests at night can be scary, so if you are, just send me a message and I can come and get you.'

I couldn't help rolling my eyes.

'Promise me, Hudson,' he said, laying a hand on my arm.

'OK, OK, I promise,' I said. I saw my dad's eyebrows rise, so I added, 'And Kenny's house backs onto the woods so we'll practically be in his garden … almost.'

'Almost,' Dad said, letting out a laugh that suggested he didn't quite trust my logic.

'It will be fine,' Mattias said. 'I'm sure of it.'

'Are you?' Dad said, 'I'm glad one of us is.' He turned to look at me, a serious expression starting to come over his face. 'Have you thought any more about your mother's request to … er … have a chat sometime soon?'

I got up to go upstairs, 'No,' I said.

'No, as in no, you haven't given it much thought? Or no, as in, no, you don't want to at all?'

I didn't want Dad to go back on his decision about the party, so I tried my best not to get mad. But I did have to leave the room. 'Going to do some homework before bed,' I said, pushing my chair in and heading for the stairs, ignoring Mattias's remark about it being the first night of half term.

When I got into bed that night I WhatsApped Kenny to tell him I was coming to the woods. Kenny's reply was short and to the point:

Great. Going to be a LEGENDARY night.

I messaged back.

Hope so

And closed my phone, not wanting to get into further chats. I'd see him before Halloween anyway, but I was still mad at him, despite his apologies and promises to set me up with Kirsten.

It took me a while to drift off to sleep, thoughts swirling around, refusing to calm down. When I did sleep, I dreamt trippy, disconcerting dreams. Kirsten was there, bending forward to kiss me. We were on a flat, expansive landscape—no trees or buildings—surrounded by lanterns, their flickering lights causing the air around us to glow. In the middle there was a circle, where Kirsten and I were laying. 'I want you to be my first,' she said to me, and tried to unbutton my shirt, but she couldn't get to it; there was something in the way. Something white, like string, but it kept sticking to her hands. She kept getting stuck, and eventually she started crying as more of the silver-white strands became wrapped around her fingers. 'This isn't how I wanted it to be,' she said through her tears. Without warning, there was a blinding light, a brief flash that dazzled me, and when my vision returned I saw that the ground was covered in rough circular things, smouldering and smoking. Tree stumps. And I could feel the heat coming off them. Extreme heat, so hot it was burning my eyes, my face, my arms, my wrist.

I woke up, breathing heavily, feeling cold and hot at the same time.

I continued to have variations on this dream each night

throughout half term. It shifted and changed each time. Sometimes it was Kirsten, trapped and bound up, sometimes it was me, as though I was cocooned, unable to move.

On Thursday morning, six days into the holiday, I woke up after one of these nightmares and got out of bed and went to the window. My alarm clock read 4.30 a.m. It was officially Halloween. I stared out, across the fields and the trees beyond that, just about visible behind the houses. Barret forest. I could see the line of them sway slightly. Grouped together, they looked like one being, one large, massive beast. Hulking. Waiting. Alive.

Chapter Seven

THE BOY

Halloween

Halloween day dragged by. I spent the morning in bed watching old episodes of *Doctor Who* on my iPad. Dad came in at one point and suggested I should get up and do something, so after a late lunch I went for a run down to the high street, about two miles from my house. Not that there was much there to make it a high street. Just a small supermarket, a post office and the local library. I decided to kill some more time by looping back through the forest. Dad didn't like it when I ran through there. He worried I'd get lost or fall over a tree root, break my leg and then die. He was always so dramatic about everything. But I figured if I was going to be sleeping in this place at night, I could easily cope with it during daylight.

After about twenty minutes, I came to the ruin of an old cottage, buried deep in the woods. Each time I saw it, I wondered why it hadn't been demolished, or why no one had put fencing up to keep intruders out. Instead, it just stood in the woods, abandoned. I'd heard some boys at my school boast about going there at night. There was evidence of this on the floor around it: roll-ups or spliffs, and a can of spray paint, although I couldn't see any graffiti on the partially collapsed cottage wall. I wasn't sure why, but something made me want to look inside, so I stepped over the broken wall and walked through into an area I presumed would have been the lounge. There was the wrecked frame of a sofa and a fireplace covered with leaves. My foot knocked against something solid on the ground and I turned it over to see it was an old VHS tape. The label on the front said *The Dark Crystal*—a movie I'd seen when I was a child. It was strange to think that someone may have once sat in this lounge and watched this video, a family perhaps, long ago. I was still looking at the tape when the lettering on the label was suddenly obscured by something black and moving. It took me a moment to realise a large spider had crawled across it and then hurried onto my foot. Before I could move it away, it had scuttled up my leg, the feeling of its legs on my bare skin sending an instant shiver through me, then continued until it went up the leg of my shorts near my thigh. 'Fuck!' I shouted, starting to kick and flail about. I wasn't overly scared of spiders, but I certainly didn't want one crawling on my skin. I pulled up the leg of my shorts but couldn't see it, then felt movement somewhere horribly close to my groin. Starting to yell in repulsion, I pulled the shorts down, my hands searching for it, slapping myself, scratching myself, not caring if I caused injury or death to the invader. The dark black-brown mass survived this assault and rushed up, seemingly out of nowhere, onto my hoodie and towards my right arm. That's where I managed to corner it, bring my palm down just before my elbow, stopping it as it headed towards my wrist and hand. I was about to crush it dead, when something stopped me. The spider had frozen completely still. In the midst of all the excitable movements, it had suddenly stopped. I did, too. I don't know whether it was a response to all the panic and revulsion or from running in the cold, but I felt a wave of dizziness coming over me. I stumbled, forgetting my shorts were still around my ankles, causing me to trip over. I fell onto my back, the thud jolting me, causing my vision to swim, even though I hadn't hit my head. Lying there, I got my breath back and then looked down at my arm. The spider was still there. On my arm, near my wrist. Part of me felt like it was looking at me. I looked at it back and wasn't afraid or repulsed anymore.

'You OK, mate?'

The voice made me jump. I looked over and near the pathway a young couple, a man and a woman, both in running gear, were looking at me, concerned expressions on their faces. It was the man who had spoken and he took a step towards me. 'Do you ... er ... need help?'

I hurried to get to my feet, bringing my shorts back up, dusting myself down. 'No, no, I... I tripped.'

The man frowned, looking unconvinced.

'I'm fine,' I said, just wanting to get out of there. Still a bit shaky, I walked out of the cottage ruins, back over the broken wall.

The man nodded slowly. 'OK, if you're sure.' He turned back to the woman and they carried on along the path. I saw them share a glance, and caught the woman pulling a face. I could tell she was amused and trying not to laugh. It must have been a strange sight, and they probably thought they'd interrupted something weird or embarrassing. In some ways they were right, though they'd never have been able to guess what it really was. As this thought crossed my mind, I hung back and waited for them to put some distance between us. I looked down at my arm. The spider had gone.

I didn't know if it was the incident with the spider that had freaked me out, or if it was a just-can't-be-bothered feeling that often set in during the autumn-winter time when it was dark, but whatever the reason, I started to wish I'd opted to spend the evening at home rather than agreed to go to a party. I'd probably have watched a horror film, then maybe read something in my room. Perhaps it was because I'd become so obsessed with the idea of not being allowed to go camping in the woods, I hadn't really stopped to consider if I wanted to.

I'd stayed out longer on my run than I'd planned and when I came in I heard Dad shout, 'That you, Hud?' from the kitchen.

'Yeah,' I called back, 'just grabbing a shower.'

Once I'd washed and dried and headed down for a quick snack, Dad told me he could give me a lift to Kenny's in the car.

'I can walk,' I said. 'It's not far.'

'I know,' Dad said, 'but it will save you a few minutes.'

I shrugged. 'Fine, yeah, great.'

I should have second-guessed his motives for this; when the time came for us to leave and we were in the car, Dad started the journey at an unnaturally slow speed, literally crawling through the empty streets at five miles an hour, giving me an embarrassing lecture on 'knowing when to say no'.

'Sometimes,' he said, doing an expression I suspected he thought made him look wise and experienced, 'there are times when you're confronted with choices—temptations, even—and although everyone might be going along with them—'

'Dad, is this about drugs? Or drinking? Or shagging?'

'All of the above,' he said, sounding a lot more blunt than he had when he started.

'Fine,' I rolled my eyes. 'I'll just have marshmallows, Fruit Shoots and I won't undo a zip.'

Dad sighed. 'Christ, you can undo a zip and put your pyjamas on—'

'Who wears *pyjamas* in the woods?'

'And you can have more than a Fruit Shoot—I've bought you two large bottles of Pepsi Max Cherry, which are currently in the boot of the car with your overnight bag—'

'Oh, my god...'

'So I'd thank you not to get prematurely sarcastic with me for caring and trying to put you in the right frame of mind to make sensible decisions.'

'Fine,' I said, folding my arms.

'I'm pleased you understand,' Dad said, nodding, as if some agreement had been reached and this whole ridiculous discussion had been worth it.

I got out the car, barely grunting goodbye. I did feel myself soften when he handed me the bag of Pepsi, especially when I saw he'd included my favourite spicy Doritos.

'Have a good time. And … just … be careful, OK?'

I nodded and he gave me a half-smile as he drove away. I tried not to be too annoyed, but it did irritate me. This wasn't a movie, after all. It wasn't like we were about to go into the woods and never be seen again, like some *Blair Witch* remake. It would be fine. This was real life. Nothing bad was going to happen.

Chapter Eight

THE FATHER

Halloween

I was in a strange mood after dropping Hudson off at Kenny's house. I didn't like the idea of that house being the starting point before they drifted through his back gate into the woods like some group of vague adolescent ramblers, without me having checked the area where they'd be setting up camp first. It all felt a bit on-the-fly and badly thought-out. I worried I should have spoken to Kenny's parents before, to check they were aware of everything. What if there was a downpour, or a storm? I had images of them waking to flooded tents, perhaps even the drowned bodies of fellow classmates floating in the swell of water rising amidst the trees.

'What's wrong?' Mattias asked as I walked through the hallway into the kitchen. I'd barely even registered driving home, as I was so caught up in my catastrophising.

'Nothing,' I said, putting my keys down on the kitchen counter.

'There clearly is something. Is this about Hudson's woodland adventure?'

I let out a bitter laugh. 'You make it sound quite sweet and charming. Like the animals of bloody farthing wood or something.'

Mattias was in the process of sorting through some papers covered in sketches on the kitchen table but set them aside when he heard my tone. 'If I remember rightly,' he said, a smile playing around his lips, 'The Farthing Wood stories weren't always sweet and charming.'

I stood in silence for a bit, not focusing on him, just staring through the glass doors into the garden, as if I'd be able to see through the fences and gardens and streets of houses separating me and my son.

'Would it help if you told me what you're so worried about?' Mattias said, coming around the table over to me.

'I don't know. It's just a feeling. I get these feelings about Hud, sometimes. That something … I find it hard to explain … something terrible will happen to him and it will be all my fault.'

'Isn't that just called parenthood?'

I rubbed my eyes. 'I suppose.'

I was appreciative of Mattias's attempts to reassure me, but I couldn't help thinking that he didn't truly know what he was talking about. He'd never been a dad. And although he made valiant attempts to be a father-figure to Hudson, it couldn't really compare to the real stress of being an actual parent who'd been there from day one.

As if my thoughts on parenthood had been some kind of premonition, I felt my phone buzz in my hand. I hadn't even realised I was still holding it and when I turned the screen up I saw a WhatsApp message. It was from Adelaide, probably wanting to know if Hudson was ready to talk to her.

Can we FaceTime?

I sighed.

'What is it?' Mattias asked. 'Has Hudson forgotten something?'

I shook my head. 'I just need to make a call.' I skirted past him and went through the door into the side room that served as my study. I turned on the screen on my Mac, signed in and navigated to the FaceTime icon.

She answered on the third run of blip sounds.

'Wow, that was fast,' Adelaide said, coming into view, sitting down in a chair in front of the camera.

'Well, you wanted to talk,' I said, sounding sterner than I intended.

'Why are you annoyed with me?' she asked, a frown creasing her brow. Every time we spoke, which wasn't all that often, I couldn't help marvelling at how English she still sounded thanks to her Surrey boarding-school education followed by Oxford, even though she was technically American. Then again, so was Hudson, and he too sounded completely English thanks to his relocation at such a young age. And after four years in Northumbria, I'd definitely started to notice a subtle morphing of the 'well-spoken' southern accent he'd acquired growing up in Westminster's Eccleston Square into something of a hybrid, with the odd vowel taking on a northern slant.

'I'm not annoyed with you,' I told her, 'I just… I don't know, I'm in a strange mood. Hudson is at a sleepover and it's just made me a bit unsettled.'

'Right,' she said, still frowning. 'Surely Hudson having friends is … a good thing, right? You've always said you hoped he would have a group of friends, so what's the problem?'

'There isn't so much of a problem … just… What do you want?'

Still looking hurt, Adelaide leaned in a little and said 'Well, I thought that would be obvious. I wanted to talk about me chatting with Hudson a bit more regularly, like properly, rather than just Christmas and birthdays.'

I shrugged. 'He doesn't seem to be keen.'

'Well, I don't see why not.' Adelaide's voice started to rise, her hands flying in the air. 'I'm so much better than I was. I haven't used drugs or drunk anything in ages, absolutely ages. I attend my groups. I enjoy going to cookery classes. I'm even part of a fucking book club, for god's sake. I know I've had set-backs, but it's been years since the last one, literally years. I have a good life, a life I never thought I could have.'

'I know that,' I said, wondering if it was wise to have this conversation when I was already feeling tense.

'I just… I wish I could make you understand how sorry I am. About what happened with us. About how I was, how … how irresponsible I was. It could have been perfect. If I'd held it all together, it would have been perfect.'

'You don't know it would have been perfect. We weren't exactly set up to be the perfect family from the start. And I've said before—you had an illness. Addiction is an illness.'

'You don't need to tell me that,' Adelaide said. 'But … well, it's nice of you to say, and I know you're on my side, Rex. But I think you got pretty comfortable with viewing me as this … this … mad woman on the other side of the world, someone you don't really need to bother about because she failed at the first hurdle.'

'Oh, come on,' I said, feeling anger starting to take hold. 'You were given multiple chances. Even if you hadn't let him wander about the desert, or locked him in a cupboard—'

'It was a large walk-in wardrobe, Rex, as you well know, and as you said just seconds ago, I was unwell. I've never properly told you, have I? The … visions that I had, especially after the terrible night in the storm.'

'Let's not relive that night,' I interjected. The memory of it still haunted me.

'The hallucinations after that…' she carried on. 'What I saw when I looked at him, what I imagined doing, what I thought could happen. I locked him in that wardrobe for his own safety as well as my own.'

'You locked him in there because you knew I was going to take him away from you,' I said through clenched teeth and a rising temper. 'It was clear he wasn't safe with you anymore.' I was feeling tired and exhausted and wanted to end the discussion, wishing I'd never responded to her message. 'Hudson doesn't want to talk to you,' I said. 'I'm sorry, but there it is. I know that must be hard to hear, but it's the truth.'

'Hudson doesn't know what he wants,' she said, shaking her head. 'He's a teenager. They blow hot and cold every moment. If he only knew how great it is here, he could come and visit, find out what American life is like. Some kids would love to have a parent in the US with a large house and lots of land. Surely he'd like a break from England?'

I heard a crack and looked down. Without realising I'd picked up a biro from my desk and had broken its outer casing between my fingers.

'It's not on the cards,' I said. 'Definitely not just now. I'll talk to him again about having more regular video calls with you, OK? But it's difficult for him, you have to accept that. His memories of you are … well, I think they're muddled. Understandably so. I'll talk to him, but that's all I can offer. Definitely don't expect any visits to the States any time soon.'

She looked unhappy, but eventually nodded. 'OK. I hate this, you know.'

'Hate what?'

'Us. Fighting. We used to be… We used to be great. Such a team. Inseparable. Don't you miss that? Don't you miss how simple things were?'

I stared at her eyes. They were wide and full of pleading, desperate for me to share her nostalgia for the past. She was right, there had been something great about our friendship. But we'd messed all that up and we've been paying for the consequences ever since. If we hadn't slept together that one time, if she'd never become pregnant with Hudson, would her mental health have disintegrated in the same way? Or would we have carried on as we were, close friends who could've gone on to marry and have children with different people? But there was one thing I did know: if I had the chance to go back in time and erase everything, there's no way I'd take that chance. Because to do that, would erase the best thing in my life. Hudson was the most important person to me in the whole world. And I wanted to protect him from the darker aspects of life. If that meant keeping his mother at arm's length, then so be it.

'I've got to go,' I said, tossing the broken pen aside and reaching for the mouse.

'So soon?' Adelaide said, looking rejected.

'Yes, I'm afraid so. Got some more work to do.'

She nodded, sadly, then told me to give her love to Hudson. I told her I would, then I ended the call. I felt unsettled at the choice that lay before me. The choice of acting on Adelaide's wishes or respecting Hudson's need for distance. And, as I turned off the computer and sat in the darkness for a few minutes, I felt sad for the fact that my once best friend viewed me as her child's jailor, rather than his father.

Chapter Nine

THE BOY

Halloween

Pre-drinks at Kenny's were a disaster. By the end, I was so close to ditching my friends and heading home.

In hindsight, I would have given anything to have done this. Changed everything. Rewritten what was about to happen.

My bad mood started when Kenny gave me grief for not drinking. I hadn't originally planned to follow Dad's instructions to the letter, but Kenny had pissed me off when he and another boy, Mark, had started laughing when I told them I wanted to drink the Pepsi I'd brought with me. 'That's not going to give you a buzz, mate,' Mark said, trying to tip some of whatever he was drinking into my cup. I told him to fuck off and then Kenny got in between us acting like he was breaking up a fight, which then caused everyone to look our way. 'Calm it down, fellas, calm it down,' Kenny said.

'There's nothing to calm down about!' I shouted, proving him wrong in an instant.

I left the kitchen and went into the lounge. Kenny's house had always been always extremely tidy, decked out with impressive modern and high-tech stuff, including things you wouldn't expect to see in an old country house next to a huge forest (like the tanning bed in the corner of the huge living room). The TV was playing some low-budget horror film and I sat down to watch it for a while so I could calm down. I had an uncomfortable prickling sensation, like pins and needles, in my hands and on the back of my neck, which made me feel both stressed and restless, like I needed to go for a long run or climb a tree—do something satisfyingly active. But nothing of that sort was possible, so I stayed on the sofa, watching the screen as a good-looking guy, who looked like the stereotypical high-school jock, started to get it on with an attractive woman around the back of a cabin in the woods, unaware a creepy, heavy-breathing creature was watching him in the darkness. I watched as the jock started getting *very* friendly with the girl, pulling up her skirt, as if it was the simplest thing in the world. He seemed so confident in the whole concept of seduction I became hypnotised by it. Then I remembered that he was an actor in a scripted film and real life was far more difficult, a lot more awkward. I needed to stop comparing myself to others, I reminded myself.

'Hey,' a voice said from the doorway after I'd been sitting

alone for a minute or two. I looked over and saw Charlene. She walked in and giggled at nothing in particular then sat down next to me. 'So ... got a bit awkward in there between you and Kenny and Mark. Lads falling out?'

'No,' I said, abruptly.

She laid a hand on my leg. Her touch instantly felt hot, as if she'd just rested a red-hot poker up against the material of my jeans.

'I liked it,' she said, whispering slightly, then giggling again, too loud and too close, causing me to lean away from her. 'Kenny told me you've been moping after Kirsten.' She moved in so close, she was practically on top of me. 'You should know, she's got bigger fish to fry elsewhere. Whereas I'm less particular.' She moved her hand up my thigh so it was literally over my dick. I didn't know what to say, so I went for, 'Er, thanks but, can we… Can I move?…'

'You don't want to move *away* from me, do you, Hud?' she asked, moving closer to me still, so that with a quick lift of her legs she was actually sitting on top of me. 'Not when we're starting to get so close.'

At that moment I heard Kenny come into the hallway, calling my name. He thudded into the lounge and said 'Wow, Charlene, you don't wait about, do you?'

She laughed and I hadn't a clue how to respond. I just sat there, with a girl sitting on my lap, wishing I could vanish into the sofa.

'Stop terrorising the poor little lamb, Charlene,' Kenny said, apparently laughing at the intimidated expression on my face. I struggled not to snap at him as Charlene sighed and made a tutting noise as she pulled herself off me. As she shuffled off me, Kenny started laughing and pointing at my crotch. 'Wow, maybe I should have left her on you,' he said, winking.

'Fuck off, Kenny,' I said, getting up, trying to readjust myself so my hard-on wasn't so visible.

'Calm down, man, Charlene's only having a laugh, aren't you?'

'Many, many laughs,' Charlene said, giggling.

I walked out of the lounge, ignoring their calls for me to return.

In the downstairs bathroom, I shoved the lid of the toilet down and sat on it. I took out my phone and saw I had a notification from Dad.

> Call me in the morning if you need a lift or if you want me to come to Kenny's house early – we could go into town?

He didn't like the idea of me drifting round the woods and seemed keen to arrange a definite end to the gathering. Judging by how all of it was going so far, it seemed likely I'd be bailing on them all pretty early tomorrow. That's if I managed to last that long. I thought about how easy it would be to just message Dad back and say, *Yeah pick me up now*. He'd come and get me like a shot and I wouldn't have to put up with any more of Kenny's jibes, weirdness from Charlene and awkwardness with Kirsten. I suddenly felt a rush of embarrassment again, thinking of Charlene's hand snaking over my leg up to my thigh, how Kenny had laughed at us, laughed at *me*, pointing at *me*.

I started to feel something—something strong and red hot, starting in my right arm and rippling down my back. The feeling startled me, even though it was over as soon as it began, replaced with a vague familiar prickling feeling. It was as if I'd been scalded, or as though something sharp had been dragged along down my neck. Images flowed into my mind, but I was unable to pin them down. It was like I was seeing colours and shapes mixed into one, as if the colour red—red mingled with brown and grey—had been glued onto my eyes and the colour was just anger and pain and nothing else.

A hammering on the door. Real life was back.

'Hud, get the fuck out of there, come on!'

It was Kenny. And for a split moment, I saw that dark red colour again. I thought of Kirsten telling me to stand up to him. What would that look like? Me shouting back? Punching his lights out? Then I took another slow, steadying breath and told myself I wasn't like that. In spite of his faults, Kenny was my friend, I reminded myself. He'd looked out for me and I shouldn't get wound up because his jokes occasionally went a bit too far. So I opened the door and Kenny pulled me out into a half-hug, half slap on the back, telling me not to be a pissy little cunt but that he was sorry for being a prick. After his half-hearted attempt to diffuse the situation, he informed everyone that it was time.

'Time for what?' I asked, confused. I glanced at my phone screen, saw that it was nearly 9 p.m.

'What do you think?' He pointed down the hallway towards the kitchen where the doorway leading out to the garden could be seen. And beyond the garden, just visible, were the trees. 'It's time to go to the woods, my friend. I've got everything set up. Tents, stuff for our campfire, drinks. Everything we need.' He lowered his voice to give it a mock-spooky edge. 'It's time to journey into the darkness.'

Chapter Ten

THE BOY

Halloween

I started to calm down when we got to the woods. Something about the atmosphere, the feeling of doing something out of the ordinary, different from the usual Friday night, all of that—it made it into an event. And although the darkness and closed-in feel of the trees may have been scary for some, in some ways I found it comforting. Almost like I felt at home here, surrounded by nature. Being at the mercy of the natural world, I decided, was far better than being at the mercy of humans and the hurtful things they could say or do. Although it wouldn't take much to feel threatened by the natural world in a forest at night, or threatened by whatever could be hiding within the shelter of the trees. There was the constant snap of branches and sticks underfoot, the rustle of falling leaves, along with a constant sense of movement caused by other sounds, perhaps belonging to animals scurrying or digging or fleeing. Nothing was still. Everything around us felt active, awake and very much alive.

I was still pissed off with Kenny, but there were other people to talk to, including a fairly new boy at the school, Freddie, who also liked sci-fi things. More *Star Trek* than *Doctor Who*, but he was at least familiar with both and I rather enjoyed our conversation while at the same time aware it riled Kenny that I was ignoring him and talking to other people. I quite liked putting him in his place a bit. For too long Kenny had seemed to think he was my owner, my fixer, the one to steer me around our social circle like a manager or something, and it was really starting to fuck me off. He came over a few times, once with Kirsten, apparently trying to tempt me back over to him with her company. 'Hey, Hudson,' she said. Her eyes… Even in the darkness, they seemed to draw me to them, catching the flickering fire light, the glow accentuating the beautiful curve of her face. 'Hey,' I replied, but left it at that. I didn't want to try to make conversation with her with Kenny watching, so stayed sitting on the log by the flat circular area in the midst of the trees that had been chosen for our camp. It was something of a designated, separated-out area, though more for picnickers than for campers, with some wooden benches with tables dotted about. After a while sitting about and chatting, we set up our tents and sleeping bags. Kenny and Alex had lit the fire in the centre using a portable BBQ and some dry wood. I thought it looked pretty dangerous and part of me thought about saying something, but didn't want to be the one to get tetchy about stuff. I didn't want to give Kenny another excuse to make me the focus of his mockery.

There was another reason I was keen to avoid making a scene. Even though I spent a lot of time thinking I was imagining it, I was becoming convinced Kirsten was flirting with me with her eye contact. She kept looking over to me and slightly smiling, seeking out my gaze, then looking away, as if embarrassed. Each time it happened, I felt my stomach lurch, and although she hadn't tried to make much conversation when Kenny had brought her over, I still got the feeling she wanted to get my attention.

Perhaps she wanted me to go over to her.

Perhaps *I* was supposed to take the lead. Had I offended her when I'd just said 'Hey'? Was I being weak? Overly sensitive? Was Kenny right, that I just needed to toughen up and be bolder about what I wanted? Kenny was certainly much better at this sort of thing, something that was clear to see when he came over and told me the tents had been divided up between the seven of us and how he had decided I was to share with him and Charlene.

'What … you and her … together?' I asked.

He winked, then laughed, 'I'm not asking you for a fucking threesome, you idiot. That's just where we'll be sleeping.'

'I… I'd prefer my own tent. You said you had enough.'

'Not enough for *one each*, you twat. Unless your dad packed you one together with your cherry Pepsi.'

'But I thought… Then maybe it could just be…'

I was going to say 'just you and me', or even offer to

share with just Freddie, who had shuffled off to go for a piss in the darkness (probably to avoid talking to Kenny, whom he'd made clear he didn't like). But then I looked at Charlene, her arm slung over Kenny's back, and although I was still embarrassed by what happened earlier, I didn't want to sound nasty or as if I was casting her out into the night to sleep alone by the camp fire. In the end I shrugged and said, 'Fine.' Then I got up and walked away, just to put an end to the discussion. There was something about the way Kenny and Charlene were looking at each other, as if they were in on some kind of joke or secretly making fun of me.

I felt a pang of that deep, intense anger again, just as I had in the house before we came to the woods. Knowing I needed some time alone, I stood up and headed into the woods, moving quickly, as if trying to get away from my own feelings.

Away from the camp, I sat down by the twisted trunk of a very large tree and fought the urge to scream. I wanted to punch the ground, to crawl through the leaves and hide. It was like my senses had gone into overdrive.

I should never have come here.

I shouldn't be here.

I should never have come here.

I shouldn't be here.

These thoughts repeated over and over in my head like a mantra or a chant, one that was broadcasting into my head, like a stream of a radio station that was impossible to turn off.

I considered calling my dad. But part of me wanted to prove to him that I did have a life. I should be free to make my own choices. Free to fuck up. Make mistakes.

I let some time pass, then eventually wandered back to where the tents were set up to find the group smoking joints by the fire. Someone had started the music on a Bluetooth speaker nestled on a blanket on the ground. The beat coming from it seemed to echo within me, like it was forcing my heartbeat to go quicker, pound louder.

'Where have you been?' Kenny asked, loping over to me. 'We've been waiting. I've got a gift for you.'

Chapter Eleven

THE BOY

Halloween

Kenny led me over to the tent that had apparently been destined for us that night. He pointed towards the opening.

'In there is a very special opportunity, my friend,' he said, in an overly serious tone. 'You can think of this tent as a transformation device. A boy will step in. A man will step out.'

My look of confusion caused an eye-roll. 'Come on, Hud, do I have to spell it out?' He stepped closer and lowered his voice, 'Kirsten is inside and she wants *you*.'

'Oh, fuck off, Kenny,' I said, about to walk away.

'No, no, serious, mate, serious.' His eyes were wide, his head nodding. 'I promise you, mate, this is for real. It's your *time*, man. *Your* fucking time.'

This almost felt too much. After my surge of anger moments earlier, I struggled to get a handle on the situation.

'She wants you, but doesn't want everyone else to think she's easy,' Kenny said, coming close to me so that I could smell the alcohol on his breath. 'So come on, man. Are you going to step up, or chicken out?'

I thought about the choice that lay before me. I'd be lying to say that my interest hadn't been grabbed. Grabbed by the throat. He definitely had my attention. And in my head, I heard those words from the week before, echoing around: *Pathetic lonely virgin. Little lost lamb.*

'Listen, mate, it's this simple: you go in; you get the job done; you come out and that's it. Virginity lost. Kirsten's happy. You're happy.'

I frowned at him. 'Why doesn't she want anyone to know? Am I that … embarrassing or something?'

Kenny laid a hand on my shoulder. 'It is not for us to untangle the whims of the female sex,' he said, putting on a posh, mock-Shakespearean voice. In his normal accent, he added, 'Mate, it's a shag. It's not rocket science.' He then produced a square piece of foil as if from nowhere. It was a condom.

'Here you go. Know how to put it on?'

I snatched it off him, 'Course I fucking know how to put it—'

'Joking. Just joking,' he said, holding his hands up. 'Right, get on with it.' He nodded at the tent.

I took a deep breath, tugged off my coat and set it down outside the door of the tent. Then I unzipped the entrance and went in. It was almost entirely dark inside. I could barely see anything.

'Kirsten?' I said into the darkness. Hands came up to meet me. Started to grasp at my T-shirt. Pulling it off over my head. I could smell her perfume, that slightly spicy, slightly floral scent that made me think of summer days. Hands were at my belt and zip and I helped her to tug off my jeans and crawled out of them.

A whisper then said, 'Lie down'. The hushed nature of her voice in the darkness, the light Irish edge to the words, all of it turned me on. I could barely believe it was happening.

There were picnic blankets and sleeping bags lining the floor of the tent, but I could still feel the knobbly terrain of the woodland floor underneath my back as I lay down. I felt her hands tug my boxers down and then without warning a rush of pleasure enveloped me and I let out a gasp.

'How's it going in there?' I heard a voice right next to me, on the other side of the material of the tent. Unmistakably Kenny.

'It's… It's going good,' I said, feeling my pulse starting to quicken, my whole body tingling as dimly in the darkness I saw a shape bobbing up and down. I rested my hands behind my head—I'd seen guys in movies doing that—and it made me feel like a real adult. Like a man. I was strong. Powerful. Capable. The opposite of a pathetic virgin. Nothing about me was pathetic. Not anymore.

'Close to finishing yet?' Kenny asked, laughing.

'Just fuck off for a sec, Kenny, will you!'

Another laugh. 'I'm sure you're doing good work to my boy, there, Kirsten, but just remember: he's not lost his virginity unless it's … y'know … full-on fucking.'

I heard a laugh and she paused what she was doing. I was tempted to say 'Carry on,' happy with just this, anything to make that amazing feeling continue. But I also knew what Kenny meant: if I'd come this far, I might as well go the whole way. I panicked for a second, realising I'd put the condom down somewhere, but then heard the crinkle of foil and felt something sliding over my dick.

'From behind,' she whispered, so quiet I barely heard her and was worried I'd misheard.

'You sure?' I said, feeling like this was too much of a step into 'adult' territory, especially for my first time doing anything like this.

'Yes,' she said, and I felt her turn and press herself up against me. I knelt behind her and I felt a hand arrive to help guide me in. My body began to take over, the rhythm of my movements determined by an urge more animal than rational, a need to keep going, feeling an end coming in sight. It might be bad to say it, but it was all about me in that moment. I barely had a thought for her or what she might be feeling; there was no room in my head for anything else apart from the mad rush of it all and feeling myself speeding towards an end goal, like an arrow aimed at a dartboard, until with a loud moan and a gasp, I arrived, the orgasm rushing through me like a thunderclap, like a million stars. I bucked forwards, desperate to feel every last moment of it, and even though I couldn't see it, I imagined Kirsten's face smiling with pleasure at what I'd just done. Impressed with me. Maybe even in love with me as a result.

'That sounded epic, mate,' came Kenny's voice through the material.

'Yeah,' I said, panting. 'Yeah, it was.' I let out a laugh at the insanity of it all. The anger and fury and sense of regret I'd felt earlier was a million miles away. I was euphoric. I could do anything. I was someone bold, someone important, someone to be reckoned with.

'I'll be over by the fire when you're finished. Going to chat to Kirsten for a bit.' He laughed again, but this time it was a strange laugh. Like he'd been holding back all this time and was able to now say the punch line to a joke. What did he mean, over by the fire with Kirsten? Kirsten was here, in the tent, with me?

'What did you say?' I called out, but I'd heard footsteps walk around the tent and off into the distance.

'Kirsten?' I said, uncertainly into the darkness. Nobody spoke, but I heard another laugh. And like Kenny's, it had a strange quality to it, like there was some joke I wasn't quite getting.

I fumbled the front of the tent and opened it up and looked out. My brain struggled to comprehend what it was seeing. There was Kenny, a little way away, sat around the fire with the others. He clocked me immediately. His arm was slung around a girl. Kirsten. She was there, with him. And then he winked at me.

Chapter Twelve

THE BOY

Halloween

'What the fuck?' I said, and jumped out of the tent as if I'd been stung.

If Kirsten was over by the fire with Kenny, who had I just been with? Who had I just lost my virginity to? I felt a burning sense of panic rush across me, as I faced back towards the tent to see Charlene coming out of it. She was pulling on her dress and laughing. I heard Kenny behind me laughing, too, getting closer. 'Fucking classic, mate. Fooled you there.'

'What? You? Why…?' I looked from Kenny to Kirsten. Kenny's smug, gleeful face visible in the flickering firelight and I felt a stab of something through the shock of it all. Hatred. White hot hatred.

'Did you like the little performance, Hudson?' Charlene

said. 'I wasn't sure I got the *Oi-rish* accent right but I tried my best.'

'What's … going on?' Kirsten asked, walking towards me. 'Hudson, where are your clothes?' She looked puzzled.

'Did you know they were doing this?' I yelled at her. I saw more faces turn towards me. Some people were laughing and pointing, but I didn't care. I needed answers. To get this nightmare clear in my head.

'Mate, you just needed to lose it, and Charlene was up for it. So we had a bet going that you'd do it if you thought it was Kirsten you'd be shagging. And I was right.' He slapped me on the shoulder. 'Now, get your clothes on before you catch a fucking cold or something and blame that on me, too.'

I heard Charlene laugh in response, and it was this that made me flip.

'You're both … both fucking *cunts*…' I said. I'd never used that word as a proper insult before and it felt weighty, ugly in my mouth, but I didn't care.

'Hey, hey, calm down mate,' Kenny said. 'Just get dressed and come over to the fire. We'll have a laugh about it.' He tapped me again on the shoulder.

'If you touch me one more fucking time…' I said through clenched teeth. Something was happening to me. A rushing across my skin, all around, onwards and unstoppable, not unlike the mounting orgasm I'd felt moments before, but this time a thousand times more powerful.

A thousand times more terrifying.

I felt as though I was going to break in two, like I was a

searing source of heat, like I had the power of a lightning strike within me.

'What's going on?' I heard another voice ask, and Freddie came into view. 'Why are you naked? Is this like an orgy or something? Are we doing a Halloween ritual?' He laughed but nobody else did. I wasn't even capable of talking anymore. Something was happening to me. Something painful. Terrible. Beyond words.

I bolted away from them all, away from the camp, the tent, needing to be away from everyone. I ran into the forest, welcoming the darkness, hoping it would swallow me whole so I would never have to face them all again.

But they followed. I heard Kenny first, shouting, 'Fucking hell, Hudson, just chill a bit, OK?'

Then Charlene called out, 'Hud, it was *joke,* honestly. I'm sorry if I was that bad a shag that you have to act all ... well ... all fucking weird like this.'

I collided with a tree.

The pain of it knocked me off balance and I felt myself twitch and convulse on the floor, unable to speak. Had I damaged myself seriously? Fatally? The pain felt like it, but mingled with the pain remained that overwhelming sense of panic and anger. It was the strongest, truest thing I had ever felt—like a physical force, consuming me completely.

'Hudson!' A voice called, but in my terrible state I couldn't tell if it was male or female. It was certainly getting closer and I heard it again as I struggled to pull myself up.

Something was wrong; something was very wrong. I wondered if I was going to vomit, and I felt myself retch, but nothing came out. My vision was distorted, but also widening, and I couldn't work out which way was up and which was down. I felt as if I was being both crushed and falling through space, all at the same time.

Then I heard the scream. High pitched. Desperate. The sound of someone scared out of their mind. I felt danger, imminent danger; a new layer over the burning fury that I couldn't escape from.

I ran towards the figure closest to me.

I got there quickly.

There was blood. A lot of it.

I don't remember everything that happened next.

Or perhaps I just don't want to.

Chapter Thirteen

THE BOY

Halloween

Searing pain. Heat. Writhing on the ground.

People were shouting. Kenny and Charlene. They were getting closer.

'Hudson!'

It was my name. I knew it. But at the same time, it was as if I didn't know it. As if it was someone else's name—no, not a name at all—a word. A word used by strangers to describe a stranger.

I felt a breaking, a snapping, tearing. I wanted to cry out in pain, but as my sense of sound started to break down, my ability to shout went, too. Any attempt at noise came out as a rasping, scratching, clicking sound and then not at all.

I was amidst the leaves, every breath I drew in brought in dust, bits of bark, flakes of it, a dry organic mixture that coated me, inside and out as I moved, bits of me jutting out, parts that didn't seem to belong to my body.

And then blackness.

Something in the blackness.

Close. Someone was close. I could feel them, hear them, no, not hear, sense them, their movement, vibrations, keep away, I needed to scare it off, get away, get away.

Attack.

Lashing out, teeth, strong teeth, stronger than anything, sharper than anything, blood.

Taste.

See. Wide, expansive, everywhere. The forest. The whole forest around me. Darkness but glowing, sparkling, alive. Alive for me. Ready for me. My home.

Hunger.

The blood. The screams. Shouts sending ripples. Vibrations.

Feed.

I liked it. Tasting my prey. Needing it. Hunger. Deep hunger.

Run.

I bundled her up. I knew how. Coming out. So much of it. White, silvery, sticking, wrapping.

Run. Now.

I ran. Took my prey with me. Dragging. Carrying.

Shelter. Needed shelter. Place to rest. Place to build. Place to feed.

I dragged the body through the darkness. Held it in my legs. Kept it close. Leaves. Blood. Screams.

It's screaming it's screaming it's waking wrap it tight wrap it tight bind it tight. It mustn't escape mustn't escape.

Must bind it.

Wrap it.

Bind it tight.

Part of my mind could make out the shouts. The shrieks in the night. Getting nearer. But my thoughts were far from clear. There was a quaking in that side of me, an energy pushing me on. Pushing me to do terrible things. Things that would otherwise sicken me.

It's moving it's moving mustn't escape it mustn't escape

Tie it up.

Tie it up.

Bite it.

Bite.

Bite.

'Charlene? Are you OK?'

I registered the shout without knowing what it meant. It was like I both heard it and felt it, like the sounds were vibrations I could pick up on, decode, without having to hear the words. I couldn't think about things clearly, even though I was trying. Try to hold on to the thoughts I know belong to me, to the proper me, the part of me who knows what I'm doing is…

Feed

Feed

Feed

Feed

Chapter Fourteen

THE BOY

Halloween

I woke up to pain. I was on the forest floor. I could feel something digging into me. Lots of things, things everywhere, harsh and sharp. And such cold. Terrible coldness, like I'd never know warmth again, never know the heat of the sun or the comfort of a fire. It was as if the core of my body had turned to a pillar of ice and the rest of me couldn't escape it.

I looked down. I could see what was digging into me. Twigs. Loads of them, digging into my skin. So much skin. Too much skin. Where were my clothes? I panicked, horrified to find I was completely naked, lying outdoors. I scrambled to my feet, although this wasn't as easy as it should have been. In the darkness, I flailed out and clung on to the side of a tree as I began to teeter forward, slowly and cautiously, towards something. A light. Yes, there was a light. I could see it in the distance. How was it in the distance? How had I drifted so far from … from what? I couldn't think. Couldn't think why I was here. Then I remembered: the camping trip, the forest, this was the forest and I was supposed to be in a tent.

A tent.

The tent.

Things started coming back to me. Kenny. Charlene. The trick they'd played. Kirsten.

What had happened after that? How long had I been out here? It was still dark—very dark, with no sign of dawn.

I forced myself to try to piece together what had happened. I'd got … angry. Rage. That's what had happened. Rage happened.

I found I couldn't think about that. Trying made my head hurt—hurt a lot—and I needed to focus, decide what to do. I needed to find my clothes, find my phone, get Dad to take me home. I couldn't stay here.

I walked carefully through the trees, the forest floor prickling the soles of my feet as I went. The fire was burning very low, so the light it was throwing over the clearing had almost reduced to nothing, but I could just about make out three sleeping bags with people inside. People had dragged them out to huddle around the fire and had fallen asleep. I went to the nearest tent. It wasn't done up and two sleeping people were inside—a boy and a girl. Kirsten. She was in there, intertwined with Freddie. I felt a stab of something. Sadness, perhaps? Anger? But I couldn't deal with that. I had to focus. I had enough worries of my own without letting my jealousy take over.

Then I noticed Kenny's tent. The one he and I should have been sharing. I heard the laughter. Not happening around me at that moment. It was in my head, but I could hear it as if someone was pressing the sound into my ears, as if a chorus of people were laughing and pointing. The prank they played, Kenny and Charlene, and the anger.

The huge, searing, scorching, *anger*.

I reached forward and undid the tent zipper. I thought I heard something as I did this—a gasp, maybe even a sob.

What was going on?

As I drew the zip across and round to open up the flap, I had a sudden feeling—foreboding, I think it's called. A feeling that I was about to step into a situation that was going to make this night weirder than it was already.

He was in the corner, swaying and shaking. Even in the darkness, I could see how he jerked and backed away as I looked in.

'Kenny?' I whispered. 'What's... What's going on?'

'Come ... come inside and close the zipper. Quickly,' he whispered back, his voice shaking and chattering.

I did as he said and crawled on my knees over to him. I felt my joins protest, an aching, straining pain, as if I had been stretched and bent out of shape. The surface of the ground beneath me changed to something soft, and with relief I realised I was kneeling on my clothes.

'What's wrong?' I asked as I tried, with difficulty, to pull on my jeans.

'I ... ran ... away.' He half-whispered, half-sobbed these words, as if saying them involved him confronting a truth he'd rather not know.

'Ran away from what?'

'Charlene. She ... fuck... I think she might be dead.'

Chills rushed down my back. 'What do you mean, *dead*? Why... Why would you think that? How could she be dead?'

'I ... saw ... an animal...' He pressed his hands into his face, as though trying to block out an image, an image that was causing absolute fear.

'What animal?' I whispered.

Eventually Kenny answered.

'A spider. I think... I know it sounds fucking insane, but I think Charlene's been killed by a massive fucking spider.'

Chapter Fifteen

THE BOY

Halloween

As soon as Kenny had said this, I heard noise from outside. The tent had been unzipped and someone looked inside. Kenny jumped and gasped, backing away.

'What's going on?' It was Kirsten's voice.

'Get inside,' Kenny hissed, 'It'll get you.'

'What will get me?' Kirsten asked, not obeying him, 'Kenny, why are you hiding in here? We've been looking for you. We thought you and Charlene had vanished into the night.'

Neither me nor Kenny said anything in relation to this.

'And where did you go after your strop?' Kirsten asked pointedly, looking at me. Her voice was stern and even in the strange circumstances, the word 'strop' stung. Like I was an unruly child.

'I … was cross. I needed space so I went for a walk,' I said.

'Naked in the woods at night? You've been gone ages,' Kirsten said, sounding disbelieving. 'Come on, what the fuck's going on? This is all very strange.'

'Did you see her?' Kenny asked in a weak first.

'See who?'

'Charlene. Out there,' Kenny said.

'No, I don't know where she is, I thought she'd be with you or Hudson. I decided to get off with Freddie.' She sniffed a little as she said this, as if she knew the magnitude of what she was telling me.

'You … and Freddie?' I stammered.

She shrugged. 'Why not? I figured if you and Charlene were getting it on, why shouldn't I have a bit of action.' She was talking fast now, her words tumbling over each other, as if she was in danger of crying.

'Where's everyone else?' Kenny whispered. 'They shouldn't be out there.'

'What are you talking about? They're all asleep after all that weed and vodka. And Alex was… He was with us.'

I blinked at her. 'Alex was … with you and Freddie…'

'Not in any participatory sense,' Kirsten said curtly with another sniff.

'Kirsten, please, I'm begging you, come inside and close the flap,' Kenny said, the distress rising in his voice again.

'Tell me what's going on,' she snapped, her voice loud and more annoyed than I'd ever heard her.

'She's dead,' Kenny said, very quietly.

'She's … what?' Kirsten asked, pulling herself into the tent properly and crawling over towards Kenny, as though sure she must have misheard.

'She's dead,' he repeated, 'I … saw her. It was … a creature.'

Kirsten just looked at him. Then she reached out and touched his forehead.

'What are you doing?' I asked.

'Seeing if he has a temperature. It's too dark to see his eyes, but I presume he's been smoking weed or taken something else.'

'I'm not fucking stoned,' he said, sounding more defensive. 'Charlene is out there. I went looking, and saw her… She's in the abandoned cottage, just along from the stream. She's… She's hanging in a web.'

Hearing the word 'web' caused a prickle to run from along the top of my skull, down my neck along my spine, like a current passing through me. Then images came to me. They were stretched. Distorted. Fuzzy and clear at the same time, as though I was tuning in and out of a picture on an old-fashioned TV.

'Hudson, what's he talking about?' Kirsten asked.

'How should I know?' I replied, sounding instantly defensive. Suspiciously defensive, I thought, as soon as the words were out of my mouth.

'Well, I'm going to look for her,' she said, moving towards the tent flap.

'No!' Kenny hissed.

'Yes, I am,' she said, sounding determined. 'This is

ridiculous. You're off your head on something and have convinced yourself you've seen something. Charlene could be out there injured or choking on her own vomit or something, and I'm not going to sit here in a tent and just hope for the best. Come on, Hudson.' She grabbed my shoulder.

'I… What?'

'Come with me,' she said, then softened her voice a little. 'Please, Hudson. Just… Just come with me.'

I stared back at her. Managing to just about make out her eyes. Pleading flecks of light in the near-total darkness.

I didn't want to go. Didn't want to see what might have happened out there. But I found I couldn't say no to her.

'OK,' I said. 'Let's go.'

Chapter Sixteen

THE BOY

Halloween

We walked out into the darkness. I could tell Kirsten was nervous as she held out her phone, using the torch to light a path away from the campsite and into the surrounding trees.

'This was the direction Kenny and Charlene went,' Kirsten said. I'd already worked that out since it was the direction I had gone in, and since they had been trying to follow me it was likely we'd end up retracing my steps. Kirsten seemed to be thinking along the same lines as I saw her glance my way before saying 'So where did you go?'

'What?' I said, playing for time. My pulse had started to increase and it was getting to a point where I worried Kirsten would be able to hear it.

'Where did you go, Hudson?' There was an edge to her

voice now. Impatience, perhaps. 'Where did you go after you slept with Charlene?'

'I didn't shag Charlene!' I yelled. 'Kirsten ... I don't think we should be out here. Kenny's right, we should go back.'

'Oh, so I imagined it, did I?' she said, 'You coming out of the tent stark fucking naked—a tent with Charlene in it. So you were, what, having a cosy chat about *Doctor Who* or something?'

I wasn't sure what affected me more: the fact that Kirsten had remembered I liked *Doctor Who*, or the fact she was now using it to make a dig at me.

'I did have sex with her, but...'

'But what? And why were you having a go at Kenny?'

'Because I thought it was you!' I shouted.

She froze. 'What?'

A bird made a loud squawking sound near us, followed by a flapping rush nearby. The sort of sound that moments later would have probably made us both jump. But in that moment, we were both entirely still, staring at each other, half of Kirsten's face in shadow, the other half illuminated bright white by the harsh light of her torch.

'I thought... I thought it was you I was having sex with.'

A couple of seconds of silence passed. It felt like an age. And for a brief period, the tension between us dissolved all my feelings of panic and disorientation and worry about what we might find in the forest, what had happened to me, what I may have done. It was just me and her, locked in that moment. Then at last she said, 'Right... I'm not sure if I should be flattered or offended.'

I let out my breath. 'It was dark and she ... well, she put on your accent. And she was wearing your perfume. I'm not sure if she borrowed it off you or bought some deliberately for the trick.'

'The trick?'

'Yeah,' I said, 'She and Kenny... They were both in on it. Thought it was a laugh to make me think ... well, think it was you.'

She was silent again for a few moments, then said 'Christ, Hudson. That's a really nasty thing for them to do.'

She took a step towards me. Put a hand on my arm.

'Was it ... um... Was it your first time?'

I found I couldn't look at her then. I let me eyes fall to the forest floor. And nodded.

'God. That's fucked up. Are you OK?'

I stayed looking at the floor. Then something occurred to me and I asked it before I lost my nerve. 'You and Freddie, tonight ... was that yours? I mean was that your ... first time?'

Another lifetime of silence. Then she said 'Well, we didn't fully... It was just a... Oh, god, this is all a bit of a mess, isn't it?'

I looked up at her then. Felt a wave of sadness pass between us. How things could have been. How it could have happened differently for both of us.

'Kirsten,' I said, taking a step towards her.

'Hudson,' she said, watching me.

Her face was near mine. For a moment, I thought we were going to kiss, like a boy and a girl would do in the movies—a boy and a girl who realise they both love each other and have done for so long that fate had finally brought them together.

But then all that was ruined. Because she screamed.

'Fuck!'

I snapped around but couldn't see anything as her torch was jerking around. 'What?'

'What is… Oh, my god…' Kirsten steadied the light and I was able to see what had upset her.

Webs. Thick. Hanging. Silvery-white, swaying in the low branches of the tree behind me. And inside the lower folds I could see something. Residue of something dark. Something that looked like…

'Oh, fuck, is that … *blood*?' Kirsten moved closer, holding the torch near to it. 'And … there's… Christ, I think that's hair. It's long…'

She swung the torch across the forest floor. More flecks of blood became visible on the leaves. And a long mark on the ground that seemed to go off into the trees and beyond. 'It's like something's been dragged…' Kirsten said.

'Kirsten … I really think we should go back…'

She didn't listen. Just started to follow the trail, calling out Charlene's name as she went, her voice shaky but determined. I followed behind her, feeling an overwhelming, mounting feeling of dread.

'Hudson,' she said, coming to a stop, 'I think… I think she's in the cottage.'

'What?' I said, though I knew exactly what she meant. It was as if the further I walked through the heart of the woods, the more the pieces slotted into place. Fragments starting to make up a whole picture. A picture that terrified me.

'The abandoned cottage… It's here… The trail leads inside.' She started to walk slowly forwards. 'Look,' she said. 'Oh, my god, no… Oh, my god, what's… What the fuck's going on?'

The shaking, juddering beam of her torch showed us a sight beyond anything I could have imagined.

Charlene. Her body partially covered, silver strands covering her, as though she'd been spun round and round. The thin webbing held her up, suspending her high off the ground as though she was in a cocoon. A cocoon with dark red stains visible, soaking through from within. Despite the matted strands of hair stuck to her face, I could tell it was her. Eyes open. Covered in blood. Lifeless.

'Oh, god, oh, god,' Kirsten said, 'Hudson, oh, fuck… I'm going to be…'

She dodged to my left and held onto the broken part of the cottage wall as she vomited noisily. I heard her gagging and the sound took me away from the present, a sound I'd heard before in the form of strange vibrations. The sound of something splashing onto the ground. The terrible choking sounds. The flailing, scratching, attempts to break free.

Kirsten had straightened up, and wiped her mouth, her hands shaking more than ever, trying to hold her phone. 'Fuck, I have no signal. We need to phone … someone. Fuck, Hudson, can you…'

'My phone's in the tent… I think it's dead,' I muttered, unable to say much more.

'Maybe there's a chance… Do you think she's still alive?'

I shook my head. By the way Kirsten said it, I didn't think she believed there was a chance, either, but she still went over to the body and put out a hand, stretching up on her toes to try and reach Charlene's neck. I knew she was searching for a pulse, but Charlene's wrists were too tightly bound in the webbing to be accessible without cutting through the spun silk. I watched as Kirsten's hands and sleeves started to become soaked with blood and decided I should step in. 'Kirsten, don't touch… Come away…'

'Why? Do you think there's a spider, too? This is obviously the sick work of some … some… I don't know … serial killer. This is his staging, yes, that's what they call it. I've seen it in … in crime series… I… Fuck, Hudson, help me get her down.' She was sounding urgent and breathless.

'We shouldn't touch anything,' I said again. 'Kirsten, come on.' I went to pull her back, but she pushed me aside, causing me to stumble and fall.

'Oh, god, sorry, I'm so sorry, Hudson,' she cried as she put a hand out to help me up. I noticed then some of the blood was on her hands and quickly transferred onto mine.

'Can't we just get out of here?' I said, getting to my feet, though feeling so faint and shaky I thought there was a danger of me falling again. 'I don't think I can stay here any longer.'

I heard the tremors in Kirsten's breath as she drew it in. 'OK,' she said, 'OK, here's what we do. We go back and get your phone. If it doesn't work—fuck, even if it does work—we wake everyone up and get them out of the forest and back to Kenny's house. Then we'll phone the police. OK?'

I continued to stare at Charlene's lifeless corpse and the tight webbing that had sealed her fate. Then I nodded.

Chapter Seventeen

THE FATHER

Early hours of 1 November 2024

Hudson's call came at 4 a.m. My phone buzzed on the bedside cabinet drawing me out of a dreamless sleep.

'Hello,' I said, picking up, feeling Mattias stirring next to me. 'Hud? What's wrong?'

'Dad, you need to come,' Hudson said at the other end. I could hear his distress. The tension in his voice. I was instantly awake, pulling myself out of bed.

'What's going on?' Mattias murmured.

'Where?' I asked Hudson, my voice harsh, blunt, desperate for information.

'Kenny's house. Come now, please. The police and ambulance are coming. I was going to ask you, but then thought I should phone them first. I thought that… I thought I should.'

The words chilled me. 'What? Why are the police needed? What's happened? Are you OK?'

'It's not me. I'm... I'm fine. Just come, please.' He ended the call abruptly before I could ask anything else.

'Fuck,' I muttered tugging on yesterday's jeans and T-shirt.

'Is Hudson OK?' Mattias asked, 'Do you want me to come?'

'No, stay here,' I said, making sure I had my wallet and phone. 'I'll call you when I know more.'

The police and an ambulance were already at Kenny's house when I arrived. I was feeling so wired, it was hard to believe I'd been asleep less than half an hour ago.

The front door was open and people were walking in and out—paramedics and police. I saw another van draw up, with the words Forensic Services on the side.

Part of me was expecting something terrible to greet me as I walked into the property, but there was nothing. Just an ordinary hallway.

'Excuse me, sir, can I help you?' A uniformed police officer stopped me, putting out her hand, not touching me, but making it clear I wasn't to go any further into the house.

'My son is here; he just called me,' I said, aware how breathless I sounded. Keep calm, I told myself. These people must deal with worried parents all the time. It's going to be OK.

'Are you the owner of the house?'

I shook my head. 'My son's friend lives here. They were out in the woods…'

'What's your boy's name?'

'Hudson. Hudson Toussaint-Ray.'

She led me through the corridor into the living-room area. A group of about ten teenagers, a roughly equal number of boys and girls, were in the room. It was a sizeable area, but I saw some dining-table chairs had been brought in to accommodate them all. I scanned the faces, desperately trying to find Hudson. At last my eyes, settled on him.

'Hud, I'm here,' I said, walking over and crouching down.

'Dad,' he said. 'I … I don't think I'm allowed to leave.' He looked around. Two police officers were talking to each other at the doorway.

'Tell me what happened.'

Hudson looked around at the others, some of them seemed to be watching us; others were staring off into space. Possibly drunk or on something. I realised then that Kenny was next to Hudson on the sofa, but had his head in his hands and didn't seem aware of my presence.

'Not here.' Hudson stood up.

We told the officers at the doorway he was going to be sick and needed the bathroom. They didn't seem to mind him going, nor me going with him. Once we got into the downstairs bathroom, I told Hudson to sit down on the loo seat. He looked grey and nauseous and I turned around to the neatly ordered sink area. There was a glass on a shelf that held an unlit candle. I took the class and filled it with water and told Hudson to take small sips.

'Now, please, Hud, tell me what's going on.'

He swallowed his water then looked up at me.

'Dad … it's … really bad.'

My imagination was in overdrive. What could be so bad that could warrant all these police? A forensic team?

'What happened? Why are the police here?'

'They're trying to reach Kenny's parents… They're in Scotland…' Hudson's words had a vague, slightly dreamlike quality to them, as if he was dazed. Or on drugs.

'Have you taken something?' I asked, unable to hide the accusatory tone creeping into my voice.

Hudson's eyes looked straight into mine for a moment. 'What? No. Nothing. I mean, I had a beer, but I wasn't drunk. And I'm not drunk now.'

'You sure? You haven't smoked anything? Nothing like … pills or anything.'

He shook his head.

'Fine. Just tell me everything.'

Hudson took a deep breath and just said 'I don't know everything. I just … found the body.'

I went cold all over. 'Whose body?' I asked.

But before he could answer someone started knocking on the bathroom door.

'Is everything OK in there?' a woman's voice said.

I looked at Hudson. He looked back at me, his eyes wide and searching. He needed me to take control, to be the adult, to save him from whatever was happening, even though I was still infuriatingly in the dark about what was actually going on.

'Yes, fine,' I answered. 'We'll be out in a minute.'

The woman on the other side of the door didn't say anything again, but I felt like our place of privacy had been rendered more or less useless. I reached behind Hudson and pulled the chain, even though the loo seat had remained closed. I was worried how pale he still looked, though, as he stood up, a little shakily.

'I'll tell them you need to go home and get some rest. No matter what happened, it can wait.'

I opened the door and found a woman standing on the other side. She was quite short, probably around forty, with brown hair and piercing blue-eyes. 'I'm afraid it won't wait until morning, I'm sorry to say,' she said. She looked round me. 'I understand you're Hudson? You found the body?'

I looked round at Hudson and he nodded. 'Kirsten and I did, when went to look for her.'

She nodded. 'OK. Well, I'm DS Ruth Scott. We're going to be taking statements from everyone, although from the state of your friends we might need to wait until everyone has sobered up. Tell me, Hudson, have you taken anything tonight? Drunk much alcohol?'

He shook his head. 'One beer. That's it. And that was … I don't know, but must be hours ago.'

'Drugs? My officers have already made a few discoveries around the campsite, so it would be good to be honest right now.'

Her voice was surprisingly kind, gentle almost, with a

soft Scottish accent. I wondered if she was a mother. I wondered if she could understand the stresses of this situation.

'I promise I haven't taken any drugs, ever.'

She looked at him for a few seconds more, then nodded and said, 'OK, let's have a chat then.' She looked up at me. 'You're the first of the parents to arrive, so it would be good to get started, while things are fresh in Hudson's memory. Let's go to the dining room.'

'I'd like to take my son home to get some rest,' I said, putting a hand out to stop Hudson from following. 'Can't we do this later?'

'No, I'm sorry,' she said with a shake of her head. 'Come with me, please.' She led us through towards the dining room. There seemed to be lots of people going through to the garden, where outdoor lights had been turned on and I could see towards the back a door in the fence had been opened, with people in plastic protective clothing making their way out into the blackness beyond.

'In here, please,' DS Scott said when she noticed I'd paused in the hallway. I did as I was told and sat next to Hudson across the table from her.

'Are you OK if I record this?' she asked, taking out her iPhone. 'Just to save me writing things down while we talk. That OK with you, dear?' She looked at Hudson. He looked at me.

'Is that… I don't know…' I suddenly wondered if I should have a lawyer with us. Throwing caution to the wind, I decided to ask. 'Do we need a lawyer?'

DS Scott looked at me, her mouth pinched a little. 'You can have one, if you want to wait for them to arrive, but I had hoped to get this bit out of the way. If you want to take Hudson home to rest, this is the quickest way forward. In terms of *need*, well, Hudson may have more of an idea of whether you *need* one.' She looked at him again. What she said wasn't a question but her voice went up at the end as if she expected an answer. And I didn't like what she was suggesting.

'My son's done nothing wrong,' I said, the words blunt and harsh in my mouth.

'Well, let's get on with discussing what happened, then—and if you want to stop at any point and reconsider the lawyer position, you just let me know. OK?'

I didn't know what to do. I hated being in the dark, hated being plunged into this situation, as though I'd stepped into some TV police drama. Only the reality was far less entertaining and far more nerve-wracking than I could have ever imagined. Still unsure, still with a thousand thoughts wrestling within me, I nodded.

'Splendid.' DS Scott nodded and offered a small smile. 'Now, Hudson, my first question isn't a nice one, but I always think it's good to get the nasty bits out of the way.' Hudson looked back at her. He looked terrified. She then took a breath and said, 'Did you have any part to play in the death of Charlene Clay?'

Chapter Eighteen

THE FATHER

1 November 2024

After that initial stark question, to which Hudson answered 'No', the police interview was over quicker than expected. Although it seemed Kenny was yet to be formally interviewed, he had openly volunteered the information that he believed there was an animal of some kind roaming the woods and the police were 'keeping an open mind' about how Charlene had been killed. I asked what animal they thought it was, but nobody seemed to be very forthcoming on this, although I noticed Hudson shuffle his feet uncomfortably and I planned to quiz him on this, and every other part of the evening, once we were safely in the car and on the way back home.

The main point of contention seemed to be the blood Hudson had on him. He explained he and Kirsten had tried to ascertain if Charlene was definitely dead and Kirsten had (perhaps foolishly) tried to pull her down from where she'd been tied up. He'd also touched one of the cottage walls when he had fallen over. Photographs, swabs and clothes were taken. Hudson went along with all of it.

Once we were in the car on our way home, I asked him, 'Are you going to be honest about what actually happened?' When he didn't reply, I added, 'Because I have a lot of questions, Hud.'

Silence once again greeted this. I glanced over at him, but he had his face turned, staring out of the window at the passing trees. We were still snaking around the edge of Barret Forrest and I wondered if that vast mass of trees would now mean something different in our neighbourhoods. Would people no longer go amidst those trees for hikes or dog walks? Would campers be afraid of what might be lurking in the shadows? A wild animal that had killed a girl and may be still out there, biding its time.

'Hud, please speak to me,' I said after a few minutes, 'I need to know you're OK.'

I thought he was going to ignore this, but then I saw his face turn away from the window. 'Yeah. I just need to sleep.'

When we got home, that's exactly what he did. Mattias came up to us as soon as we walked in and Hudson rushed up to his room without saying anything.

'What happened?' Mattias said.

'In a moment,' I muttered, then called up to Hudson, not

wanting to postpone our conversation further. He had closed his bedroom door, but I didn't hesitate to open it again and found him tugging off the baggy tracksuit the police had given him to wear during the forensic processing.

'I'm going to bed,' he said. His voice was low and emotionless.

'We need to talk about what happened,' I insisted again.

'I just want to fucking sleep!' he yelled at me, making me jump. I took a step backwards, alarmed by the sudden outburst. I half expected him to dissolve into tears and tell me he was sorry for shouting, but no such thing occurred. No tears arrived. He just looked extremely pale, with a strained look on his face. He buried himself under the covers and settled his head down on the pillow, not saying another word.

I admitted defeat. With one last worried look towards my son, I left the room, wishing I could turn back time. Wishing I'd refused to let him go anywhere near Barret Forest on Halloween night.

I filled Mattias in when I went downstairs. He absorbed all the information without interrupting once, although I could tell from his expression he was confused by some aspects. I couldn't blame him.

'So ... you're concerned Hudson had something to do with the girl's death?'

I widened my eyes at him, 'No, that's not what I said. My concern is that Hudson has been disturbed by what he's seen and is too traumatised to confront it, and that's going to make him look suspicious.'

Mattias frowned. 'But the police let him go. So they clearly don't think he … well, killed anyone. And if it was an animal …well, it's the woods, who knows what might be lurking in the dark.'

I nodded, rubbing at my chin. I could feel the harsh bristles of stubble and was aware my hair was probably untidy having practically leapt straight from bed and into the car. Perhaps I needed to sleep, too, but I couldn't shake the nagging feeling that there was something wrong about how the morning had gone. But when I said this to Mattias, he laid a hand on me and said, 'Of course something is wrong. A girl has died. That's awful, no matter who or what attacked her.'

I nodded. 'I know, I just mean… I feel like there's a detail I'm failing to see.'

I could tell from Mattias's face he didn't understand. I leaned forward, kissed his cheek and pulled him close. 'I'm going to go back to bed for an hour or two,' I said. 'But if Hudson wakes, will you come and get me?'

He assured me that he would. Although, once I was in bed with the curtains drawn, I knew at once there was no hope of me drifting off. I couldn't get Hudson's face out of my head—his face when we'd gone into the downstairs bathroom at Kenny's house, when he'd been about to tell me something. Something that seemed to be causing him immense pain and anguish from within.

I got out of bed and marched straight to Hudson's room. He was under the covers and stirring. If he'd been fast asleep, perhaps I could have convinced myself not to wake him, but the sound of the door opening had woken him. Or perhaps, like me, he had failed to drop off at all.

'Dad ... I said I'm tired—' he started to say.

'No,' I said, firmly, 'this can't wait.'

He avoided my eye, pushing his head back into his pillows. I marched forward and pulled the duvet off him.

'Dad! What the—'

'There's something you're not telling me Hudson,' I said. I half expected him to get off the bed and run, but instead he rolled over and turned away from me. That's when I saw his back. Scratches. Not major, but there. As if he'd been running through undergrowth. Or perhaps even scratched by someone.

'Hudson, how did you get these scratches?' I asked, reaching out to touch him. He flinched when my fingers met his skin.

'Get off!'

'Hudson, tell me everything. Right now.'

I realised, with alarm, that he was shaking. When eventually he turned around, I saw the fear in his eyes.

'Dad,' he muttered quietly. 'It's bad. Really, *really* bad.'

It felt as if a cascading rush of ice-cold water was making its way down my back. I was terrified of what he was about to tell me. Horrified that the worst was possible. But I had to hear it.

'Tell me,' I said, gently.

Hudson's face had that taut, strained expression. For a second, it reminded me of something—something I couldn't quite put my finger on. A memory. Then I realised. He reminded me of Adelaide, during some of her more fraught moments, when she was trying to come off the drugs. She'd sometimes describe it as like trying to swim with no arms and no legs, but still desperately trying to keep your head above water.

'I killed her, Dad,' he said, very quietly. 'I killed her.'

I knew he was going to say it. I'd guessed. Of course I had.

'Just you? Or you and Kenny?'

He shook his head. 'Just me.'

I frowned, puzzled. 'Then ... why was Kenny talking about an animal? Was he lying?'

Slowly, Hudson shook his head. 'No, he wasn't lying.'

'But...' I said, struggling to understand, desperate to get my head around what sort of confession my son was making to me. 'Both things can't be true? Either Kenny saw some ... some ... *creature* attack Charlene, or he saw you?'

'That's the thing, Dad,' Hudson said, a single tear now slipping from his right eye and falling sideways down his face. 'Because both things can be true. *Are* true. I killed Charlene. And I was the creature. I was a spider.'

Chapter Nineteen

THE BOY

1 November 2024

I watched Dad's face as a I told him. Told him I was the one who had attacked Charlene. That an animal had killed her, but not a wild beast. It was worse than that. The stuff of nightmares. Something so strange and unexplainable, the very concept made me feel sick to even say it out loud.

I was the creature. I was a spider.

I saw the consternation in his eyes at first. Then something closer to panic. 'No… What? You're … imagining things, Hudson. You must have… Christ, your drink must have been spiked.' He leaned back, away from me, hands going to his face, rubbing his eyes, as if he could wipe away the worry and confusion.

'My drink wasn't spiked, Dad,' I said, trying to keep calm.

'You're not making sense,' he said, getting up. 'I

understand you may *think* that's what happened, but it can't … *can't* be true. You do see that, don't you?'

'It's true,' I said, simply. 'It… It's so weird. I can barely remember it. But I can remember the feeling. The prickling sensation … like static electricity. Like when you get a shock off something, but all over my body. The burning feeling in my fingertips, the heat rising over my arms and legs. I wanted to crawl out of my skin. The pain was unbearable.' I thought back to the moment this had happened, the moment I realised those feelings weren't confined to just my skin, but my mind, too. The heat, the prickly, the searing pain—it was all happening inside, as well. And in many ways, that sensation was much worse.

Dad was looking at me, slowly shaking his head. 'This can't be happening…' he said, staring at me.

I pulled myself up. 'What do you mean?'

He opened his mouth, then closed it again. Then he said, 'I just mean … what you're saying can't be true.'

'No,' I said, watching his twitching, panicky eyes, 'you said "*This can't be happening*". As if *this*, specifically *this* was … something you … understand?'

He shook his head, but I could tell he was trying to recover himself. 'I definitely *don't* understand it, Hudson. All I can think is that something terrible happened in the woods between you, Charlene and Kenny, and you boys—probably him—started … I don't know … a scuffle or fight of sorts, and he ended up hurting her and you were caught in the aftermath.'

'It wasn't Kenny,' I said again.

'Hudson, it *must* be,' he said, 'because you wouldn't … you … you just *wouldn't*… Surely you know that? And all the animal … the spider hallucinations … I can only think it must be drugs. That's the only explanation.'

'You don't understand,' I said.

'Then make me understand, Hudson,' Dad cried, almost shouting.

'How can I when I don't properly understand it myself? I don't know what happened to me out there in the woods, but it did happen and it was horrible. It was the worst thing I've ever gone through and no matter how much I try, I can't bear the thought … the *feeling* … of what happened.'

Dad looked disbelieving. 'That's probably just the after-effects of the hallucinations. I've read what LSD can do…'

'I didn't take fucking LSD.'

'And … MDMA … high strength cannabis-induced psychosis… All of this could be matched to a whole raft of symptoms and side-effects.'

'Dad, I promise you, I didn't take any of those drugs last night. Never have. What happened came from. From … *inside* of me.'

'No,' he said, getting up, 'You didn't do it. That awful boy Kenny killed her, whether by accident or out of malice or something, but I refuse to believe you did anything. He's just managed to scare you enough to believe his crazed delusions.'

He walked out of the room, slamming the door behind him.

I stayed in bed for most of the day. Thinking. Trying not to think. Trying to forget. Trying to pretend it was all a nightmare. When it got to 3 p.m., I went to the bathroom and took a shower, then decided to brave going downstairs.

Dad was sitting alone in the kitchen. 'Where's Mattias?' I asked, before he could say anything or start berating me again.

'Newcastle. Gone to his studio.' Dad stretched and got off the breakfast stool and came over. 'Is that OK?'

I shrugged. 'I don't care. I just wondered.'

I went to the fridge and took out some orange juice and a dish containing cold macaroni cheese.

'Would you like me to heat that up for you?' Dad asked. I got the feeling this was his way of saying sorry for getting angry earlier. I nodded and then went into the lounge. I knew he'd try to talk to me again, try to ask more questions. I understood why. I'd shaken his world when I told him what had happened. I wondered if he'd suggest taking me to a doctor. Or the police, even. Or perhaps an institution. Have me sectioned, decide I was completely insane.

I turned on the TV while I waited, hearing the hum of the microwave from the kitchen. The screen filled with a local news programme, the reporter stood against a backdrop of trees. Even though the sound was muted, I knew it was Barret Forest. Then a familiar face appeared on screen and I turned up the volume

'... joins me now. Could you tell me what happened last night in these woods?'

Kenny looked paler than usual, but he still gave an enthusiastic nod for the cameras. 'Yeah, sure, it was messed up. My friend Charlene was attacked by an animal. No jokes, there is a full-on *creature* in those woods. People aren't safe.'

I listened as the reporter tried to tease out some more details, asking him to talk viewers through what had happened and why he and his friends had been in the forest on Halloween night.

'We were just camping out and having a laugh. The creature snuck up on us, in the darkness, with ... y'know ... stealth, right? Then it just went for her. It was awful.'

The reporter then moved to Kenny's mum, the camera moving to show her standing next to him. 'If my Kenny says that's what he saw, then that's what he saw,' she said, belligerently.

'God, I can't believe they've gone on *television*,' Dad said behind me. He came into the room and placed the steaming bowl of pasta on the table. 'That's... It's...'

'It's what?' I asked, actually interested in his opinion. I certainly knew mine.

'A bit ... distasteful,' he said. 'I mean, surely the police won't be happy about that.'

I shrugged. 'Typical Kenny, trying to grab his share of the limelight,' I said.

A thought suddenly occurring to me, I pulled my phone out of my pocket. I hadn't looked at it when I took it off charge earlier, and I now saw a mass of WhatsApp messages and missed calls. All were from school friends, with the majority from Kenny. I didn't get round to reading most of them because the most recent one made me freeze.

Hope you didn't mind me mentioning you but people are commenting on this one now and someone's tagged you in it so you might want to answer them so it doesn't look weird.

I followed the link at the bottom of the message. Kenny's face arrived on my phone screen, a video auto-playing from a tweet posted by a local newspaper's account.

Classmate of deceased girl talks about their night of horror in the forest was the text. I didn't turn the volume on. I could tell Dad was watching me. But the video had been subtitled and I could see the words there on the screen in bold under Kenny's moving mouth.

'We were just camping, having fun in the woods for Halloween. It's awful what happened. It's awful. I didn't know Charlene well but my close friend Hudson did - he was having sex with her just before she was killed so he may have seen more than I did.'

I was horrified.

'Fuck,' I said, without even thinking. Dad moved towards me quickly, trying to see the phone.

'What is it?'

'Nothing.'

'Hudson, what is it?'

'I need to talk to Kenny,' I said. I pressed call and held the phone to my ear. He didn't reply. I then tried FaceTime and WhatsApp video call. Nothing.

'That fucking prick,' I muttered, starting to type.

'Hudson, what's with all the swearing?'

I paused for a moment, looking up at Dad, unable to believe what I was hearing. '*Swearing?* You're worried about me fucking swearing?'

My dad made a grab for me phone just as I sent the message.

'*Why the fuck did you say that?*' Dad read aloud from my message to Kenny, '*About me and Charlene. I only fucked her because you lied to me. Why did you say that to a fucking journalist?*'

Dad lowered the phone. I thought his face was serious before, but now his expression had something else in it. Fear. 'Oh Hudson, what have you done? Did you... Did you have sex with that girl just before she died? Christ, the police are going to...' He trailed off, shaking his head.

I stood up, 'I already told you. But you accused me of being delusional and covering up for Kenny. Do you know how ... how hard it was for me to tell you everything?' I felt my voice starting to crack with the strain of everything.

Dad opened his mouth for a moment then something seemed to catch his eye on the phone. 'Kenny's typing,' he said.

I snatched it back and he didn't try to stop me. I read the reply, quickly and silently.

Well, it's true, you did fuck her. Didn't you tell the police that? We should talk, compare notes about that night. Can I come over?

I thought about this then messaged back.

No, meet me at the quarry. By the large rock. Come alone.

I looked up at Dad.

'I'm going back to bed,' I said, making up my mind about something. I knew the best way to play this, having a sudden moment of clarity I'd been struggling to get hold of before.

'What? You've just come from there? You've been sleeping all day. What… What did Kenny say?'

I put my phone in my pocket. 'He said sorry.'

Dad spluttered in disbelief. 'What? Kenny saying *sorry*? I don't believe it.'

I walked away. Of course, he followed, talking all the way about how if I needed help—legal or medical—he could find it, we could work through this together.

I just said, 'OK.' And when I reached my room, I closed the door on him.

This didn't stop him, of course. He opened the door straight away just as I was getting into bed.

'Hudson! Can we just—'

'We've talked enough,' I snapped. 'I've told you

everything I know. And now I just want to rest. I barely slept earlier. I promise you we'll … we'll go over it all again.'

Dad crouched down by my bed. 'Hudson, the police are going to find out you had sex with her. It's going to change things. They've got your DNA. And no fanciful story about a monster that you and a drunk Kenny cooked up together is going to save you.'

I stared back at him. 'Is that really what you think we're doing?'

'It seems to me like the only option, from where I'm standing.' He drew himself up and raised his hands. 'OK, we'll talk later. But if we're going to get ahead of this, I think we need to think strongly about going back to the police and you being the one to tell them the full details about last night.'

He went to leave, then paused just before he closed the door. 'Oh, and remember, everything you send to Kenny on that,' he pointed at my phone, 'is a trail of evidence. Just keep that in mind when you're saying sorry to each other via WhatsApp.'

He closed the door.

I messaged Kenny immediately. Waited half an hour, then walked very carefully out onto the landing. Silence. Then I heard something. Dad talking. He sounded like he was in his study. I walked as quietly as I could down the stairs and into the hallway. He was certainly talking to someone, presumably on the phone. It occurred to me he might be talking to the police. Then I heard another voice, slightly distorted and realised he was having a video chat with someone. And the more hard-to-make-out words I heard, the more I realised who it was. It was Mum.

How much was Dad telling her? Would he tell her everything? And I wondered about that moment—the moment I'd seen in Dad's face something other than shock and confusion. Something closer to dread.

It can't be happening.

I couldn't shake off that feeling: the feeling that he knew more than he was telling me. I tried to edge closer to the door of his study without making a sound, convinced this sudden video call with Mum might shine a light on something. Something key to what was happening here. But no matter how hard I tried, all I could hear was muffled noise and Dad occasionally saying 'OK' and 'I don't know' and 'Why?'

I suppose that was the ultimate question. *Why?* Why did Charlene die last night? What caused that to happen? What led to a change in me so horrific, it bent my understanding of the world and everyone in it out of all proportion?

Eventually I left the hallway, remembering I had another situation to deal with. A situation involving Kenny, waiting by a large rock in the nearby quarry.

A situation that, I think I knew in my heart, even at that point, wouldn't end well.

Chapter Twenty

THE BOY

1 November 2024

It was still light when I set out for the quarry, but only just. It was some distance away, on the east side of Barret Forest, and in other circumstances I would have cut through the trees to get there. Today, though, I thought it better not to go deep inside. I wasn't sure I was ready myself, and I worried the police would still be searching for evidence. I didn't want to risk being caught or dragged in for further questioning. I knew it would probably come. I knew my lies and my secrets would catch up with me. But for now, I just needed to find out what Kenny knew, what his plan was, and persuade him to leave me out of his many public chats about what happened last night.

The light was getting low as I approached the small chalky-mud pathway that led up to the quarry's edge; a sheer drop that would have been a great diving site if the mass of empty ground had been flooded. Sadly, it remained dry but out of use. Another stretch of ground where teenagers like me kicked about and drifted with friends while adults looked on, presuming we were up to no good. Like the forest, there had been a number of stories about the place—attempts at creating horror out of accounts that may, at some point, be based on a grain of truth. I remembered hearing once that a child's body had been found in the centre of it, surrounded by stones and rocks in a circle. I wasn't sure who told it to me, but I remembered trying to look it up online and found no results other than the well-documented case of a young girl's drowning in the nearby stream in the 1980s, which was the likely source for the story. I figured people liked the idea of making an already unsettling place feel even more strange and dangerous. Perhaps if they were the ones inventing and spreading scary stories it gave them a sense of control. As I got near the meeting spot, I wondered if anyone was really in control of anything, or if we were all at the mercy of the terrible secrets that lurked unseen in the darkness. Or inside us.

A strong breeze started up as I walked through the last of the trees. Through the falling leaves I saw him standing there. He was leaning up against the rock at the side of the ground's edge, his face illuminated by the cold light of his phone, cutting through the grey twilight. He looked up when he heard me approach.

'Kenny,' I said.

'About fucking time.'

'I had to sneak out,' I said, feeling awkward and unsure.

Kenny scoffed. I knew he would think the idea of having to sneak out ridiculous, but I didn't want to get into that. Instead, I went straight for the topic at hand. 'Why did you say on camera that I had ... that I—'

'Fucked Charlene?' He shrugged. 'Like I said, it's the truth.'

I took a step towards him. 'Because you *tricked* me. You and Charlene tricked me.'

'Oh, come on,' he said and I saw him roll his eyes. 'You were desperate to lose it to anyone, it was so obvious. You'd have done it with a fucking sheep if I'd set you up with one.'

I felt something shift within me as he said that. A change. One that was just about noticeable. But there. A flick of something.

'Shut up,' I said, quietly, my words probably drowned out by the gust of wind and the background, white noise of the swaying trees.

'I don't remember you complaining when you were getting your dick sucked, all thanks to me and my skills of persuasion—not that I got any fucking thanks.'

'Shut up,' I said again, louder now, but Kenny carried on.

'*Oh yes ... ahhh yessss ... fuck yesss!*' He made an exaggerated groan and I realised he was mimicking what he'd heard. It was too much. I felt something snap, like an electric shock going off within me. I lashed out and slapped him, hard across the face.

Momentarily shocked, Kenny stopped and took a step back. He raised his hand to his face where I'd hit him. Then he laughed. 'Christ, you're slapping me like a fucking girl in the playground.'

'You're horrible,' I said, breathing heavily, the sudden action shocking me almost as much as it had Kenny. 'My dad's always said it, but for some reason I was too stupid to see it. But now I know. I shouldn't have come here.' I turned to leave. Then Kenny said something which made me stop.

'At least I'm not a murderer.'

I paused for a moment, trying to calm my breathing. Then, slowly, I turned back to face him.

'What did you say?'

'You heard.'

I stared at him. He stared at me, his lip curling. 'You disappeared into the forest. I went looking for you, then suddenly Charlene was screaming. Anything could have happened in the darkness. I didn't see where you went. Or what you did. You probably took her to that cottage to fuck her again, didn't you? But maybe she didn't want it, again. Is that what happened? Or maybe she just thought your dick was too fucking small the first time. Perhaps you were too pathetic to give her the pleasure she needed. Maybe she wanted a real man.'

That fizzing, prickling feeling was back, running across my skin. My hand hurt, my wrist was throbbing, presumably from the force of the slap. I tried my best to keep my words slow and calm but there was a force rising within me now. Rising. Rising. Impossible to ignore.

'What about the creature?' I said, taking a step towards him.

Kenny looked momentarily afraid again, and I saw the ghost of that shaking, cowering boy huddled at the back of the tent. 'I imagined it. I was drunk.'

'Really?' I said, moving closer. 'Because you were so sure, yesterday.' I couldn't disguise my heavy breathing and I could see Kenny noticing it.

'What… What's up with you… What are you doing?' he said, his eyes darting around.

'It's interesting,' I said, cracking my knuckles, the prickling starting to turn into something else, something closer to pain, 'that you chose to meet someone you suspected of a violent murder in a place like an abandoned quarry.'

I felt my shoulders contorting, my arms starting to crack and reshape.

It was happening again.

Happening again.

Happening again.

'It's happening,' I said, out loud, not meaning to but at the same time impossible to avoid.

'You're a fucking weirdo,' Kenny said and before I could stop him he punched me, straight in the face, knocking me backwards. With a speed I didn't know I had, I punched him back, pushing him up against the large rock while he scrabbled to steady himself.

He tried to come at me again.

I was too strong.

I was changing.

My vision was *changing*.

Widening.

Widening.

I could see everything. Everything. The trees. The path. Kenny. Moving. Getting closer.

I lashed out.

He fell.

Hands clutching dirt. Trying to hold on to the side.

Sheer drop.

Fallen.

Fallen.

He's the last thing. Last thing I see.

Before it is complete.

Kenny's face. As he goes over the edge.

A look of terror.

Total terror.

Chapter Twenty-One

THE BOY

1 November 2024

I'd changed I know I'd changed I could walk run even or I could if I wasn't trapped

Trapped

Trapped

Can't move.

Ripping

Tearing

Clothes

Trapped by my clothes

I was free and moving running scurrying faster than I knew faster than I even thought possible I could cling on cling on easily no need to struggle full easy movement down the side of the quarry to him

The body

Body

Food

So hungry hadn't eaten hadn't eaten needed food had been too long too long too long

It was everywhere suddenly it was everywhere but I knew what to do knew how to wrap and bind wrap and bind wrap and bind

He was wrapped now the body was wrapped dead body completely wrapped

Fangs going in

Deeper

Penetrating

Pushing through flesh

Pushing through bone

Mouth clamping sucking liquid

Sucking liquid

Streaming

Feeding

Feeding

Feeding

The flow

But then the kicking

Still alive

Still alive

In spite of feeding, parcel still alive

Writhing

Web coming up

A hand coming out

Clamp jaws tighter sucking drinking all flowing out warm and bits hard bits but still liquid more liquid

Parcel wriggling twitching moaning

Then still
Still
Drink
Flowing gushing
Feed
Finish
Blackness
Needed to sleep
Needed rest
Darkness

When I came round, I was confused, hurt, and for a few seconds I wondered if it was Halloween again. It felt the same, but also different. Less peculiar. I wasn't as weak. I could sit up and stand quicker.

Steadily more thoughts began to order themselves. I wasn't in the forest. Well, I was, sort of, the trees around me, towering tall, made that clear. But not like last time. The ground was harder, rougher, rockier, more powdery.

The quarry. I was in the quarry.

The cold hit me. The frozen November air. I wasn't sure how long I'd been on the ground but it had been too long. I looked down and saw I was naked, just like last time. My clothes were nowhere to be seen—not that I could see much around me. I could make out the trees against the night sky, and the edge of the quarry. And the mass. The shape, a few metres away.

Feeling a twinge of fear, I got to my feet, feeling less shaky than I expected, and walked over to look.

In the gloom, I could make out two things; first, there was a lot of blood, and second, the person was definitely dead.

It looked like the body had fallen apart. There was webbing around it, but a dip was visible in the centre, near where the stomach would be. That part had been opened entirely. Or dissolved. A thick, glutinous mixture, which had spread and dripped across the dusty, gritty floor. There were also puncture marks across the wrapped body, some which had torn the webbing. One of these looked as if the neck had been the target, but it had resulted in a tearing of the face. In spite of the jagged flaps of skin, I could still see it was Kenny. Or *used* to be Kenny.

A flash of a memory came to me. A rich, meaty flow of liquid and other things.

Feeding. Drinking.

I suddenly felt myself retch, but I put a hand to my mouth, forcing whatever it was rising inside of me back down. I couldn't be sick here. I needed to get home.

I suddenly felt much less strong and able than I had a few seconds ago. Shaking even more, I turned and looked up around the high quarry walls, made up of rock and chalk and sharp, jagged edges. Something I had managed to scale during my altered state. My many legs sticking and gripping, carrying me down, as if I were able to defy gravity. There was no way I could climb back up. I'd have to go the long way round, through the other side of the quarry. That exit would set me on a path that looped round through the main heart of the forest then back round towards home. It would be a long walk, but I didn't have much of a choice. Get my phone. Get my clothes, or whatever was left of them. I remembered breaking free, hearing something tear.

I was suddenly overwhelmed by the number of problems I was facing. No matter how much I stopped myself being sick, there would be something left of me here. The WhatsApp messages, the phone placing my location, traces of me on the broken mass that used to be Kenny.

I couldn't think about all that. I just had to move. Had to start the journey out of this enormous hole in the ground.

I walked down to the far end where I knew there was a more gradual incline and steps to get up to the forest. The ground was harsh against my bare feet. When I got to the top, I was glad for the softer surface of the woodland floor, though before long the twigs and occasional stones started to cause a constant sharp pain. I trod the well-worn path into the trees that I knew looped round the edge of the quarry and eventually came out the other side to the large rock on the ledge where I'd met Kenny.

Walking slowly through the trees, trying to see through the darkness and stick to the path, I gradually became aware of a low grumble. It sounded like voices, human voices.

Voices in the distance.

People were here. In the woods, at night, somewhere close to me.

A laugh cut through, making me jump, a lot closer than I'd expected.

Then I saw a flicker of light, like a flame fluttering into

life, then going out again. I continued, walking past some larger tree trunks and eventually I could make out a cluster of figures up ahead of me. Another light, this one colder and harsher. A phone screen. Then the torch of a phone, and the flame—again—which I could now see was from a lighter. A group of boys was in front of me, four of them, two of them were on bikes, another two were seated on a fallen tree. I could smell weed and cigarettes. And because I could see them, they could see me.

'Fucking hell, what's this?' one of them said, laughing and pointing at me.

'Er, mate, where are your clothes?' One of the tree-trunk boys laughed. I recognised him from school; he was in the year above me and I presumed the others were, too.

'Yeah, why you butt-naked?' another said. 'You a tree-shagger or something?'

'More like he was doing some slag in the bushes. She still around? Can we all have a go?'

More laughter.

'I need… Can I borrow a phone?' I asked, my voice raspy.

'Fuck off,' the closest guy on the bike said, leaning over the front of his handle bars. 'You might run off and nick it.'

'Please,' I said. 'It's … an emergency.'

The front one laughed again. 'An *emergency*' he said, copying my southern accent, making it sound even posher than it was. 'Who d'you need to phone? Your mammy?'

'Nah, he wants to phone his bird,' the other biker said. 'Make sure she's keeping her bra and knickers off so he can go back for a round two.'

'Fine,' I said, 'I guess you'll say no, but can I borrow a jacket or a hoodie or something? I'm freezing.'

'Not surprised you are,' the front biker said. 'But ... er ... let me think, that's a big fucking "no", you weirdo. I'm not giving you my clothes.'

I looked around at the others. 'Please,' I said again.

They all just stared back at me. Not one seemed to waver. Not one wanted to show some mercy, some kindness, some inner sense of doing the right thing.

'You shouldn't be wandering around these woods at night,' the front biker said. 'People die in these woods.'

'Someone died here,' another boy said.

'Yeah,' said the front one. 'We've seen police, up at the other end. Girl got slashed, apparently. Heard on the news it was an animal.' He took a puff on his cigarette then jerked his bike forwards, making me jump and step backwards. He threw his cigarette at me. It missed, falling to the ground. But it was enough. Enough for me to tune in to something that had started without me properly noticing. A prickle of rage.

'You scared?' the boy asked, then laughed. The others joined in.

'No,' I said. 'But you should be.' My voice was quivering, shaky, but not from the cold or from fear. This time, it was power. A power I felt I'd come to know well, even after this short time. And in this instance, instead of letting it take hold of me against my will, I did something I'd never done before. Never dreamed I would or could ever do.

I welcomed the darkness in.

Chapter Twenty-Two

THE BOY

1 November 2024

It was a dizzying festival of carnage in the woods that night. Although I experienced the ripping, the tearing, the drinking, the feeding all while it was happening, I was shocked how vivid the memories were when I found myself back in my human form once again. It was as if the gulf between my normal mind and my animal mind was getting smaller and smaller. And I had access to things I hadn't before. Vivid, terrifying images. I lay there for a moment, the senses in my skin starting to return. Dry leaves and bits of broken twigs against me. And I allowed my mind to roll back as I opened my eyes. A severed foot lay in front of me. It was almost whole, but with a rip near the ankle exposing the Achilles tendon, the skin around it jagged and torn. I wasn't certain which boy it belonged to, but the foot looked quite large so I suspected it was the first, the guy who had belligerently refused to help me or let me pass. I remembered him trying to run. All of them trying to run. But the webs stopped them. The strands came out of me without me having to decide, having to do anything; it was as if my body knew what to do without pausing to think, without me instructing.

I got to my feet. I didn't ache as much this time. The transformation had been smoother, easier. Not painless, exactly, but without the same discomfort as before. I looked around at the nearby trees. Folds of webbing swayed in the wind. Blood still dripping down some of the bundles, just as it had done in the cottage, where Charlene had been partially wrapped, only this time it was on a grander scale. The sky had cleared, and through the trees, rays of silver moonlight illuminated the scene, and for a split second I couldn't help think it looked strangely beautiful, like a painting or an intricate sculpture.

I couldn't remember how many boys there were before the transformation and the carnage that followed. But I quickly realised that I must have missed one as I looked at the wrapped bodies hanging from the trees. Because a hand reached out and grabbed my ankle.

I jumped backwards and fell hard to the ground. Sitting there, I looked at where the hand had come from: a nearby fallen tree. The boy was inside the trunk. He was still mostly intact, although some of his fingers were bent back unnaturally and he had several large large gashes across his face. I could tell he was staring at me, and as my eyes made out the details in the shadows away from the moonlight, I saw the gashes had ripped off part of his cheek so that the left side of his jaw was open and visible, his tongue moving in his mouth.

He was trying to talk but he was unable to form any words. Where his lips used to be was a mangled lump stuck to the bits of flesh that were still there, flapping at the sides of his teeth. Even so, I thought I could guess what he was trying to say. His outstretched hand. He was either asking for help. Or begging for mercy. I pulled myself up. Got to my feet.

I waited for the horror at what I had done to hit me. The feeling of regret and anguish and dismay, the wave of revulsion. It didn't come. I felt strangely neutral. Not completely out of touch with my normal human emotions, but at the same time unconvinced they'd be entirely useful at this moment. And in a way I was glad. It allowed me to think practically and clearly about what I needed to do in that moment.

I walked up to the boy where he clung to the broken edges of the tree branches. He must have been hiding behind them after sustaining his injuries during the attack. He probably watched as his friends were bitten and bound-up into the webbed packages above him. He must also be in terrible pain. I didn't care. I just stood above him, looking down, watching as tears fell from his eyes, mixing with the earth and blood. Then I just said, 'I'm going to need your clothes.'

He made rasping, moaning sounds, a mixture of ill-defined words and sobs, as I roughly pulled him out, dragging him along the forest floor, and then forced him out of his hoodie. His sobs became higher pitched when it got bunched around his face, and I suspected more of his broken cheek was dragged back and torn off when it finally came away. Still, I didn't care. I just knew I needed clothes to walk back, to keep me warm; just a practical survival instinct I had no plan to ignore. I tugged his T-shirt off him, which resulted in sounds that were more like screams. Then I started on his jeans, which were more difficult, with his legs kicking and jerking, arms scrabbling, clearly with attempts to crawl away from me, though apparently without the strength needed for it to be effective. I, however, was very effective. It was as if I had been freed from basic, unnecessary things like emotion or sadness or pity, things that would have delayed me in my task. I wasn't embarrassed for him as I stripped him down to his pants, as he crawled amidst the leaves and the twigs and earth and the blood of his friends. Once I'd pulled on his clothes, I saw his movements becoming less wild and energetic. He was slowing, tiring. As he twisted on the ground he rolled onto his back, and that's when I saw the slit in his stomach and the blood leaking out of it. I felt with my fingers at my own stomach at the corresponding part of my torso and felt a rip in the T-shirt that I hadn't spotted when I'd pulled it on. He clutched one of his hands to it and in the darkness, I noticed the blood looked deep black, like oil or dark treacle. He flailed around a little more, then came to a rest on his back, staring up at the sky. The trees. The stars. Maybe he noticed, in his last moments, how bright the moon was. How the sky was dazzlingly clear and pricked with sparkles. Or maybe he didn't see anything, at all. It didn't really matter, I thought, as I turned away from the now lifeless body.

It hit me as I walked home via the nearby the fields, edging around the forest. It was gradual at first and then cataclysmic, causing me to fall to my knees. The magnitude of what had happened. What I had done. All the feelings of horror and revulsion I had felt so free from now flooding into my mind like a terrible, painful drug. It was dizzying and nauseating, devastating and tortuous. I needed to get home. Get away from this place. I had to keep things small. Manageable. The only way I was going to get home was to put one foot in front of the other and try not to remember all the things I had done. Things I worried would drive me mad within minutes if I focused on them too much.

So I carried on walking. Slow but determined. Ducking behind the trees if I saw someone. I was aware that to my left through the darkness was Kenny's house. His parents would be inside, wondering where their son had got to. Wondering why he hadn't come home. I presumed they hadn't yet discovered his absence. Or perhaps they were out there, in the forest now, trying to find him themselves.

The anxiety and emotional pain I had tried so hard to press down resurfaced again as I arrived home. Dad hadn't phoned the police, but he claimed he'd been minutes away from it as a last resort. According to him, I'd been missing for hours. It was nearly midnight. He and Mattias had been taking it in turns to drive around the roads looking for me. They wondered if I'd returned to the scene of the crime, but the police presence in that part of the woods stopped them from looking.

'You'll never know how worried I was,' Dad said, pulling me towards him when I walked through the kitchen door. I'd had this deluded hope I'd be able to sneak upstairs. Take a shower. Get into bed. All this without Dad ever knowing. Of course, that's not how it went.

'I'm sorry,' I said. I was trying to think what else to say, what excuse to give. Whether I should tell him what I'd done. How much of it to be honest about. Which pieces of the truth to hide. I pulled away from him. 'Dad...'

He looked down at me, clearly realising something. 'Hud, these aren't your clothes, are they?'

I shook my head.

'Hudson, you're freezing. Why have you been wandering outside in the dark? Where did you get these clothes from? And they're wet... They're...' He pulled a hand away. It was bright red, the florescent light of the kitchen making the colour gleam on his fingers.

'Christ, Hudson... What...'

I suddenly thought of something. 'Where's Mattias?'

'He's out looking for you...' Dad said, looking from his hand, to me, then back to his hand. He sounded a bit dazed.

'I need to tell you ... something.'

'Yeah, Hud,' he said, swallowing, lowering his hand but

holding it away from himself so as not to transfer the blood to his own clothes. 'I really think you do.'

I told him it had happened again. Twice. This time, Dad listened, keeping quiet. He let me talk, even when I said words I thought he'd object to —words like *transformed, spider*—and when I told him what I did to Kenny.

'I... I drank him, Dad. I knew what to do. It was... It was easy. And his body, or what's left of it, is still there. I spun a web around him. He's trapped inside. But it's not just that. The second time it happened tonight was worse, I think.'

'Why was it worse?'

I took a deep breath. Then I said it. 'I killed four people. Four boys. In the woods. They wouldn't let me pass. They were ... jeering at me ... making fun of me. And I wanted to show them I wasn't pathetic. That I wasn't someone to be pushed around. I... I wanted to hurt them.'

There was silence for a while after I said this. Then Dad, rubbing his face with his hands, said in a muffled, tired voice, 'Are you sure? Are you sure they're really dead?'

I swallowed hard. 'They're ... in pieces.'

Chapter Twenty-Three

THE FATHER

Early hours of 2 November 2024

We got back from the quarry at 3 a.m. Once again, I struggled to sleep and instead lay on my back, staring at the ceiling. I thought about what I had just done. How I had knowingly broken the law. Helped disrupt a crime scene. Removed evidence that might incriminate my son. I had no idea if what I had done would be enough. Or even if it was right. Up until that moment, when I'd gathered up Hudson's torn clothes on that ledge above the quarry and pocketed his phone, I thought I knew the difference between right and wrong. But since Halloween, I'd been thrown into an ocean of grey. Not knowing which shade I should be choosing. The most terrifying colour of all, it seems. And nobody was there to tell me what to do.

The decision to not tell Mattias about what was

happening with Hudson was reached after my Zoom conversation with Hudson's mother. Adelaide had been on my mind ever since Hudson had said that word. That one word that completely changed everything. I don't think I'd ever known until then what people meant when they said their blood ran cold. I thought it was just a cliché. But from that moment on, I knew what it meant.

Hudson's mother's words echoed through my head as I laid in the darkness. Conversations we'd had just before I left Texas with Hudson. Dreams she'd relayed to me. Fragments she'd mentioned about the hallucinations she'd had when she was off her head on whatever mixture of pills she'd taken, or during one of her doomed self-imposed attempts to get clean. I'd dismissed everything as a symptom of her addiction. But I was having to face up to the fact that elements of what she'd said were starting to fit like puzzle pieces into something a lot more terrifying. But how could she have known, I asked myself, again and again. How could she have known what might happen? Could she have sensed something in Hudson that was invisible to me? Had there been a mother-son bond between them I'd failed to appreciate and had presumed was part of her disturbing chemical-induced behaviour?

No easy answers came to me. Mattias's slow breathing next to me—usually a soothing sound—made me feel tense, pressured even, making me increasingly aware of another problem I was going to have to deal with. I knew at some point I would have to tell him what was going on. And, understandably, he was going to think I was going insane. Perhaps, I thought, I was going insane. Perhaps I, Hudson and his mother were falling victim to one of those collective delusions, where we become so convinced about something we keep reinforcing each other, picking up on signs that just aren't there, things that could potentially have a reasonable explanation.

They're in pieces. I killed them all. I wanted to hurt them.

I got up and went downstairs. As I got to the lower part of the staircase, the old polished wood creaking loudly under my bare feet, I saw a dim light coming from the living room. Inside the small table lamp at the end of the room was switched on, and sat in the single-seater armchair next to it was Hudson.

'Hud, why are you down here all alone?' I asked. It was such a redundant question. It was obvious why he couldn't sleep. The night's events had shaken us both. How could they not?

'Leave me alone, Dad,' Hudson said in a quiet voice. In all of what had happened, I hadn't heard him talk like that. It was a small sound, like he'd sounded as a child when he'd done something wrong or hurt himself whilst playing.

'Hudson,' I said moving closer through the room.

I noticed then there was something in his lap. A pile of something. In the darkness, I couldn't see what it was. The light from the lamp was causing stark shadows and no matter how hard I looked I couldn't tell what he was holding close to himself.

'Hudson, what have you got there...?'

He moved and something fell to the floor. It was a box. A box of tablets. I recognised the packaging. Ibuprofen and Codeine. Several sheets fell out of it when it hit the ground. Then another box fell off his legs. And another down the side towards the edge of the sofa.

'Christ, Hudson, how many... How many have you taken?'

I started to walk quickly towards him, but then something made me freeze.

I turned on the main light and now the boxes of pills had fallen away, I could see Hudson's hands. They were clasped in his lap around a knife. A kitchen knife. Long and professional, well used but kept sharp. Very sharp.

'Oh fuck,' I muttered and stepped forward.

'Please ... don't come any closer,' Hudson said, moving suddenly to raise the knife to his left wrist.

I froze. 'You're not going to do this, Hudson,' I said, quietly. My heart pounded in my ears, my senses on fire.

'Why not?' he said, his voice coming out as a sob. Tears started to roll down his face. 'I'm bad, Dad. There's something terribly wrong with me.'

'You're not bad,' I said, my voice loud and forceful.

'I am,' he said, raising the knife and his wrist a little. I saw a droplet of blood fall onto the white material of his boxers. Red and harsh. The blade glinting in the light.

'I *wanted* to hurt them,' he said, his voice now just a whisper.

'Not you,' I said, 'And ... I think there's something I need to tell you.'

His eyes looked up at me now. He'd been focusing on the middle-distance, his expression glazed, dreamy almost, but now I had his attention.

'Tell me what?'

'Something... Something about what's happening.'

I saw hurt in his eyes then. Betrayal, even. 'You've known something about all this, haven't you? And... And you didn't tell me?'

I knelt down in front of him. 'Hudson, I think this has something to do with what happened ... something that happened ... when you were very young, in America. Something to do with your mum.'

Hudson kept his eyes on me, I could feel him staring deep into mine but he dropped the knife. I grabbed it from his lap and placed it behind me on the coffee table. My eyes then fell on to the boxes of tablets again and I picked them up. One of Ibuprofen and Codeine, another of Paracetamol. 'How many of these did you take?' I asked again. Pulling out the sheets.

'Two Ibuprofen and Codeine. I thought it would ... stop the pain.'

'Nothing else?'

He shook his head.

'Good,' I said, letting out a long, heavy breath.

'I knew there was something you weren't telling me,' he said. He didn't sound angry. He sounded relieved.

'Everything that's happened ... all the horrible things ... there has to be a reason. And you know that reason?'

'No,' I said. 'But I have a suspicion. And we can try to work that out together, OK?'

'You know what's going on?' Hudson's voice was raised, the sobs were back, sounding less calm, more agitated.

'I don't *know* anything, Hud, not for sure, I just—'

'Why didn't you tell me?' He stood up. 'I've been going *mad*! Insane. The whole thing is so fucking insane. That's why I just wanted to die! That's why I want all this to be over. How could you have kept this a secret?'

I reached forward and took his shoulders in my hands. 'Hudson, I promise you I'm just as confused as you are and— Christ, you're burning up.' His skin was hot, extremely hot. I took my hands away, but it was like the whole of him was radiating heat, as if he was charged with electricity.

I became aware he was breathing heavily. Very heavily. As if he had just been running. 'Dad, leave the room,' he said, panic in his voice. Loud and pleading.

'Be quiet, you'll wake Mattias,' I said. 'Just... Just calm down.'

'I can't ... I can't...' he said. I took hold of him, pulled him into my arms to hold him still, make him feel safe, but again but he pulled away. But even so, I was horrified by the change in texture that had occurred—his skin had become different, rougher, the hairs on his back and shoulders coarse and wiry.

'I don't want you to see this,' he cried. Then he fell to the ground.

For a few moments I continued desperately to try to help him.

Then I couldn't move at all.

I was backed against the coffee table. Trembling. Nauseated. Utterly terrified by what was happening to my son in front of my eyes. It was, without question, the worst thing I had ever seen in my life.

Chapter Twenty-Four

THE FATHER

2 November 2024

I could barely comprehend what I had just witnessed. I think part of me had still hoped—desperately hoped with all my heart and soul—that none of it was true. Imagining Hudson had been having a psychotic breakdown was easier to stomach than the truth. That none of this had any basis in reality. That it was all a fragment of our imagination. In fact, I *believed* none of it was true.

Now I didn't know what to believe. The world I lived in wasn't the world I thought it was. A thousand questions crowded my mind.

Why is this happening to my son?

How will this affect our lives? His future?

I tried to pull myself up off the floor, but my legs didn't work.

Legs. The sound Hudson's legs had made. Then more of

them had ... arrived out of him. More than I could see or count, though I knew how many there would be. Attached to a body. A horrible, sickness-inducing mass, the size of a large dog.

I managed to stand. The tattered remains of the boxers Hudson had been wearing were on the floor. I stumbled over the packets of pills, the cardboard collapsing under me as I tried to get my balance. I had to find him. I knew I had to go after him. But the thought of seeing that ... *thing* ... what he'd become, it made me almost heave with revulsion.

Then a hideous thought crossed my mind. *Mattias.* Asleep upstairs. Alone. Vulnerable to something crawling up to him in the darkness.

I ran. Shaky and scraping the door, but running and making progress, through the hallway, up the stairs, onto the landing.

'What's going on?'

Mattias was in bed, pulling the covers off him, starting to climb out. 'Go back to sleep,' I said.

'Why? Is it Hudson?'

'Yes, but he's fine,' I said, dashing to Hudson's doorway. I froze at the entrance, suddenly feeling something that I was ashamed to acknowledge. I was scared.

It's still my son. *He's* still my son.

I moved closer, edging my bare foot over the doorway. And then the other foot. I was in the room.

He's still my son.

I took a breath.

'What are you doing?' Mattias said. 'Is Hudson OK?' I

could hear him getting closer. But my eyes were drawn to something. From the moonlight coming in from the bedroom window, I could just make something out from underneath the bed. Legs. Spider's legs.

I left the room. 'I said go back to bed,' I said to Mattias, but he was out of the room now, walking along the landing. I moved over to meet him, physically turned him around. Thankfully, he didn't fight me and allowed himself to be guided back. I went with him, not knowing if what I was doing was right. Not knowing if I was abandoning my son or saving my husband. Or both.

We got back under the covers. Mattias slept, but I didn't. I waited an hour. Then another. Eventually, at about 4.45 a.m., I edged as quietly as I could out onto the landing. At Hudson's door, I looked at the spot on the floor just under the bed where I'd seen ... what I'd seen. The legs.

There was no longer anything there.

I walked in. My heart was beating a cacophony again. I felt sweat breaking out on my brow. 'Hudson?' I whispered as quietly as possible. Nothing. Then again. 'Hudson ... are you there?'

The sound of unmistakable movement. Coming from under the bed.

I took a step back away from the source of the noise. Then a sound came that made me feel weak with relief. Hudson's voice.

'Dad...'

I forced myself to breathe normally. Swallowed. Waited a few seconds. Then said, 'Oh, thank god. You're... You're...'

'Me again. Yes, I am,' he said, his voice muffled, although he didn't sound upset or in pain. 'I'm... I'm sorry, Dad. I couldn't stop it. I felt so... I couldn't...'

'It's OK,' I said, lowering myself to peer under the bed. But I couldn't see Hudson fully. Amidst the darkness I could, however, make out something, something blocking my view, something coating the underside of the bed like a white wall.

Webbing.

'I'm... I'm not ready to come out yet,' Hudson said. 'Can you go ... just for a bit? I'll come out when I'm ready.'

Slowly, I rose to my feet. 'That's... That's fine,' I said. 'I'll go.' At the door, I looked back and started to say, 'Hudson, it's all—'

'Don't say it's going to be OK, Dad,' Hudson said. 'I know why you're saying it, and it's kind of you. But ... I don't think I believe that's possible anymore.'

I wished I had words to the contrary to tell him. But none came to me. So I left the room, unable to offer my son the comfort both he, and I, so desperately needed.

Chapter Twenty-Five

THE FATHER

2 November 2024

The next morning, Mattias became more of a problem. My husband's clear wish was to help—to help make everything better, to aid me in my attempts to iron out this clearly distressing time for Hudson. But he didn't know the half of it. Not even a fraction. And that was the way it had to be. There was no point in letting him think he was going mad. Or that I was mad and Hudson beyond delusional.

'Tell me again what went on with Hudson last night,' Mattias said when I stepped out the shower to find him waiting for me, arms crossed.

'Why? Where is he?' I said, quickly, looking down the landing to his room. His door was closed.

'Still asleep, I presume,' he said, frowning at my reaction. 'Rex, is there—' he lowered his voice '—I get the feeling there's something I need to know. Something going on here that you're keeping from me. And I feel like it's something serious.'

I looked again over at Hudson's door. Then back at Mattias. 'Let's talk in our room.'

Once inside, he sat down on the edge of the bed and I in the occasional chair by the window. 'Hudson is … upset,' I said, choosing my words with care. 'Upset about what happened on Halloween and what he saw.'

Mattias nodded, but was clearly unsatisfied with this. 'Well … yeah. He found the body of his classmate. A girl was brutally murdered.'

I held up a hand, 'We don't know that. There's… There's reason to believe it was an animal attack.'

'Yeah, OK,' Mattias said, his brow creasing, 'But … that doesn't really explain your behaviour.'

It was my turn to frown. 'My *behaviour*?'

'Yes,' Mattias said, leaning forwards. 'God, Rex, it's obvious. You're trying to cover something up for him, aren't you?'

I avoided his gaze.

'Rex?'

'Hudson just… He… He found the girl's body,' I said. 'He *found* Charlene's body. He's upset about that. That's … enough, surely?'

Mattias raised an eyebrow. 'That's a strange way of putting it.'

I half shrugged, getting impatient now. 'Well, that's how it is.'

'In which case, maybe we should think about therapy?'

I shook my head. 'Hudson doesn't need therapy. He just needs us to give him time to work through ... whatever it is he needs to work through.'

I went to get up but Mattias laid a hand on me. 'I don't understand why one minute you're placing a lot of importance on what happened to him in the woods, then the next minute downplaying it.'

'I'm not,' I said, 'I just need things to calm down. With all of us.'

Mattias stood up to face me. 'It isn't fair. It isn't fair that you're making me into a problem here. You can trust me.'

I stared into his deep, green eyes. Then pulled him close to me.

It took all the effort I had not to break down in his arms. But I held it together. Swallowed hard, blinked, took a deep breath. Then I said in a quiet voice, 'I'm not making you into a problem. I'm trying to protect you.'

Mattias drew back. He seemed to be deciding something. 'OK. But ... if there's anything I need to know, I can trust you to tell me.'

I nodded.

'Things aren't as terrible as they seem, sometimes,' Mattias said. 'I'm sure Hudson will get through this.'

I didn't say anything. I was thinking about what I'd seen during the night. What had happened in front of me. Then the feeling of revulsion I'd had when I saw under the bed. The webs. The movement behind them.

'Rex ... are you there?' Mattias reached out and gave me a little shake.

'Sorry,' I said.

I saw something cross his face then. Something closer to annoyance rather than concern. 'I just want to say,' he said, 'when we spoke on our wedding night about us being both perfect parents for Hudson, about a united front, about how we would both be dads to him ... well, this doesn't feel like that. Not at all.'

He then left the room. I heard him go downstairs. And a bit later, I heard the door close without him saying goodbye.

I sat still in the chair by the bed. I lost track of time. I felt I should go and check on Hudson again, but I hadn't heard any noise from his room and didn't want to disturb him unless I had to. And, if I was honest with myself, I wasn't in a hurry to confront what we'd both been through last night and discuss the likely ramifications of the incident at the quarry.

A buzz from my phone on the side of the bed jogged me out of my thoughts. I wondered if it would be Mattias trying to make peace. Or Hudson, asking me to come to his room. But it was neither. It was Adelaide.

I need to talk to you. Urgently.

It was barely 9 a.m. It must be the middle of the night in Texas. I picked up the phone and messaged back.

What's wrong?

The reply came instantly.

It's happened again, hasn't it?

My fingers trembled as I typed back.

How do you know?

I waited a few seconds. Then her next message appeared.

Video call in two minutes. There's more we need to discuss.

Chapter Twenty-Six

THE BOY

2 November 2024

I woke up lying on the carpet under my bed. It was surprisingly soft. I guessed it hadn't been trodden on much, with the bed on top of it. When Dad bought the house, it was an old, creaking, ramshackle old place. He still had some money left in his budget after selling our Westminster home for a lot of money, so he had all the bedrooms and living room re-carpeted and done up nice. To make a home. A warm, safe, peaceful home—that's what he said at one point. I think he felt guilty about us moving, about losing a lot of his savings on a bad investment with an old school friend.

But the home was no longer a warm, safe, peaceful place.

Nothing would ever be safe again.

Not so long as I was alive and in the house.

The webbing under the bed was thick and hard to push

through. I thought I remembered walling myself up, but the memory was hazy and tinged with something, like a fuzzy, bright-red sheen across it, as if I had a filter on my mind or a piece of plastic over the lens of a camera. I think I was scared. Scared that Dad would follow me into the room and look for me under the bed while I was still … as I was. Still capable of producing strands of silk like the curtains of it that swayed a little around me. Still capable of hurting someone I loved, potentially without even meaning to.

I didn't dare try to tap fully into my feelings up until this point, but I was aware things were changing. My moments of transformation still came from moments of extreme emotion, but once I had changed, my thinking was becoming clearer. I was able to properly remember more now, when I looked back. I didn't want to remember, but the images were recorded in my mind like unnerving little clips playing on a loop.

I could remember Dad's face as I changed. His look of horror as I fell to the floor. As my body began to shift and contort into something so far beyond the boy he knew, it must have terrified him past anything he'd ever seen before. How could it not have?

I pulled myself out of the webbing and crawled out from underneath the bed. It was like I was being born again, but into a world I already knew was terrible. A world I wanted to opt out of. A world where I was the monster that needed slaying.

When I stood, I spent ages rubbing my skin, trying to get

the strands of web away from me. I had a piece caught around my right wrist that wouldn't come off right away.

It was quiet outside. I hadn't checked the time, but I could tell by the light it was later in the morning. After continued silence on the landing I walked straight out of my room, to the bathroom, and into the shower. I let the water pour down on me, not waiting for it to warm up. Then I wrapped a towel round me from the pile on the side near the bath, inhaling the scent of washing powder. Something normal, something nice, something an everyday human would use and appreciate. Ordinary people going through ordinary lives.

I went back to my room to dry properly and dress, then headed downstairs, a heavy feeling of nervousness about seeing Dad. About what state he might be in. I briefly wondered if there would be an army of scientists waiting for me, lab technicians, police, army personnel, like the last part of *E.T.* where people start to experiment on the alien and the boy who found him. Would they do the same to me? Turn the house into a laboratory, putting flaps of plastic up and quarantine zones, in case Dad and Mattias had become infected by being near me.

No such scene greeted me downstairs. No scientists, no police, no army. But I could hear Dad talking. Like the day before, I could hear him speaking to someone in his study. And again, I heard a woman's voice. Mum's voice.

She sounded agitated, distressed even, much more so than when I'd heard her talking before. Then the voices stopped and the door opened. Dad stood there, looking dishevelled, his hair all sticking up.

'Hud,' he said, startled to see me standing there in the hallway. A few seconds of silence passed between us. Then he said, 'Are you … OK?'

I nodded. Then I asked, 'What's wrong with Mum? What's going on?'

I was aware this must have something to do with what Dad had said last night. What he'd been telling me, or trying to, when I … lost control.

'She's…' he said, then stopped himself, clearly deciding how much to tell me, '…. troubled. She's troubled by what's going on.'

I drew in a shaky breath. 'Did you tell her? About last night?'

Dad reached out and put a hand on my shoulder. 'Let's sit down and have a chat. A … calmer chat.'

We went into the living room. Dad directed me to sit down on a different sofa to the one he'd found me on last night. 'Hudson, you're going to have to bear with me—I'm still trying to digest everything that's happened. Everything that … I've seen. And I don't know what to do about the police. I don't know, from what you've told me, how close you are to arrest, if you are indeed a suspect. It sounds awful, but I think you must be. To be honest, I'm surprised they haven't done some DNA match or something already. They're probably going to turn up today if they've seen what Kenny said on social media about you … well, you having sex with Charlene. But that's only half of our worries.' He closed his eyes, pinched the bridge of his nose between his eyes. 'Your mum's suggested we go to Texas.'

I leaned forwards, surprised. 'Would we be allowed to?'

He shrugged. 'I doubt it.'

'Then why…?'

'I'm just trying to think, Hudson,' Dad said, a little harshly. Then looked at the floor. 'Sorry. I didn't mean to snap. There might be a way. I'll … think about it.'

'What? Dad, I'm not getting mad… I'm not going to … change right now, don't worry … but I'm really tired of you not telling me things. Things I think you and Mum know.'

He nodded. 'OK. But it's less about keeping things from you and more about trying to get things in order in my own head.' He sighed. 'I imagine you're hungry, as well. You've barely eaten anything in days.'

This wasn't entirely true. But I didn't want to draw attention once again to what had happened the previous day. to what I had done. But it was true, I was extremely hungry. I only properly realised it when he mentioned it.

Dad started clattering around the kitchen looking for something to eat. I saw tension in his face. He was stressed, agitated and becoming more so with each cupboard he opened.

'There are no cereals, no bread. Mattias finished the milk this morning.'

'It's fine. I'll wait,' I said.

'Fuck,' Dad swore. This unsettled me even further—he didn't usually swear, at least not when I was there. 'I'll go and get something from the shop around the corner,' he said, grabbing his keys from the counter. There was a small corner shop two streets away, barely a couple of minutes in the car. He then paused and looked at me. 'Or maybe I should stay?'

I shook my head, 'I'll be fine.'

'You're not to leave the house, you understand, Hud?'

I knew what he was really saying. What he was worried about. *Don't go out and kill anyone else.*

'And if the police arrive?' I asked.

He sighed. 'Well, let's just hope that doesn't happen.' He went to go and then paused, 'Tell you what, if they do arrive, it's unlikely they'll have a warrant to smash down the door. So just don't open it. If the door rings, you stay completely still and wait until they've gone. And stay away from the windows. Understand?'

I nodded.

'OK.'

Dad came towards me then and kissed me on the forehead. He then paused and looked at me, putting a hand on my shoulder and giving it a little squeeze. He didn't try to tell me everything would be fine, not now. We'd reached an understanding that we were too deep into this strange new world to kid ourselves any longer that the way forward would be smooth. But I knew he was there for me. And that was enough for now.

Barely a minute after Dad had left, the door opened and someone walked in. I had gone up to my room to watch some *Doctor Who*-themed unboxing video, trying to introduce a sense of normality into this very abnormal day. When I heard the sound, I went out onto the landing, laptop in my hands, and peered down, wondering if he'd forgotten something. But it wasn't Dad. It was Mattias.

He saw me looking down from the stairs.

'Hudson. Where's your father?' He looked worried. Something seemed to have unnerved him.

'He's gone to the shops. Why are you back? I thought you were getting the train to Newcastle?'

'I forgot my wallet,' he said, distractedly.

'Whatever,' I muttered, hoping he'd just go.

'I wanted to talk to your dad before I did. It's important. It looks like there's been more murders.'

I felt a chill descend around my shoulders.

'Oh?'

He looked up at me, eyes narrowed a little. 'Yeah, there's a police cordon, around the corner of the forest near the quarry.'

I continued to stare at him. 'And why do you need to talk to Dad about this?' I asked.

Mattias closed his mouth. He looked grave. 'Where were you last night? When you went walkabout, scaring the wits out of your father and me?'

In other circumstances I'd have been snarky about his attempt to make it sound like he and Dad were a shared parental unit, equally worried about me and my welfare. But in this instance, I stayed silent.

'Well? Hudson?' he said, his voice now loud, borderline shouting.

I thought of all the many things I could say. The excuses, the lies. But no matter what came to mind, everything was underpinned by one thing: my resentment and frustration that Mattias was even here in the first place, pushing himself in when this was something that only concerned me and my dad, and maybe Mum, too—though I hadn't got to the bottom of that side of things yet. This wishy-washy pretty boy with his blond hair and perfectly cut nails and his obsession with art and painting, even though it earned him hardly any money. Why had Dad brought him into our lives? How could he think he loved someone so … so … *dull.*

'Hudson?' Mattias said again and started towards the stairs.

I walked around the landing railings and began to walk down the stairs towards him. 'What? What are you really trying to ask me?'

'It can wait,' he said, his eyes still narrowed.

'Fuck you,' I said, turning away from him.

'What did you say?' he shouted back.

'I said fuck you!' I yelled, swinging round to face him, not hiding my anger at him anymore. My laptop fell from my arms and cluttered down the stairs, lodging about halfway along.

'Hudson, I know you're very well practised in this sullen-macho-lad shit but don't forget that I live with you and your father and I know you're just a frightened little boy who'd rather be watching your weird little YouTube videos about Star Trek nutters than actually doing normal stuff like a normal fucking teenager.'

It was the first time I'd seen him properly angry. Really angry. His naturally olive-tanned face was more flushed than usual, his eyes had gone from narrowed in suspicion to wide and flared with anger.

He paused to take a breath then shouted 'Did you kill them? The bodies they found in the woods? And that girl on Halloween? You did, didn't you? Your father doesn't want to believe it. Doesn't want to believe that his son is a deranged psychopath, but I've got you fucking sussed, Hudson.'

He started to move towards me, marching up the stairs. I didn't know what he was going to do, if he was going to attack me, restrain me somehow and call the police, or just wanted to yell his suspicions at me, face-to-face. I didn't wait to find out. I bolted across the landing and closed my bedroom door behind me.

Mattias was shouting at me from the other side. How he was going to tell my father everything. That he was tired of tiptoeing around us when it was plain as day what was happening.

'You have no idea!' I shouted back, feeling something—that prickling, fuzzing feeling, spreading from my arm, up to my shoulders and neck, down to my other arm.

No. No. No. No.

The thought came to me like a puzzle piece slotting into place.

A simple idea. So simple.

All I had to do was to open the door.

And so I did.

I opened the door and stepped back.

Mattias walked in, still shouting, although now I couldn't

hear him. All I could hear was my own heartbeat. And the buzzing, humming sound.

Without saying anything, I walked over to the door and closed it. Then I took off my T-shirt. My breathing getting heavy. My vision changing.

'Hudson ... what are you... What's... What's going on?'

Heavy breaths. Prickling. Prickling.

I looked up at Mattias.

'This won't take long.'

Chapter Twenty-Seven

THE FATHER

2 November 2024

As I drove down the street, flecks of rain coming from the dark afternoon sky, I contemplated turning back, telling Hudson we'd both wait until Mattias got home and send him out for food. But I carried on, part of me gaining some strength from just being outside in the daylight, going somewhere as normal as the shop. In spite of this, I couldn't help imagining what might be happening to Hudson at that moment. What if he left again and harmed someone else? It would be my fault. Or if he transformed and left the house without meaning to—even if he didn't harm anyone, him just being seen would cause panic and god knows what other issues. Or perhaps the police would arrive and they'd see him through a window or hear him moving about.

In the shop I paid for the basket of items I had chosen and left as quickly as I could. I raced home, not caring about speed limits, and just as I was indicating to turn into the driveway of the house, I saw a woman walking on her own towards the house. It was DS Scott. I thought this strange. Why didn't she have a lower ranking officer accompanying her? Part of this made me feel a bit better: if she was coming to arrest Hudson, surely she'd bring others? Uniformed officers to take him away, putting their hands on his head as he got into the car, as I'd seen on TV. But nothing like that seemed likely here with just one lone detective walking on her own towards the front door.

DS Scott turned around as she heard the car coming close to the house.

I got out. Tried to control my facial expressions. Tried to look calm, collected.

'Er… Hi,' I said, getting out of the car.

'Hello Mr Toussaint-Ray. Is your son home?' She didn't sound very calm or collected herself. There was something bothering her, I could see it immediately.

'What's this about?' I asked.

'Can I ask where you've been?' she said.

'Shopping,' I replied, bluntly.

She looked down at my empty hands.

'Oh, yes, I…' I turned awkwardly and reopened the car and pulled out the carrier bag.

'Is your son home?' she asked again.

I didn't know whether to lie, to prevaricate, to stay silent, tell her she'd need a warrant to come in. Or to act casual. Keep up the act that we, as a family, had nothing to hide. Happy to help the police with their enquiries. I also knew news of what Kenny had said on social media about Hudson and Charlene would reach the police's ears at some point.

Part of me hoped it was that. And not something else. Like what had happened in the woods near the quarry the night before.

'Please can I come inside? Hudson isn't in any trouble,' she said. The words surprised me. 'Please, Mr Toussaint-Ray, I just... Let me be honest with you. My colleagues don't know I'm here and I could be in a lot of trouble if they did. There's something ... strange ... going on here. Something that might be potentially explosive in terms of the media, in terms of ... well, everything we understand to be possible. I think an information blackout is likely to follow so I wanted to try to talk to you both before things got more uncomfortable for you both.'

She knows. The thought appeared in my head and then flooded my brain like poison in a glass, spreading, merging with my thoughts. *She knows what's happening to my son.*

'Please can we go inside? I want to talk. That's it.'

I nodded. 'OK,' I said, not knowing if I was being stupid to trust her. But I needed to work out what she knew. Needed to find out how much of our secret, our terrible, life-changing secret had become known to someone outside the house.

Inside, I could immediately tell something was wrong, although it took me a second to work out what had made me stop. Then I saw the stairs. The laptop, open and wedged halfway up it. And the webs. Thick folds of them, hanging down like horrible curtains placed intermittently around the stairway, hanging from the ceiling and banisters above. Whatever was beyond that webbing was shrouded in darkness, and for a moment I felt as though I was staring down the entrance of a long, dark tunnel with no light at the end of it.

I turned to look at DS Scott, attempted to hide the worry from my face, hoping she hadn't seen the horror in my eyes. 'These are … Halloween decorations,' I said.

She looked concerned as she started to nod. Her eyes then rested on the laptop on the stairs. My mind continued to whir as I looked at it, too. It must have been dropped. Hudson must have dropped it. If he had been in a hurry. Or distressed. I picked it up quickly. 'I'm always telling Hudson to stop leaving things on the stairs,' I said, trying my best at a calm, normal-parent sort of tone. *Get her out*, I thought to myself. I needed to get her out of the house.

'Shall we go … outside,' I said, 'We could talk in the garden?'

If she wasn't suspicious before, she certainly would be now. The cold, grey, drizzly November air wasn't an inviting prospect for a chat.

'Or maybe the kitchen?' DS Scott said, eyebrows raised. For a moment, I felt like telling her this wasn't her house and I'd decide where we'd chat. But instead, I gave her a vague nod and led her down the hallway. I saw her pause at the door, look back into the hallway, at the webbing hanging down around the stairwell.

I let my eyes scan the kitchen but I couldn't see any

evidence, at least not in that room. No discarded, torn clothes. No disturbed furniture.

I was still thinking about this, my senses on high alert, when DS Scott started talking. Her first sentence took me by surprise.

'To cut to the chase, I think the boys were right about an animal.'

I blinked at her.

I shook my head.

DS Scott leaned forward a little across the kitchen table. The room was dark and I could hear the sound of rain starting to patter against the windows. Even in the dim light, though, I could see something new in her eyes that I hadn't seen previously. Something closer to fear. 'I think Hudson and Kenny saw something truly astonishing that night. Something that ... people ... they're going to want to hush it up. So, not to cause panic, but I have a duty to the memory of Charlene and her family to get to the truth. I don't want this covered up. People *need* to know what happened.'

I was so tense, I thought I could hear a ringing in my ears. I was clenching my teeth so hard, I felt a sharp pain when I released my jaw to speak.

'What's prompted this?'

The fear in her eyes seemed to magnify. This woman, who must have seen her fair share of nastiness in this world, seemed close to unravelling. I just needed to find out how much she knew. Whether she was aware of the real reason she should be afraid.

'Something has been found,' she said, quietly.

'*Something*?' I repeated back.

'Something … strange … in the quarry. A body … or rather what's left of one.'

Kenny. They'd found Kenny.

'We have found five bodies in total, four in one location within the forest, and a fifth in the quarry. And there are things … details … about the state of these bodies that is … disquieting.'

I bet it is, I thought to myself. I hadn't seen what Hudson had done to Kenny's body, but from the few brief descriptions he'd given, I guessed it hadn't been a pleasant discovery. And it explained why DS Scott looked so shaken. Because anyone who had found such a disturbing mixture of skin and bones bound tightly in webbing would understand that nothing about this whole situation was simple. Or normal. This was something else.

'And you think … what?' I asked.

'I think there is something out there. Something truly terrifying. And because everybody is scared, things are going to get left behind. Like the truth, like honesty, and it's all going to be lost in the midst of either secrecy or hysteria. I've seen it happen before, and I'm tired of lying. Christ, I was so close to just handing in my badge today.' She let out a half laugh, half sound of annoyance, and raised a trembling hand to her face. Something had shaken her. Whether it was what she saw in the quarry, or the orders she was now being given from up above. Whatever it was, I felt the dynamic between us changing by the moment.

'What I'm saying, Mr—'

'Call me Rex.'

'What I'm saying, Rex, is that … there are things out there that you wouldn't believe. Things that happen in this world that we're told never to disclose to the public. And when these sorts of things come up, a very specific set of people are brought in to control the narrative. So the truth of the situation is never revealed to the public. To avoid panic. Keep things tidy.'

I stared at her. 'What sort of narrative?'

She laid her hands flat on the table between us. 'One that people would easily believe. A teenage boy who tried to have sex with a girl, perhaps without her consent, then when she fled he attacked and killed her.'

The look of shock on my face must have been obvious, '*What?*'

'And then, when his friend threatens to tell the police, he pushes his friend into the quarry where he falls to his death.'

'But … that…' I spluttered, trying to find the words without giving away how much I already knew. 'That didn't happen. Hudson wouldn't—'

'Believe me, I don't think he did it. But very soon, a decision is going to be made about how much to tell the public. And a teenage serial killer is a lot more of a palatable explanation than the one that might be closer to the truth.'

I forced myself to breathe slowly. 'And what, according to you, is the truth?'

DS Scott paused. She cast a look over to the kitchen window where the darkening sky had started to rumble with distant thunder over the fields. 'That somewhere out in the woods is a monster.'

We stared at each other for a few seconds. Then there was a thud upstairs.

Both of us looked at the ceiling. Then DS Scott's expression changed. 'Who's up there?'

'Nobody,' I said, an obvious lie.

'You said Hudson wasn't… Is he up there?'

'No,' I said, standing up. 'I… I think you should go.'

'I need to talk to him,' she said, also standing and making her way for the kitchen door.

'Stop… Just wait,' I said, but she ignored me, walking down the hallway with purpose.

'I need to speak to him. I need to find out what he *really* saw that night,' she said.

I reached out and grabbed her arm.

'Hey! Get off me!' she said, shaking her arm free and starting to climb the stairs. 'Hudson!' she called out.

'Stay where you are!' I shouted.

I wasn't sure if my command was to her or to my son. But regardless, she stopped, standing on the third step. Her arm stretched out. Touching one of the hanging strands of webbing.

'These aren't—' she took her hand away quickly. 'These aren't Halloween decorations, are they?'

I didn't answer. There wasn't time. I barely had a second to register the look of horror—or the worst of her dreads confirmed—flash across her face when the legs took her.

Closed around her head and upper body and pulled her into the darkness.

I think I shouted something. It may have been 'No!' or something less distinct, I'm not sure. Whatever it was, it was drowned out by the screams. Screams echoed around the house. Then they became muffled, like something had covered her mouth.

Then there was a snap. Then another. And another. Then the sickening sound of something splashing—a liquid sound. Spraying. Dripping. From my position, backed up against the wall in the hallway, I noticed flecks of something landing on the stairs. Deep red flecks.

Then nothing. Just the sound of a hurried scurrying, scuttling, along the floor above me. Followed by silence once more.

Chapter Twenty-Eight

THE BOY

2 November 2024

The mental numbness I felt as I crawled from the bedroom floor to my bed was expected, this time. I didn't try to override it. What was the point. I hadn't acted badly, I thought as I lay on my bed, waiting for my strength to return. I'd just defended my territory and eaten because I was hungry. It was what practically every living being does on a daily basis. Nothing wrong in that. In fact, the whole idea of wrong felt like an odd, unnecessary thing. I decided not to think about it. I just lay there, on top of my covers, not minding the fact that my body and the sheets underneath were sticky with blood.

I did start to mind, though. As I felt myself slowly returning. My mind slowly sliding back into its usual shape, with my usual feelings and emotions, taking longer than before, the time passing and the daylight from the window growing dim. Things were getting back to normal. Though really, normal didn't exist anymore. Not in any way that mattered.

I cried this time. I think before it was the shock that stopped the tears. But it was the thought of having to tell Dad about Mattias that overrode that. I didn't know how I was going to say it. How I would tell him. And what I would leave out. Like the way I wanted him to come into the room so I could shut the door. Trap him in here as I changed. As I attacked. The sound he made as he tried to fight me off while my fangs punctured him. How he moved and jerked as I opened the wound in his stomach wider and started to drink.

I wouldn't say any of that. In the end, I didn't have to say much, at all. I just walked out of my room and down the stairs, my legs clicking a little as I went. I tried to not focus on the hanging webs, the bloody mess along the stairs.

I didn't care that my bare feet were leaving marks on the floor. I just needed to keep moving. To face this awful moment. To tell him what had happened.

'Dad,' I said, the sobs rising again as I walked down the hallway.

'Hudson!' he called out from the living room.

I walked in, and as I did so, I knew he already knew. He was sitting on the single-seater sofa by the fireplace, the small lamp on the table next to it the only light in the room.

'I'm so sorry, Dad,' I said.

He looked at me. 'Mattias…' he said in a quiet voice that

still seemed to cut through the air and into my heart, like an icy blade.

I just looked at him, not bothering to brush my tears away from my face as they fell.

'Is he...?' Dad whispered.

I nodded.

I saw something break in my father's face at that moment. Something that couldn't be fixed. And I was responsible. I had broken him.

He got up off his chair and came over to me. I sobbed into his chest as he put his arms around me.

Neither of us said anything, not for a long while. We just clung on, both of us struggling to comprehend what had happened. And what we would have to do next.

Chapter Twenty-Nine

THE FATHER

Early Hours of 3 November 2024

I hugged my son because I didn't know what else to do. I'd sat there for hours, waiting for him to come down. My mind terrorised me about what might have happened to the man I loved.

I'd seen his keys. Just after the death of DS Ruth Scott. With the sounds of the blood splattering down the stairs still in my ears, I had turned to see his keys lying in the dark-blue oval bowl on top of the small table near the door. That was when I knew he'd come back while I was out. And if he wasn't downstairs, he must have gone upstairs and likely suffered a fate similar to the one I had just witnessed.

I tried to compute the situation as I sat in the lounge. But I don't think I really believed it until Hudson came in, covered in blood, tears running down his face. A look in his eyes that made me want to crumble and fall into a thousand little pieces.

So I held him in my arms.

Then I told him what I was going to do. A decision I had made during my time sitting there, waiting for Hudson to return to his normal self.

'I'm going to contact my father.'

Hudson drew back away from me, worry in his eyes.

'What? You... You're not going to tell him...?'

I shook my head. 'No. But ... he's going to have to be told something. And I think I know how to do this.'

He looked worried and confused, but didn't argue.

'I want you to go and shower while I phone him, OK? Don't touch... Don't go anywhere near... Just leave the bodies. OK?'

He nodded. I think we both knew how difficult it was for me to refer to Mattias as a 'body'—one of two corpses somewhere above us.

'Shower, wash all the blood off. Use a lot of shower gel, then do it all again. Scrub hard. Then once you're clean go into my bedroom and sit on the bed. Don't go back into yours and don't tread in any blood on the landing. Put on some of my pyjamas and get under the covers. Keep warm. I'll come and find you when I'm done.

Hudson nodded, then left the room as instructed, eyes red. Hands shaking. Once I heard him go upstairs and the bathroom door close, I dialled a number I had saved on my phone but hardly ever used.

'What's wrong?' came my father's curt answer. No

'Hello' or warm greeting. I wondered how he answered the phone to his other son. The one he had with his wife. The one that wasn't the result of an affair.

'There's ... something I need help with,' I said. 'I'm sorry to phone out of the blue. I know it's been a while.'

'Tell me what this is about.' He didn't sound annoyed, but the curt nature of his tone made it clear he wanted me to get to the point quickly. Cold and businesslike. That was how he'd always treated me.

'It's about ... something I can't talk about on the phone.'

A few seconds silence passed between us. Then he said, 'If that's the case, I think you really must be in need of help. We can meet in person.'

I put my hand to my face. I hadn't thought this through. There was no way I'd be able to drive all the way to my father's house in central London. I couldn't leave the house as it was, especially with the body of a missing police officer. Her colleagues could have already started looking for her. And Hudson. If leaving him for under an hour had resulted in multiple fatalities in the home, it was inconceivable I could drive hours away to another city.

But to my surprise, my father provided a solution to all this without me having to explain.

'I'm in Newcastle,' he said, simply. 'I trust you haven't moved without telling me.'

'No. I mean, I haven't moved.'

'I'm at the Hilton Newcastle Gateshead. Room 383. Don't be long.'

The line then went dead.

I told Hudson where I was going. I said I needed to meet my father, who was staying nearby, and he would sort everything out. I wasn't sure if what I was saying was true or even possible, but I decided to say it and hope for the best. Then came the difficult part.

'I'm going to shut you in, Hud,' I said. 'I'm sorry. But I think it's for the best, OK?'

From inside I heard a murmur of agreement. I locked the bedroom windows and pocketed the keys. The bedroom door didn't have a lock on it, so I dragged, with some effort, the unit of drawers next to the wardrobe out of the room. Outward opening doors to the bedrooms had always been something we'd talked about altering due to their awkwardness on the landing. Now, when it came to imprisoning my own son, I was glad we'd never had them changed.

Once the drawers were up against the door, I called out to Hudson letting him know I was going to be as quick as I could.

I hovered for a moment, before I turned to go down the stairs, looking at the doorway into Hudson's room. I knew I would eventually have to go in there and see what remained of my husband. I couldn't put it off forever. But I decided now wasn't the time. I had to get a handle on the situation. So I looked away, keeping my eyes fixed forward, avoiding the webbing and blood as I trod slowly and carefully down the stairs, opened the front door and left the house.

Chapter Thirty

THE FATHER

Early Hours of 3 November 2024

The forty-minute drive to Newcastle city centre went by quickly. I followed my father's instructions when I got to the hotel. Nobody stopped me at reception, no key card was needed to access the stairs. I just went up to floor 3 and located room 383. As I neared, I could hear voices coming from within.

The door opened after my first knock and there he stood. My father, Michael Allerton. Looking as blank and unreadable as always. I noticed his once-blond hair greyer than when I last saw him a few years ago. The rest of him, however, was unchanged. Tall and slim, smartly dressed in a shirt and tie as if he were in his office. He looked at me briefly, his phone clasped to his ear, then motioned me inside whilst saying 'Yes, that is very clear, thank you. No, he has no right to complain. If he had stuck to his guns, rather than having an emotional crisis in the dock under cross-examination, he wouldn't be in the mess he's in now.' In other circumstances, I may have been interested in the subject of his phone call and wondered who he may have been talking about. Which rich but disreputable member of society was paying for his consultancy company to fix their problems. But today I didn't care. Today I needed him to fix *my* problems. And I would have bet everything I had in the world, he'd never had a client come to him with a situation like the one I was facing.

The hotel room was more like a suite, with a separate living room leading off from the door. He gestured towards the sofa, and I took that as a sign he wanted me to sit. I sat as he went over to the desk near the window. He closed an open laptop and said, 'The price has gone up. You're his lawyer; you can be the one to tell him. If he wants miracles, he's going to have to pay for them. Yes, absolutely. That's fine. We'll talk tomorrow.' He tapped the phone and pocketed it. We stared at each other for some moments, then he crossed the room without speaking and began to pour a glass of Scotch from a bottle. 'Would you like some?'

I shook my head. 'I'm driving back after this.'

My father sighed and sat down in the desk chair so he was facing me. 'And *this* is ... what? What could be so bad you had to drive to see me tonight, for the first time in years? So terrible you couldn't possibly mention it on the phone?' His voice was as deep and penetrating as ever, like a finely tuned laser going right through me.

'It's something ... awful,' I said, weakly.

'Well, then you're lucky I was in the vicinity,' he said.

'Why are you?' I asked.

My father narrowed his eyes. 'A difficulty with a client of mine. Though, needless to say, my work is confidential.' He then got up and walked over to a small table to the left of the window and picked up something from its surface. A newspaper. He unfolded it and handed it to me. 'Has your sudden contact and visit anything to do with this?'

I looked at the front page.

FOREST DEATH HORROR: TEEN GIRL DIES IN HAUNTED WOODS ON HALLOWEEN

I stared at him, astonished. 'How did you know?' I asked, my mouth open, staring at him.

'I didn't, until now. I guessed. Your house is very close to the murder scene. It mentions a group of teenagers who were in the forest at the time. You were unwilling to talk on the phone, presumably in case the police were listening, suggesting you or someone close to you is suspected of a crime. Am I right in thinking you're here because you believe your son is involved in some way?'

I was startled by his deductions, although the more I thought about it, the more I could appreciate how he'd joined up the dots. On my way to the hotel, I'd decided to tell him the barest minimum. His suppositions actually helped me in framing the situation in a way that left out the most unbelievable and horrifying aspects. So I nodded.

'I see,' my father said.

'More people are dead,' I said. 'A group of boys. A police officer. And … and Mattias.'

I saw flicker of something like surprise in my father's face. 'Your husband?'

I nodded.

'Dear me,' he said, quietly, 'I'm very sorry to hear that. And Hudson … was involved?'

I nodded again, aware my lip was quivering. 'It's bad,' I said in barely a whisper.

'Yes, it's bad,' my father said. 'But nothing is so bad to render it unsolvable. Why don't you start at the beginning.'

I told my father a story. I framed my son as a murderer—a boy who had lashed out and killed a girl during an argument, then killed other boys in the forest when they discovered his crime. I said he killed a police officer and my husband during a scuffle when he was confronted with his crimes. It was neither an outright lie nor anywhere near the full truth. My father listened, his fingers interlinked in his lap, his eyes on me. He didn't interrupt or question or test what I was saying. Only when I finished did he sit back in his chair and look at the floor, apparently thinking. Then he straightened up and said, 'I presume, by telling me all this, you're asking me to commit a crime and help you cover it up?'

My heart started to pound against my chest. We were

reaching the knife edge of my visit, the pivotal point that would decide Hudson's fate. My fate. 'Yes.'

He nodded slowly. 'I *could* do that, yes,' he said, slowly. 'It would be difficult, but not impossible. And with no guarantees.'

'I'm sure you've committed various other crimes in your time,' I said, not worrying if I sounded blunt. I saw him raise an eyebrow.

'Oh, is that so? You know that, do you?'

I stared back at him. Then I started to speak, once again choosing my words very carefully. 'I've played the game. You've always kept my existence secret from your family. You covered up your affair. You paid off my mother to keep her quiet and didn't even attend her funeral when she died. I haven't complained. I took the money you gave me and did as I was told. I'm now asking you, begging you, to do everything you can to help.'

I saw the surprise return to my father's eyes and for a moment I thought he even looked rather impressed by my little speech. Then he said, coolly, 'There's always another option. A much simpler one.'

'What?'

'You pick a good criminal lawyer and then phone the police and tell them everything. Or I can recommend one. I can ask my good friend, Jacob Wakefield, for example. I'd cover his costs.'

'That can't be an option.'

'It's a serious one,' he said. 'And one you should contemplate before you decide to do otherwise.'

'OK, let's say I've thought about it and have decided I don't want my son to go to prison.'

Another pause. Then he said 'Well, you made the right decision in coming to me, then. But once we start down this path, there's no going back, you understand?'

'I understand.'

'Good,' he said.

I wondered if he would be saying 'good' if he knew the true horror behind everything that had happened. The real reason I couldn't tell him the full truth of what had occurred in my home.

'The house is a crime scene,' I say. 'There are … bodies and … blood.'

'I know people who can sort that,' he said, as calmly as if he were recommending a plumbing firm or a team of decorators. 'In terms of you and Hudson—I suppose you have ideas in terms of the next steps?'

'Yes,' I said, 'I need you to get us out of the country. I need to you bribe and blackmail and threaten whoever you need to, pull any strings, call in any favours, spend any money, whatever it takes.'

Another few beats of silence. Then he asked, 'Where do you want to go?'

I took a deep breath. But I didn't need time to decide on the answer to this. I've known where we'd end up for a while now. 'Texas,' I said. 'Hudson and I are going to Texas. We need to see his mother.'

Part II

HOME

Chapter Thirty-One

THE FATHER

3 November 2024

We left our home that night. I knew we wouldn't ever go back. That it was impossible. That this was an evacuation. Our home was no longer safe for my son. Years ago, we had arrived for a fresh start. Away from the bad experiences of my money worries in London. Away from the lingering memories of Texas. But in the end, we'd just swapped one feral, dangerous landscape for another. The wilds of Northumberland hadn't provided safety for us, but rather a canvas upon which the darkest parts of Hudson could thrive. Now, I was left with no choice. We needed to go back to square one. No more *new starts*. Perhaps that was my mistake in the first place. Maybe if we'd stayed in America, all those years ago, whatever had happened to Hudson wouldn't have felt the need to break out and disrupt his new surroundings. Maybe it—*he*—would have been at peace. I had no way of knowing.

My father had arranged for us to stay in a halfway house. A car arrived outside our house within a couple of hours of me coming back from seeing him. We were picked up by a grey-suited young man who introduced himself as Ezra. He carried our bags out to the car without complaint or questions. I wondered how much my father had told him. Probably very little. But a couple of times I saw him glance in the car mirror, an expression of worry on his face that made me think he was doing more than checking the traffic behind him. Maybe he knew he was helping to transport a murderer. If only he knew the truth about what this boy was capable of, I thought to myself as the car turned towards the motorway, the hulking mass of Barret Forest disappearing from view. He would probably get out of this car and run as fast as his long legs in his skinny suit could carry him.

As we travelled through the night, my mind replayed what I had done when I'd arrived home from Newcastle.

I'd called out to Hudson that I was home but needed to sort some things before I let him out. I had been relieved when he answered. No argument or complaint. But at least he was human again.

I'd set about trying to detangle the webbing—the bloodied strands, the hanging folds of silk, and put them in bin bags. I'd sobbed over the broken corpse of my husband as I'd laid him down after breaking him free from the sticky, silver cocoon that had trapped his final moments. Parts of him had remained upstairs, even after I'd bagged him up and moved the body to the hallway. His body had been in so many pieces that there were times I'd had to stop, the stench of bloody remains too overpowering. I'd had to go and be sick. Pausing to remove the kitchen gloves I was wearing, wash my face, wipe my eyes. Look at some pictures of Mattias on my phone, try my hardest to remember him that way, to keep the person in my mind rather than the lumps of flesh, blood and bone to be hidden and destroyed. After that, I'd turned to the scattered remnants of DS Ruth Scott. Her broken limbs spread haphazardly across the landing. The house looked like something out of a horror film. I could never have imagined the reality of how much blood and flesh stained a crime scene following a murder. It had clung to the walls and light fittings, brain matter seeped into the carpet, and I'd found it hard to believe that just a few hours ago these two people had been alive. I gagged on the overwhelming smell that surrounded me, too afraid to open the windows for fear of our neighbours getting a hint of the rancid decay beginning to form, and laid out the hefty binbags, ready for my father's contacts to come and dispose of.

When I'd finally finished, sweat dripped down my forehead, and as I called out to Hudson that it was time leave, I was surprised at how meekly he came along. I had asked him to quickly pack a large travel case of things he'd need to bring if we were going on a long trip. He only asked one question. 'Where are we going?'

I gave him the only answer I could.

'Home.'

The house we were taken to was dark and dusty. It only had one bedroom with a singular bed. Ezra told us we needed to stay there for a day and another night while my father 'sorted things'. I told Hudson to take the bed. He didn't argue. I spent every waking minute worrying about him. How he was going to react to the slightest thing. How we'd survive on a flight. What could happen if things went badly wrong when we were flying through the air in a pressurised metal tube with a collection of strangers. I told myself that all I could do was to try to calm Hudson down.

I slept on the sofa while Ezra dozed in the armchair in the lounge. The whole place looked like the sort of house occupied by elderly people in the 1970s, the sort you see on TV sitcoms or depressing episodes of old soaps. I didn't know who owned it or what my father normally used it for. And honestly, right now I didn't care. I made sure Hudson was settled in the bedroom on the creaking old mattress, then dropped myself onto the sofa and slept. Unlike the past few nights, sleep came instantly.

We were on the plane. Hudson next to me, the aircraft speeding down the runway, take-off fast approaching. But with each incremental gain in speed, the boy's hand I was gripping started to feel different. I turned to look at Hudson but he was vanishing before my eyes. And it was his eyes I couldn't stop looking at. All eight of them. Passengers screamed as he flew from his seat. He dashed over to an old lady first, to the right of his seat. She screamed as he went for her neck. The blood streamed and sprayed everywhere all around the cabin. More screams. So loud. He was moving fast. Scurrying over to others as they tried to get out of their seats and back away from him, but they weren't fast enough. None of them were. I tried to get out of my seat, but someone stopped me. A strong hand on my arm from the person in the seat to the left of me. It was DS Ruth Scott. She leaned in to speak to me, her voice surprisingly calm. '*There are things out there that you wouldn't believe.*' Even though she was whispering, I could still hear her amidst the roar of the plane. The screams of the passengers. '*Things that happen in this world that we're never told the truth about…*' I tried to move again, but her grip was firm. In the end, I just had to watch the carpet of the aisle between the seats. As it slowly turned from grey to a river of red. Then there was nobody left to scream anymore. The aircraft was falling. Falling. Falling.

I woke with a jolt so hard I fell off the sofa. It was 8.30 a.m. Ezra was gone from the armchair. I scrambled up to my feet, eyes sweeping the room. No signs of a disturbance. No torn clothes. No wrapped and bloodied body on the floor.

I rushed upstairs. The bedroom door was open and I could see Hudson stretched out, the covers half on, half off, fast asleep. I heard the sound of a tap running and stopping. Then the door to my right opened and Ezra walked out, a toothbrush in hand.

'Sorry, did you want—' he said quietly, pointing at the bathroom.

'No, no, it's fine… I was just…'

I didn't finish the sentence, but instead glanced back at

the bedroom. *Checking my son hadn't tried to kill and eat you* probably wouldn't help the situation.

When Hudson woke, an hour later, I brought him a shop-bought sandwich that Ezra had procured for us.

'I'm not hungry,' Hudson said, sitting on the edge of his bed, running his hands through his hair.

'I think... I really think it would be good for you to eat,' I said, patting his knee and pushing the cardboard packet towards him. He looked at me. Then picked up the sandwich. He knew what I was thinking. I didn't have any proof at the moment, but I had been wondering if the danger of him wanting to ... *feed* ... the other way might be lessened if he was more satisfied in his current state. We didn't discuss it. Just sat in silence with our sandwiches.

Hudson read books all day. He would normally have been on YouTube or tapping away on his laptop, but I'd made him leave all his devices at home. I told him it was important we didn't use them. Just in case we were being tracked. I didn't think we were, not at this point anyway, but I also didn't want Hudson researching stuff about the killings in our neighbourhood online. Reading whatever speculation there might be. Any news about the identification of the bodies found in and around the quarry. Any tearful to-camera statements from parents. I felt a pang of guilt when I thought about what Kenny's parents must be going through. Then tried to push it away, focus on my own problems, my own son.

We got word from Ezra that my father had secured us safe passage out of the UK into the US. I didn't ask how. I didn't want to know. Ezra said the passports would arrive that evening, for use on a flight the next day from Manchester Airport. I was surprised to see my father bring them in person. He walked into the house with the confidence of someone who had been there before. But his face turned grave when he handed over the passports.

'I'm sorry you're in this position,' he said in a tight, curt way. 'And I'm sorry how things have been with us ... in the past. I... I wish you both well.'

I'd never heard my father falter in a sentence before. Even in my early teen years, when he'd come to see me and my mother for fleeting moments and I'd tearfully ask why he never stayed very long, why he barely spent any time with us. He had just bluntly said 'Because I have another family elsewhere.' And that had been it. I'd grown up feeling he was invincible, indestructible, unshakable. But when it came to saying goodbye to me, perhaps forever, I think I saw a little crack in his armour. Small but just about visible.

I took a look at the names and photos. The pictures were the same as in our passports, but the names were different. Hudson had become Ethan Watson. I had become Brian Watson. My name had gone. And Mattias's surname with it. I was no longer double-barrelled. Brian Watson didn't have a husband. He just had a son, a boy he'd do anything to protect. That was the way I had to think of this now, I told myself.

'When you start on this path,' my father said, 'there's really no way off it. I have seen this sort of thing enough times to know that.'

'You've never seen anything like this, Dad,' I said, realising that, all of a sudden, I was trying not to cry. 'Not like this.'

He looked at me. I could see sadness in his eyes, too. 'Something tells me this is the last time we'll see each other. And my instincts are rarely wrong, so…' He held out his hand. I shook it. In spite of my complicated relationship with this man—in spite of all the resentment and anger I'd felt towards him in the past—I was grateful. Grateful to him for helping us. Grateful for him making me feel, in some small way, that I wasn't entirely alone in this nightmare.

'Would you like to see Hudson?' I asked. 'He's upstairs.' I was aware he had only met Hudson once, when Hudson was twelve, at a restaurant in London when, by sheer chance, we'd happened to be seated at a table next to my father and his wife. When she had gone to the ladies', I had said hello to him and introduced Hudson. My father had replied with a quick hello, shaking the confused boy's hand. Then he had walked off quickly, probably to settle the bill and intercept his wife before she came back from the loo. I wondered what excuse he'd given her for their quick exit from the restaurant. Whatever it was, I know it wouldn't have been the truth, that an unseen part of his life was sitting at the adjacent table.

A closed-off look came over my father's face. 'Perhaps not. I remember him as that shy, polite boy I met a few years ago. If he's done what you think he's done, I don't think I want to see that boy. I'm content with the memory I have in here.' He nodded his head at me, turned towards the door, then walked out of my life, perhaps for ever.

When the time came for us to leave for the airport, I found Hudson sitting on the bed, staring at his hands. 'I'm worried about the flight, Dad.'

'I know,' I said. I didn't tell him I was, too. I got the feeling he needed some certainty from me. 'It will be fine.'

'Will it?' He looked up at me. 'You still haven't properly told me. Not everything. About why you think this is happening to me.'

I went and sat next to him on the bed. 'Because it isn't really my story to tell,' I said, slowly. 'I might get it wrong. And I think it's best she explains it to you face-to-face.'

He looked at me, his eyes pleading. 'Can't you try?'

I took a breath. 'Your mother foresaw this,' I said. 'She seemed to know about ... what you are ... even when you were a baby. It was one of her main delusions. It turns out she may not have been as deluded as I thought. And what I said before ... about something that happened in the desert with you and her ... I think that might be where all this began.'

Chapter Thirty-Two

THE BOY

4 November 2024

I was terrified about the aeroplane. Worried I'd lose control. That I'd do something terrible. Dad said we should go and I didn't argue. I wanted to talk to Mum, too, and I agreed with him about going back there. Back home. It might help us to make sense of what's been going on. Return to everything. And the more I thought about it, the more I felt that something was pulling me back. Memories of something. The scent of burning. A rough texture. Small fragments floating around my subconscious. Perhaps they would start to connect and make more sense when I was back in the place of my birth.

But first we had to get there.

Dad said it would be fine, but I knew he was lying. Or stretching the truth. Stretching whatever confidence he had in me. I got that he was trying his best. That he must be struggling to keep it together after what had happened to Mattias. What I'd done to him.

I hadn't been able to stop the moments before Mattias's death from going round and round in my head. The moment I reached out and closed the door, trapping him. And the look in Mattias's eyes just before it happened.

Feeling immensely anxious, I took a seat in the back of the suited-man's car so he could drive us to the airport. Dad turned around in the passenger seat and gave me a small smile. He was checking I was still calm. I understood why.

Dad was clasping two passports and printed-out boarding passes in a plastic folder file. He said goodbye and thank you to the man driving us and then he handed me one of the passports. 'Here, take this. You've got a new name.'

I looked at the picture. It appeared to be the same as my old passport, just with the name Ethan Watson instead of my real name, and a birthday that was a week before my actual birthday.

'Learn those details. The name and the new date of birth,' Dad said as he put my bag down in front of me. 'You OK doing that?'

I nodded. 'Are you going to have to call me Ethan?'

'I'm afraid so,' he said and looked sad. 'I'm sorry you didn't get to choose it.'

So was I. But I didn't say anything. Just pick up my bag and said, 'OK, shall we go then?'

Our tickets were first class. I was surprised by this. I'd flown first class before, back when I was much younger and Dad had a lot more money than he did now. But I had presumed, because this was being done quickly and in secret, we'd be flying economy. Apparently not.

When we boarded the plane, I was in a sort of daze.

I began to count backwards from one hundred. It was helping me to stay calm, but when I got to zero I felt a flash of panic, my mind suddenly filling with all the things that could happen if everything went wrong. If I failed. If I lost control.

As I fastened the seat belt, I leaned back and watched the other passengers board the plane. A kind-looking lady with a little girl. She called her Anna and handed her a pencil case as she took her seat. I heard her telling her that once the plane had taken off, she could have her colouring books.

I felt sick.

I clenched the arm rests, telling myself to be calm. I began counting down from one hundred again. Trying not to focus on the other passengers taking seats around us. What I could potentially do to them.

Dad reached over to me from his seat and unclenched one of my hands. 'You're fine,' he said, 'Just ... stay calm.'

I nodded and tried folding my arms instead.

Eventually, all the passengers were seated and the plane doors were secured for take-off. No one had arrested us. No last-minute police officers had dashed onto the plane. Nobody had looked suspiciously at our passports or tried to catch us out with our names or dates of birth. We had made it.

Now I just needed to make it through the flight.

I slept through most of it. I ate the meal put in front of me—Dad must have ordered for me while I slept. He'd made a good choice: Hunter's Chicken. It tasted good and for a few moments I felt as if we were going on holiday and everything was fine, as though when we landed we'd get to a nice hotel and I'd put my trunks on and spend the day in the pool while Dad lay on one of the sun loungers reading.

But this was no holiday. And no matter how many times I reminded myself of that, it didn't lessen the pang of shock and unease when I saw her. When we disembarked the plane at El Paso airport, we went through border control and out into the bright heat and light of Texas where she was waiting for us, standing by a dark-green SUV.

'Hello, Hudson,' she said, walking up to me. She paused, arms jerking a little, perhaps unsure if she should hug me or not. In the end, she decided to just stand there and smile, her hand giving an awkward wave. The warm wind rippled around us and I caught a scent of her perfume. Flowers, but a bit sharp and citrussy, bringing back memories I didn't know I had.

'Hi, Mum.'

Chapter Thirty-Three

THE BOY

4 November 2024

Mum drove us to the ranch. It took about an hour and she didn't speak on the way, other than to say how glad she was we'd come. It was strange watching her, seeing her as a living, physical human after all these years. Someone I'd got used to seeing in photos or, very infrequently, on a computer screen in a video call on my birthday or Christmas. She didn't ask questions, nothing about what had happened, or about the years since we'd seen each other face-to-face. Dad didn't try to make conversation either. There seemed to be an accepted silence among us. As if we'd all silently agreed that our predicament was so weird that it was beyond the need for casual chat to fill the silence.

As we drove out towards the desert, the landscape felt stranger and more surreal. I wasn't sure I remembered it from my childhood or just from films I'd seen, but I knew one thing: it looked harsh and brutal. Dry and orange and brown, although still with something exciting about it. It was the direct flipside of the green Northumberland trees and fields I'd been surrounded by for the past few years.

I didn't realise we were on the drive up to the ranch until I saw a rusty metal fence separating it from the road. I'd forgotten how rural and expansive the whole area was. Regardless, I knew without a doubt that this used to be my home. It didn't unlock just memories, but a cascade of feelings. A mixture of familiarity and fear. As if my body knew something had happened here, or nearby. No matter how young I was, this building had left its mark on me. The grey, weathered wood on the outside and the shaded veranda that ran around the whole of the building. I know most people would probably feel a bit strange if they were to come back to the place they once thought of as home, years later, after so much had happened. But for me there was something else swirling around inside me. A feeling of rediscovery. Like this dry, harsh, unforgiving landscape that stretched out around us was an integral part of me. A part that I'd never truly recognised until now.

There were a few trees dotted about, giving the front yard a bit of shade. An evidently broken and heavily rusted truck sat to the left of the property.

The building was tidy, nicely furnished, everything neat and orderly, with throws and new-looking cushions and white rugs over the brown polished wood floor.

'Wow … this place looks different,' Dad commented as he dropped the bags on the floor and stared around him.

'You didn't expect me to not redecorate at all in the decade and a bit since you've been here, did you?' Mum asked.

'It's just… Well, it's nice … less…'

'Less shit than it used to be, is that what you mean?'

For a moment I thought she was annoyed, but I turned to see her deadpan face starting to break into a smile.

'I was going to say less rough and ready,' Dad said.

Mum shrugged, 'True. I'm not the same woman I was when I was twenty-two. Shocker.'

'I guess that makes sense,' Dad said. 'Can I sit down? I'm so exhausted I feel as if I might collapse on the floor.'

Mum sighed. 'You don't have to ask. You used to live here.'

Dad sat down, muttering something about that feeling like a different lifetime and a different world.

Mum turned to me and said, 'So, Hud … you're OK me calling you Hud?'

I looked at her. It was still weird seeing her in front of me like this. She was shorter than I'd expected. From photos and talking to her occasionally on Zoom, I'd built an image in my head of her being taller. She took a step towards me. Brown hair floating a little in the warm breeze from the open door. Her face was kind. Caring.

'I… I…' I stammered, then found my words. 'Dad said I have to use the name Ethan now.'

She looked over at Dad on the sofa. 'Is that true?' she asked.

'It was the only way for us to get here. Our passports have new identities to avoid trouble.'

She shrugged. 'Well, you're here now, so I guess it doesn't matter.'

Dad leaned forward. He really did look tired and I felt sorry for him having to explain all this again. 'How did you think we got here, Adelaide? My father set all this up and there wasn't time to be choosy about the details. You've been begging us forever to come back here and live with you. Now it's happened. But let's not pretend the name change is the difficult thing here. Because really, in the grand scheme of everything that … that's happened…' I heard his voice catch. He swallowed. 'I just think perspective is needed here.'

Mum nodded. 'You're right of course. I'm sorry. I know I said it on the phone, but … well, I really am sorry about Mattias.' I saw her eyes move for a moment over from Dad to me. Then she said, 'OK, let's bite the bullet. I'll get us some lemonade and then we'll go out onto the veranda and have it all out.'

Dad's eyes looked wide in panic. But I decided was time for me to talk. To have a say in all this.

'Yeah, I think we should. I think I need to talk about it all. And I have questions.'

Mum looked at me. I saw surprise in her eyes, but my words didn't seem to trouble her. 'Good. Come on. Let's get started.'

We did as Mum said. Before I'd unpacked, before I'd even seen my new bedroom, we left the interior of the house and went out onto the veranda. I sat next to Dad on a grey wicker seat and Mum took a seat on one of the other chairs and starts to talk. 'There's no pretending this isn't all just ... well, weird and awful. But we just need to park that for now and deal with facts. Your father has given me a general idea of what's been happening. But now I want to hear it all from you, if you feel capable of telling me. I understand the details may be ... upsetting. But I think it's important we face them. The three of us. Together.'

She nodded as she finished this little opening speech. I nodded, too, although something about it felt a bit odd, as if she was selecting words she thought would keep me calm. Trying to make this into a manageable situation, as if I were a kid who'd stopped doing his homework or was recovering from some traumatic situation like a car crash. But of course, this wasn't anything like those two things.

'And once I've done that,' I said, 'you'll explain everything?'

'I will,' Mum said. 'But Hudson, I can only tell you what I know and what I suspect. The rest is something we'll have to work through and figure out. Together.'

I told them everything. Or nearly everything. I told them about how it felt when the change happened. The transformations. The rippling, prickling feeling that gave way into searing pain. The feeling of parts of me breaking and reshaping. The murky, hard-to-define memories I had after each time it occurs. I went through each one, avoiding looking anywhere near Dad when I reached the situation with Mattias. And I held back a key detail there, too. The key detail that sent a burning ache of shame through me each time I thought of it. The fact that I wanted it to happen. In that moment, I wanted to kill him. The same way I wanted to kill those boys in the forest. But I hid that, too, making it sound like it had happened in an entirely involuntary way.

Mum was quiet throughout all of this. Then, after I finished speaking, she reached forward to the little table and poured out some lemonade for each of us. We drank it in silence, digesting all the strange, horrible things I'd just said out loud. Then I looked at Mum and said, 'Please, can you just tell me what you know? Dad seems to think that you … that the reason… I just want to know why this is happening to me. And how to stop it.'

She watched me for a moment, apparently considering. Then stood up. 'Wait one moment.' She disappeared into the house. I sat there, still trying not to look at Dad. I was doing OK; I was calm. But if I looked over and saw him crying or even looking at me at all I worried, I knew I'd lose it. Lose control.

Thankfully, Mum returned almost instantly.

'Years ago, shortly after your father took full custody of you, I had a therapist who advised me to write down any memory I found upsetting or disturbing. To give as much detail as I could. I'm no writer, but I think I rather nailed the whole experience in this journal here and I want to read it out to you. Is that OK?'

'Yeah,' I said, leaning forward, looking at the book she

was holding. It was deep purple with a black bookmark and a fabric-look to the cover. She opened it and turned to the centre, showing pages of neatly written text. 'So … when you say "experience" … this is…?'

'This is the story of what happened to me out there, fourteen years ago.' She pointed to her right, over the veranda, past the trees, out towards the rocky, desert terrain. 'To put it simply, I think this is your origin story.'

Chapter Thirty-Four

ADELAIDE'S DIARY

31 October 2010

Rex has a date. He pretended he didn't, that it was just a friend he was meeting, but I knew it was a date. The way he wouldn't look me in the face whenever he talked about him. He said his name in a vague way, as if he could hardly remember it. I knew he was doing it to be kind. To save my feelings. Make me feel less awful about not having any kind of love life, sex life, social life. I haven't slept with anyone since I'd slept with Rex that night almost three years ago. A mistake. Such a mistake. We should never have done it. A heterosexual woman and a gay man—how could it have ever worked? Well, it did work—the sex itself. The mistake. But drunk, foolish people often make mistakes. No matter how many times I write about that night in here, there's no undoing it now.

So Rex went off on his date, although before he went he made a point about being able to smell marijuana. I assured him I had only smoked a small amount, just a few puffs. He asked me about tablets and I told him I'd barely taken anything all week, that I was better, that I was doing as I promised.

I lied. The moment he was gone, I reached for the stash of pill bottles I'd hidden down the back of the sofa. I needed them so I could be a good mother. Needed them so I could be myself, otherwise I was a mess, useless. These were the stories that got me through from one tablet to the next.

It was such a lovely evening. Fall in Texas is often warm and suddenly I felt a need to be outside. I picked up Hudson and guided him to the push chair. He didn't cry or complain. He was getting a bit big for it now, but settled in happily enough. I was going to take him on an evening stroll, then put him to bed and have a nice long bath.

I packed the pill bottle. Oxycodone. And a bag of weed in the stroller, just in case I needed them. Another little lie I told myself. 'Just in case'. There was no just in case. I'd spend every step thinking about them. As I pushed that stroller, every turn of the wheel said to me, 'Is it time, yet? Surely it's time? You've gone without some for so long … at least four hours … or four minutes … but it's the same difference, you tried, that's what mattered… Now treat yourself… Go on…'

So I did treat myself. I parked the pushchair under the shade of a tree, took out a blanket from the back, laid it down and began to roll a spliff. Pulled out a bottle of vodka I'd put in there, too, just in case, of course. And the bottle of tablets. Rattling. Taking one out.

The roll of thunder. I think it was then that I heard it. But it sounded distant.

Just another swig from the bottle, then I'll take us back in, I thought. The thunder's miles away. It must be. No rain was forecast.

A long, long drag on the spliff.

So relaxed. I'd been so stressed, with Rex watching me the whole time, telling me my 'substance use' was getting out of control. I just needed something to calm me down.

Another long drag.

The blanket was so comfortable. You'd never guess how hard this ground was. How dry. In need of moisture. Liquid. I had liquid. In the bottle right next to me. I'd have some, I thought. Just a bit more.

I don't know how long I was asleep for. But when I opened my eyes, I was confused at how bright things were. And then darkness. Then more light, then it went again. Then the huge crash. That properly woke me up.

A storm was happening around us. A huge, electrical storm, although there was no rain. The ground was still dry. Parched. Cracked. Broken. I stood up, walked over to the stroller. That was when I saw it was empty. He'd been taken. Someone had taken him. And now it was dark, in the middle of a lightning storm, strips of shining white light illuminating the horizon. It was like, every other second, the world was set on ablaze by the brightest fire that's possible to imagine. Then it would go again, only to return even brighter. The sight was astonishing, but I couldn't stop to look. I had to find my boy. Had to…

He was there. A short way away from me. Toddling along the ground that merged into the desert floor.

I was about to shout, but the words left me with barely a sound. I couldn't speak—I could only watch. Watch as the ground started moving.

It was like it was rippling. Folding and unfolding. The movement was strange. Uncanny. And Hudson was in the middle of it. In front of something. A tree stump. He was in front of a tree stump in the midst of the moving, shifting floor. I forced myself to take a step forward, but an unusual feeling had come over me. It was like my whole body was tingling. Buzzing.

Then a flash of lightning illuminated the ground in front of me. The ground surrounding my boy. And that was when I saw why it looked like it was moving.

Spiders. The whole ground was alive with spiders. All roughly the same size, around the same as the palm of my hand.

I called out to Hudson again but struggled to get purchase on the words. It was like my mouth had been filled with treacle. My limbs paralysed with a drug.

How many pills had I taken? Was this an hallucination? But it felt so real. So real.

Hudson approached the tree trunk. I managed to take another step closer and I could see from another flash of lightning that there was an opening within the trunk. A hollow. And the spiders were coming out of it. Pouring out. And Hudson, in all his child-like innocence, seemed captivated by this. So he reached out a hand.

An astonishingly loud crack broke the sky. I had time before the flash to see the lightning bolt come down like a thrown javelin, finding its mark. Striking at the tree stump just as Hudson stretched out his hand to touch the hole. The hollow. The nest.

The screams cut through the night air more powerfully than any thunder. And suddenly I could walk again. Run, even. Running over to my boy as the spiders on the ground around me followed me. Changing direction.

Scurrying.

Scuttling.

Screaming.

But the screams weren't coming from the spiders, they were coming from my son. As I reached him, the screaming stopped and he went very quiet. Just lifted up his hand—the hand he'd used to try to reach into the hole in the tree stump. He looked at it. Then he collapsed, his little legs falling beneath him.

I had a horror of the spiders engulfing him. Swarming over him. Devouring him. But they didn't. Within seconds they disappeared, and by the time I'd hauled Hudson into my arms, the last of them had scurried up the gnarled edge of the tree stump and disappeared into the hole.

I called Hudson's name again and again, trying to get him to wake up. I shook him. Tapped his head. He didn't look as though he was in pain. He looked like he was sleeping. And for a terrible moment I thought he was dead. So I cried. Cried and cried, clutching him to me. But I felt his breath against my neck and I saw his chest going up and down.

I got back to the blanket and laid him out, checking him for injury. His skin was clear from damage, as far as I could make out, save for one small mark. A mark on his wrist. The wrist of the hand he'd touched the tree stump with. It wasn't a cut or a bruise. More a small line, like a scar from an injury he'd acquired years ago. It hadn't been there before, though. I was sure of it.

Then came the rain. A massive crack across the sky, accompanied by more lightning, brought a sudden, extreme downpour the like of which I'd never seen. I fled. Wrapping Hudson up in the blanket, I bundled him into the pram and made my way back to the house.

Inside, I grabbed my phone. Tried Rex but he didn't answer. So I phoned 911.

The words of the 911 operator were muffled in my ear, but I couldn't distinguish them. I was distracted by the sight of Hudson in his stroller.

He'd sat up. Awake. Calm.

A smile on his lips.

Chapter Thirty-Five

THE BOY

4 November 2024

I found I couldn't speak after Mum finished reading. I looked down at my hand, my wrist, run my finger along it.

'You still have the mark,' Mum said. It wasn't a question. A statement.

I nodded.

'I have it, too,' she said, and held out the wrist of her right arm. At first I couldn't see it. But then, as I peered closer, I could see a slightly raised, darker area, almost impossible to see unless you were looking for it.

'I've had it ever since that night,' she said. 'Perhaps it's less pronounced compared to yours because I was further away from the lightning strike and the trunk of the tree. I don't know.'

'I think I knew it was something to do … something

connected to what was happening,' I said. 'When I... When I change, I feel a strange feeling, like a fizzing ... and I think it comes from here.'

I held up my hand, pushing my wrist outwards.

'What happened to me that night?' I asked, suddenly feeling panicked. Afraid.

'All I know', Mum said, 'is what I wrote here. I have theories of course, but...' She trailed off and shrugs.

I was silent for a few moments, then I asked, 'The bit about me being a mistake...'

A sad look came over my mother's face. 'I didn't mean it like that. I'm sorry, I should have left that bit out.'

I shrugged a little. Tried to brush it off. 'I suppose it was honest ... if that was how you felt.'

I looked over at Dad, 'And how did you know what happened to me was something to do with all this? Did you know what had happened ... out there in the desert?'

I saw Dad glance at Mum, then he said, slowly, 'I knew there was a chance you had been struck by lightning. You were taken to hospital because of it. I felt awful that I'd gone on a ... to meet a friend... I left my phone in the car by mistake and when I got back I had missed calls from your mum, that you'd been taken to the hospital. But because I'd had alcohol I couldn't drive, so had to wait for a taxi. When I got there, you were OK, but it ... caused changes.' He looked awkward.

'Changes in me?' I asked.

'No, no,' Dad said. 'Changes as in ... your custody.'

'As in taking you away from me,' Mum added. At a look

Dad gave her, she held up her hands. 'I'm not starting an argument; I was just stating facts. And I couldn't understand how at the time, but the incident ... unsettled things. It unsettled me. I began to have...'

'Have what?' I asked, frowning at her.

'Visions.'

'Visions of *what*?' I felt a prickle of frustration run over me. But it stopped there. No rage. Not at this point at least.

Mum reached forward and took up her glass of lemonade. She took a long drink, then set it back down and sighed. 'I started to lose my grip on reality. I kept trying to give up the drink and the pills, then suffered panics and withdrawal and went back on them again. I even started injecting at some very low points. In the end I had to go and stay in a rehab clinic in central El Paso.'

She paused, as if negotiating some memories that had come back to her. I knew what that was like. But there were more questions I needed to ask. 'What was in the visions?'

She waited a few more seconds. Then she said, 'I would dream that I was pregnant with you again. I knew it was you, not another baby. In the dream, I went to have the ultrasound ... all very normal, and I was delighted, I remember that vividly. I remember smiling at the nurse as she did the scanning and was looking at the screen, and she smiled back, asking if I wanted to know if it was a boy or a girl. I told her I knew it was a boy and that he'd be called Hudson. And then she stopped smiling. She started looking closer at the screen. I asked what was wrong and she said 'There are too many...' And in the dream I remember thinking she meant I was pregnant with twins, or even triplets. She ran from the room, saying she needed to get her colleague. I turned over to look at the screen. She… She was right. There were too many legs. I couldn't believe what I was seeing. But it was unmistakable. It was a spider. Its legs bunched together, as if it was closed up and asleep. But I must have leaned too far as I fell off the bed and landed on the floor and something … broke… I felt it and it was so painful. I screamed and the nurse came back with one of the colleagues and almost skidded from the blood. The blood that was coming out of me… And she screamed that I was about to deliver. She bent down and said it was starting. And I could feel things … and then her face contorted and she started screaming. Backing away, blood all over her from kneeling on the floor. That was when I woke up.'

I stared back at her, horrified, thinking about what she had just told me. Then I said, 'But … that was just a dream.'

'It was a dream,' she nodded, sounding uncertain. 'But it wasn't the only one. I kept having them about … about you. About your life. But each time, you were replaced with … this *thing*. This animal. A… A spider.'

I felt Dad shift next to me. 'An important detail here is … the drugs … the alcohol. It was obvious—or obvious at the time—that these were just hallucinations. That the incident involving the spider's nest and the lightning had caused some kind of breakdown.'

Mum held up a hand. 'I know, and I thought the same. I'm not trying to make excuses or blame you for not taking them seriously—*I* didn't take them seriously. I couldn't. *But*, and again, I'm not trying to qualify this in retrospect, but a part of me did know there was something different about these dreams. That's why I called them visions, just now. Because they did feel like movies that had been inserted into my head, or real-life memories that I had, rather than the vague, shapeless nightmares or hallucinations you can get when off your head. There really was something different about them—like I was trapped, being made to watch Hudson's short life being rewritten. Rewritten as a horror story.'

I looked over at Dad. 'So … when I told you about what had happened, and when you saw it yourself … when I changed in front of you … you remembered what Mum had told you about these visions?'

He nodded. 'That's why we're here. It seemed too much of a coincidence.'

I looked at Mum. 'And you believed Dad? When he told you?'

Mum nodded. 'It was almost as if I'd always known something like this would happen. I can't explain it any better than that. It was as if I just knew.'

I looked down at the mark on my wrist. I touched it. I didn't know if it was my imagination or if I could really feel it, but I thought I could feel a tingling sensation, very lightly, underneath the pad of my finger. And part of me liked the sensation. I looked up to see Mum watching me. She reached forward and laid a hand on my arm.

'Are you OK?'

I nodded slowly. 'I think I can remember parts of what

happened. The blinding flash. And the sound. The sounds the spiders made as they scuttled across the dry ground. I don't know how much of it is memory or just coming from what you've told me.'

Mum and Dad were silent. They didn't have the answers. How could they? Then I asked another question. 'Is it going to happen again?'

'Do you want it to?' my mother asked. I was surprised by the question. I wondered if she could tell I was even more conflicted, even more troubled, than I dared to show.

Then I thought about the bodies, the bloodshed.

The look of fear in Mattias's face before he died.

The way Kenny's body moved and twitched as I drank him from the inside out.

The screams from those boys as I tore into them.

The warmth of Charlene's blood when I punctured her neck.

I felt sickened, disgusted.

I looked up into my mum's eyes. 'No,' I said. 'I never want it to happen again.'

Chapter Thirty-Six

THE BOY

December 2024

Over our first few weeks in Texas, I was aware of my parents watching me. Cautious. Nervous, even. As if they were waiting for the horror to return. Waiting for me to lose control, for my body to start contorting, for the worst to return. There were times when I saw panic clear in my dad's face if I got up too quickly or ran to my new bedroom for some trivial reason. I knew he thought, for a few terrible seconds, that it was all about to unravel. But it didn't. Amazingly, I actually felt the chance—the possibility, even—of such a thing happening fading away. It was like we hadn't travelled to the US by plane, but actually by boat. A slow-travelling ship that was gradually sailing away to new lands, with the terrors of our previous home gradually getting further and further away in the distance, covered by mist and out of sight.

Out of sight, but not completely out of mind, of course. Although I started to feel confident I wasn't in danger of another imminent transformation, it took a lot of work not to be tortured by the memories I had. I sometimes woke screaming in the night, waking up scrabbling at my face, as if I could feel thick, dark liquid running down from my mouth onto my neck and chest, or bits of flesh or bone coating my mouth. Sometimes Dad would come into my bedroom, shake me awake, and try to calm me, but I'd pull away from him, turn on the light and dash across the room to the mirror. To check it wasn't real. I'd touch the skin of my chest and feel that it was human, free from splashes of blood. See that my mouth was normal and clean.

Mum was surprisingly good in these situations. She'd take me into the lounge, sit me down and teach me breathing exercises. How to count and hold in my breath and let it go at certain stages. I wasn't sure at first but went along with it, and soon realised it actually helped. It did calm me. 'There's always a calm way out of a situation,' she said on one of these nights. 'Choosing not to panic and choosing tranquillity.'

These words were useful in the daytime as well as the night. It was agreed I would start school in the new year, so in the days leading up to Christmas I was free to explore. It took me a long time to feel confident enough to do so. Although I started to go for running sessions down the long desert road and back, I didn't go into the nearby town or any other buildings. I got the feeling Dad thought this wise, but as we passed four weeks of being in the US and with no sign of any transformations, Mum suggested I should start to go to more public places. Get me ready for school.

'I think we should rethink the school plan,' Dad said one Sunday after dinner. Mum had left the table to decorate the Christmas tree. 'I'm worried that we're rushing into things.'

Mum came over, two silver snowflake ornaments in her hands. It felt odd seeing decorations so evocative of winter in such a different environment and climate. If the situation hadn't already been so strange, I'd have found the prospect of a very different kind of festive period quite unsettling. I'd have worried it wouldn't feel like Christmas at all. Now, though, that seemed like the least of my worries.

'Rex,' my mother began, her voice gentle, 'Hudson's been cooped up in and around the house for weeks. He needs to go out, needs to meet people his own age.' She looked over at me. 'Don't you?'

I looked at her, then at Dad. Eventually, I nodded. 'Yes, I do.' I saw Mum smile at me. I found it strange, living with her and feeling a connection to her, when it had always been Dad I'd lived with and turned to for advice. But I had this sense, this inner feeling, that Mum understood this situation a lot more than Dad did, even though he was the one who had witnessed it more fully. I put my hand on my arm. Felt the mark on my wrist. It hadn't prickled or caused me any pain or discomfort for weeks. I looked at Mum and our eyes met. I understood, at that point, why she could be so much more relaxed and understanding. She had felt it, too. A diminishing in sensation, the reduction in any feeling or discomfort. She knew when I was in peril, or a peril to others. And she knew now that I was becoming safe.

'I'm worried we're just … pretending,' Dad muttered, his face in shade from the main light and the twinkling of the Christmas tree. 'Pretending normality is … possible.'

'It was your idea to come here,' I said, 'And we did it. In spite of everything, we did it. Now we must … move on.'

Slowly, Dad nodded. Then he turned to Mum. 'Why are you so confident?'

She looked down at the ornaments in her hand for a moment. I saw her eyes move and I was sure they had, for a moment, settled on her wrist, where the faint version of my mark was. Then she looked up. 'Because I have battled addiction and won. Battled a dark part of myself that I thought would take me over, control me forever, and I proved it wrong. Proved to myself I could be master of my own demons. I'm sure our boy can be, too.'

She smiled at me. I found myself smiling back. Just a small smile, but I think it was my first in a long time.

'And besides, I don't know if this is important,' Mum continued, 'But I think it might be. It's no longer Halloween.'

'What does that mean?' Dad asked, frowning.

'It means,' she said, 'I think we might be out of the danger zone.'

Dad nodded. Then he said, quietly, 'Or it means we have just over ten months until we're back in it again.'

We tried our best to build up our lives again. We agreed that, in order to make my transition to US life feel like a new start—and leave the horrors of England behind us—I would adopt the name Ethan permanently. It had taken both my parents a while to get used to it, but both thought it a good idea. Initially Mum argued I should be able to keep Hudson and that, as a dual British and American citizen, I would have certain rights when it came to living here. But Dad said my grandfather had sorted that out and it would complicate matters to try and untangle the work he'd done. I was also very much aware that we were getting money off my grandfather and I knew Dad was conflicted about that. So I went along with what he thought was best. I didn't actually mind. I liked the idea of becoming someone new. And it helped me. It helped me to think of those terrible things as something another person did. A person I used to know, perhaps. A person I had ceased to be.

In the early weeks following our arrival, Mum talked a lot about her journey to recovery. Her journey away from addiction. How she managed to stop the alcohol and the drugs completely and find, what she called, 'her inner peace, inner balance, inner tranquillity'. She said she would teach me to control my reactions to things. Be more in tune with my emotions and learn to understand that just because I felt something, didn't mean I had to act on that feeling. It didn't mean I was at the mercy of that feeling. And it didn't mean I was out of control. So we worked together, every morning, sitting outside on the veranda, talking through practices she'd put in place to help her conquer her own demons. We didn't talk about the 'how or why' when it came to what had happened to me or what I had been through. We avoided wondering or speculating. We just dealt with the central aim: to regain a sense of control and move on with my life.

And it worked. I didn't have an instance of transformation. Days and weeks went by, putting distance between me and the last transformation—that terrible day I brought Mattias into my room knowing I wanted to transform and hurt him, knowing a part of me wanted to be unleashed. But it was *Hudson* who made choices like that. *Ethan* would know better. So I woke up every day with the resolve of knowing better than my past self. Being better.

It was agreed I would start going with Mum to the shops. These were trips to the supermarket; an event I'd have found dull had it been back home in England, but I found examining the varieties of American food I wasn't familiar with oddly entertaining, and soon the trips started to feel carefree, risk free, almost fun. I went to other shops with her—clothing stores, a shopping mall. Being around other people at the food court. One evening, the three of us went to see a film—a Christmas comedy—and I sat and ate popcorn and laughed and enjoyed myself, almost as though I was a normal teenager. A normal boy doing normal things.

So I started to journey out alone. I went for walks into town. Picked up milk and cereal, went for runs in populated areas and even borrowed books from the library.

It was in the library that I first properly spoke to someone in Texas who wasn't related to me or a shop worker. Someone I could have a proper conversation with.

He was sat at one of the desks in the corner of where the science fiction and fantasy sections met romance and general fiction. I'd only glanced at him, acknowledging he was about my age and seemed engrossed in what looked like school work. I was about to go past him to see what new sci-fi books the library might have had come in since I'd visited the week before, when I felt something on my arm and heard a thud behind me. I looked around and saw I'd knocked off some of the books the boy had balanced on the table next to him.

'Oh, sorry,' I said, bending over to pick up the books. 'Here you go.'

'Thanks,' the boy said, smiling. I turned to go but he then followed it up with 'Hey, are you British?'

I paused, feeling slightly awkward, 'Er, yeah. Well, sort of.'

'Sort of?' he said, eyebrows raised.

I wasn't quite sure how to explain, how much I should publicly admit, but I figured there was no danger in being mostly honest. 'I was born here, but moved to England when I was young. I've just moved back.'

'Ah, nice,' he said, 'You back here for school or college or something?'

I nodded, 'School. I start at The James Whiteford Academy in the new year.'

'Sweet, I go there, too,' he said, grinning even wider. 'Be prepared for all the homework, that's all I'm saying.' He nodded at the work in front of him and laughed.

'Ah, thanks, I'll … be prepared.' I looked at the book I'd

knocked to the floor. Frank Herbert's novel *Dune*. 'You a fan?' I asked.

I saw excitement light up his face. 'God, that would be the understatement of the century,' he said. 'I've read it, like, three times, and have loads of my own copies, different editions, you know, but I take a library one to school so I can keep mine nice. You read it?'

'Yeah,' I said, 'I liked the film, too.'

He tilted his head, 'The film's OK. Gets some things right, some things not so right, but that's just my opinion. Hey, this might sound weird, but since you're from the UK I wondered if there's a chance you've heard of a show called *Doctor Who*?'

I struggled not to laugh at the way he'd worded this, 'Yeah, I've very much heard of *Doctor Who*.'

He looked like Christmas had come early, 'Oh, god, man, you need to sit down.' He removed his bag from the other chair at the table, 'I'm Elijah, by the way.'

'Nice to meet you,' I said as I took a seat, setting the books I was holding down on the table. 'I'm Ethan.'

Chapter Thirty-Seven

THE BOY

December 2024

Elijah and I were instant friends. Our shared love of *Doctor Who* and other science fiction was like an instant glue bonding us together. We never ran out of things to talk about. That first conversation we had in the library lasted over an hour and passed in what felt like a few seconds. It was a match made in platonic heaven. He was funny, kind, and oddly flirtatious—on the second time I met him, in the same spot in that quiet corner of the library, in the week leading up to Christmas, he unzipped his pencil case in a fake-seductive way and pulled out a sonic screwdriver, whispering to me, 'I don't show this to all the boys before the first date.' I laughed so much, I earned a frown from the librarian who was shelving an armful of Danielle Steel novels in the nearby romance section. Elijah wasn't actually flirting, though—he was into girls, namely Ava, a girl who apparently lived two doors down from him, who had a home cinema where they'd go after school to 'watch movies'.

'Did you have a girlfriend back in England?' he asked, sneaking out a green-and-white coloured candy cane from his back pocket and snapping it in half. With half an eye on the librarian who was still a short distance away, he slipped the long stem of sugar from its plastic wrapping and offered me the hooked half.

'Thanks,' I said, taking it from him and biting off a chunk. His question about a girlfriend had caused a flicker in alarm in me. Whenever I went too close to *those* memories of England, I felt cold and nervous, as if I needed to retreat under a duvet and shut out the outside world. I was tempted to ignore the question, but didn't want to appear rude or embarrassed, so I just said 'Yeah, hundreds,' and laughed. Elijah laughed, too, and the conversation moved on.

Two days before Christmas, after hanging out with Elijah a number of times, I met Ava. Elijah and I had moved from the library to a nearby Starbucks. He was meeting her to go to the cinema afterwards and she was apparently keen to meet me. When she came in, I was surprised by how 'alternative' she looked. Elijah was always very smartly dressed, with a rather preppy look to his clothing and a brown leather satchel bag, whereas Ava had vibrant purple hair and a tattoo of a snake down her neck and arm.

'So this is the guy you haven't been able to stop talking

about,' she said, sitting down at a spare seat next to us. 'Nice to meet you, Ethan,' she said, smiling widely and slapping me on the shoulder. 'I'm Ava. I doubt he's mentioned me once.'

'I have,' said Elijah, rolling his eyes, 'Well, at least twice.'

'Twice, wow, I'm so fucking flattered,' she said with another eye roll.

'Definitely more than twice,' I said, grinning.

'You know, you should meet Scarlett,' she said. 'She *loves* British guys. She's obsessed with that show.' Ava didn't mention what show she was referring to, but suddenly stood up. 'Shit, just realised the time, we're going to miss the movie if we don't go. Want to join, Ethan?'

I looked at them both. 'You sure?'

'Yeah, come,' Elijah said, his eyes bright and eager.

I didn't even bother asking what the film was. 'Sure,' I said, 'If you don't mind me tagging along. Would love to.'

It was my fault for forgetting to message Mum and Dad. I remembered halfway through the movie and nipped out to the loos. I saw I had two messages from Mum and eight from Dad, including four missed calls. Mum's first was, 'Are you going to be home for dinner? No problem if you're with your new friend!' followed by 'I presume you're eating out with Elijah?' Dad's were more blunt and grew to borderline hysterical, with the last saying, 'Where are you? This isn't on and it's not fair on me or your mother. Call us now. I'm going to drive through the town looking for you, message or call when you get this.'

'Fuck's sake,' I muttered to myself. I messaged them both.

I'm fine, have gone to the cinema with Elijah and his girlfriend, will walk back after.

Then I put the phone away and went back to my seat in the auditorium.

Dad, however, wasn't content with this. He was waiting in his car outside the cinema. I said a hurried goodbye and 'Merry Christmas' to Elijah and Ava, nodding at their suggestion to meet up soon before New Year. Dad was furious with me the whole ride back to the ranch, saying how I'd put him and Mum through hell and he was terrified what might have happened. 'Nothing happened,' I said in a small voice. I knew Dad was scared. I knew he was scarred by what he'd gone through—what I'd put him through—back in England. I knew he was grieving for Mattias. But that didn't stop me being angry with him. Angry for not appreciating that me making new friends and going to the cinema was a big deal for me. A major step forwards. In many ways, I thought, this was a cause for celebration. A glimmer of hope, the sign I might be able to have a new, normal life here. But instead, he had to turn it into a drama.

Back at the house, Mum was a lot calmer. 'You do need to tell us, when you're staying out,' she said, laying her hands on my shoulders, 'But that doesn't take away from the fact that I am pleased you're making friends. I think it's a really important step and it's especially good if they're going to be at your new school.'

I saw Dad thud down on the sofa still looking angry. Then he got up suddenly and I was alarmed to see tears in his eyes. 'I can't do this right now,' he said and went to walk away, then reached back and took the open laptop that was on the coffee table with him.

'He's upset,' I said, suddenly feeling even worse. 'I've upset him.'

'He's just... He'll be OK,' Mum said.

I don't think I spotted that there was something else going on that evening—some other ingredient I wasn't aware of. But I soon found out when I went to the room Dad had started to use as an office. I'd intended to say sorry, but became distracted when Dad suddenly clicked off something as he spotted me in the doorway.

'What was that?' I asked, nodding at the computer screen.

'Nothing.'

'Dad, come on,' I said, walking into the room.

Dad sighed and pulled the browser back up. It was a news story. A British news story, on the ITV News website. I realised what it was as soon as I saw the unmistakable sight of Barret Forrest in the image at the top, the main entrance, the trees, the sign displaying its name outside the closest thing it had to an official entrance. All of it so familiar and immediate and still like a distant memory, like a place I'd read about once in a storybook a long, long time ago.

'They've made an arrest,' Dad said, although I didn't

need him to. The headline made it clear. Although I couldn't properly focus on the words—the letters of ARRESTED FOR MULTIPLE MURDERS swam in front of me.

'No!' I shouted, or tried to shout, but the words were a strangled, gasping sound.

I ran. Terrified of what was coming, I ran across the hallway to the bathroom. I vomited in the sink, the room feeling as though it was spinning right and left all at once, my reflection in the mirror shifting, changing…

'Look, it's fine. He's waking up now,' I heard Mum say.

I was on the sofa in the lounge. I saw her, eye level, crouching beside me, Dad standing above her, the lights of the Christmas tree shimmering behind him. I focused on the lights, the way they twinkled and changed, the pulsating pattern somehow stabilising me. I pulled myself up. 'What happened…? Did I…? Have I…?'

I felt myself over, tapping at my torso, but my clothes were there, still intact, with no sign of webbing or blood. Everything did seem to be … normal. I hadn't transformed.

'What happened?' I asked.

'You fainted,' Mum said.

'Just… Just that?'

'An ordinary, very human faint,' she assured me. 'Dad told me you saw the news report. About the man being arrested in England.'

It all came back to me then. Or rather, the small amount of info I'd discovered. Just a headline. I needed to know more. 'I want to read it,' I said, now in a sitting position. 'Where's my phone…?'

'I don't think that's a good I idea, I shouldn't have—' Dad started to say, but I cut across him.

'Please, just bring me my phone, it's in my room, I think, or your laptop or something. I want to read it all properly. Then… Then we can talk about it.'

Dad brought his laptop in. It still had the news report on its screen. I rested it on my lap and scrolled down the page, taking it all in.

It said an arrest had been made for the murder of Charlene and of the boys in the forest. Police could apparently place a man, Owen Beecham, at the scene of Charlene's death due to a discarded cigarette near her body and his DNA on one of the boys. Kenny's murder was later added to the charge. He had also been arrested for a number of serious assaults on other teenagers in nearby Newcastle. DS Ruth Scott had interviewed him at his home shortly before she had gone missing, and although no body was found, it was strongly suggested in reports the man was responsible for her disappearance, too.

'I've been keeping a close eye on the British media and Newcastle news sites,' Dad said. 'I… I assumed you might have been, too. But I didn't want to ask in case you hadn't and started to go looking.'

'I hadn't,' I said, 'I… I think I didn't want to accept that things were carrying on there. I just wanted it all to be over.'

'That's what we both thought,' Mum said. 'We didn't want to distress you by it.'

I looked at Dad and said 'What about Mattias? The report doesn't mention him.' After I'd asked the question, I saw something in my father's face that made me look away. I think I was afraid that the mention of Mattias's name might make him upset again.

'I don't think anyone knows he is missing. My father… He… He had his people sort everything out in terms of his work and gallery contacts. I think there's been a false trail made about him going to work abroad. Since he doesn't have any other immediate family, there's nobody to report him missing. I don't want to go too deep into what my father's company does, but I don't think this is the first time they've had to create a … well, a fictional disappearance.'

I nodded, as if I understood and this was all fine, but the truth was it was anything but fine. I *felt* anything but fine. It was as though I had made some headway with slipping into my new identity as Ethan Watson, rather than Hudson Ray. And all this threatened to destabilise that. And there was another moral dimension I found I couldn't ignore.

'But … an innocent man. An *innocent* man is going to go to prison, perhaps for ever, for something he didn't do. How can you stand there and tell me that's OK?'

Mum and Dad looked at each other. Then Mum said, 'It isn't as simple as that. I don't think it's something you have to worry about.'

I frowned. 'What do you mean?'

Dad looked and took a deep breath. 'There are other news reports that go into more detail. Rather horrible detail that I don't think you need to read. Basically, because of the nature of where his DNA was found on one of the boys' bodies—one of the bodies near the quarry—he was obviously an evil man… He's committed other crimes against teenagers and children'

I let this sink in. Dad then crouched down so he was at the same level as Mum. He laid his hand on my arm, looked at me imploringly. 'Just believe us when we say that he is no loss to the world. In fact it's probably a good thing, a very good thing, that he will be locked up for a long time.'

I knew why they were keen on this. It meant we were safe. It meant nobody was coming to find us. It meant we were free. It also proved Dad right about something. He'd mentioned that, during his last conversation with DS Ruth Scott, the police officer had implied that not everything was as it seemed with the investigation into the deaths in the forest and the quarry. She was worried the murders would be pinned on me, even though the authorities knew there was something else going on. Something the public would find terrifying. There was no way anyone discovering Kenny's body could think he was the victim of a 'normal murder'. I knew this. Dad knew it, too. So I decided he was right. And I gave myself permission to be glad. Permission to be glad they were pinning it on someone. Permission to be thankful that it wasn't me.

'I hope it doesn't sound awful to say it, and I'm not pretending I don't find a lot of this … very upsetting … but this is sort of the breakthrough we needed.' Dad looked very earnest as he said this and gripped my arm a little tighter. 'Let's use this moment to move forwards,' he said, nodding slowly, as if desperate for me to accept what he was saying. 'I really think we should see this as a gift. Perhaps the best

Christmas gift we could ever have hoped for at the end of this difficult time.'

Mum nodded, too. 'I think your father's right. We should see this as a gift. A gift that will enable you to live your new life. A gift that lets you be free.'

I then saw her eyes travel down to my arm, the part just below where Dad's hand rested, and settle where the mark on my wrist was visible. Then she added, quietly, as if almost to herself, 'For now, at least.'

Chapter Thirty-Eight

THE BOY

January 2025

When I started at my new school, I found it a little hard to adapt to the way they taught in the US and the different exam system, but I got the hang of it. I had been provided with all the documents I needed to start school, presumably from my grandfather, and had been learning all the dates and facts I needed to remember to make my fictional history believable. During the first week, Elijah and Ava very much took me under their wing. We were mostly in the same classes, and even the ones I had to find my way to alone weren't too daunting. The teachers were either openly welcoming and enthusiastic (the very loud English teacher Mrs King kept telling me how much she 'loved *Downton Abbey*', how I sounded like I'd walked off the set of that show and asked if I knew anyone that had been on it) or they were generally neutral and barely acknowledged me in an over-worked teacher sort of way.

As well as Elijah and Ava, I made a small group of other friends, people who were far more welcoming than Kenny or Kirsten had ever been back in England. Although Elijah remained my closest friend, I also became close to a boy called Axel, who enjoyed running like me and encouraged me to join the track running club. After a Friday evening session, while we were in the showers and talking about what we were doing at the weekend, Axel dropped into the conversation that he was having a party and I'd be welcome to come. I jumped at the chance to hang out with my newfound friends.

I could've predicted my parents' reactions when I told them about the party later that night. Mum was gently encouraging but Dad was hesitant. Despite his uncertainty, I wasn't forbidden from going and when I arrived at Axel's large house in a very posh part of town, I felt relaxed and eager to have a great night. It was my first party since arriving in the US, and although I was nervous about the memories it might trigger, I was determined not let that stop me. I wanted to make new memories, ones that would replace all thoughts of past parties.

Inside, I found Axel, who was playing some kind of drinking game, sat on the island counter-top in the enormous kitchen. The music was loud and pumping. Elijah was there, too—Axel had said he'd invite him so I'd definitely know someone else—and I saw he'd brought Ava.

'I want you to meet Scarlett,' she said, dragging me over

to the living room area where a Taylor Swift video was playing on the screen, even though the song playing from the invisible speaker system around the house was Dua Lipa.

Scarlett turned out to be an extremely attractive girl. Her flowing, dark-brown hair, gorgeous natural tan, full lips and piercing eyes (of a colour that I was unable to see in the darkish room, but I liked to think it was grey-green) instantly made me attracted to her.

'Oh, here's the English boy,' she said, coming over, her voice smooth but with a more notably Texan drawl than Elijah or Ava.

I was tempted to correct her, say that I was actually American, but realised that might diminish my perceived attractiveness in her eyes.

'Hi, nice to meet you,' I said, 'I've … heard great things.'

'*Great* things. God, I hope I haven't been oversold.' Her eyes wandered to Ava and Elijah, who were lingering nearby. 'I'm not great. I'm blunt and bold,' she said, getting close. 'I think I'm what you English boys would call—' she leaned in close to my ear and then whispered '—*very* forward.'

She stepped back, probably to assess the effect she was having on me, which was likely to be very visible, with my wide eyes and half-open mouth and glazed expression. 'Come on, let's go chat upstairs in Axel's bedroom,' she said, in such a low, quiet voice that I thought I must have misheard her. But she grabbed my hand and I only had time to see Ava laughing and Elijah say 'Have fun, man,' as I was led off through the house, upstairs, and through a door. I didn't comment about how she seemed very familiar with which bedroom was Axel's. I went with it. Right up until the moment she tried to pull me down onto the perfectly made double bed. Then I froze.

My heart was pumping. Memories were stirring. I thought I could smell perfume. Scarlett's perfume, probably, but in my mind it transformed into another scent, sweeter, more floral. And suddenly I felt I could feel the uncomfortable forest floor beneath my knees, even though I was still standing on soft carpet.

'What's wrong?' Scarlett asked, raising up from the bed and coming over to me. 'You look… You sure you're OK?'

'Yeah, fine,' I said, feeling my heart-rate quicken.

Please don't let it happen… Please … I don't want it to happen.

'I know what might relax you,' she said, as she dropped to her knees.

'I'm not … sure,' I said as she worked to undo my zip.

'Oh you're about to be very sure, English boy,' she said, tugging my jeans down. Before she could actually do anything, however, a shaft of warm light from the landing cut through the gloomy bedroom.

'Oh, shit… Scarlett, *really*?'

'Piss off, Axel,' she said.

'Piss off? This is *my* room!'

'It's OK. We're done,' I said, hastily zipping myself up.

'Sorry, man, I'm not mad at you. It's Scarlett here who takes liberties at times.'

'Keep up your moaning, Axel, and I'll have to tell your mom about your vodka and stash of fake IDs.'

'I think I'd better go,' I said, feeling very awkward.

'No, come with me,' Axel said, 'There's something I wanted to show you.' He came over and grabbed me by the hand and for the second time that night, I found myself being dragged somewhere through the house, feeling as though I was a new plaything for these bored teenagers.

'This way,' he said, ushering me in to a room down the end of the hallway. Inside was what looked like another version of the living room, only with a gaming chair, an even larger television, bookshelves crammed with paperbacks, and a desk at the end of the room by the window with a laptop, two desktop monitors and a row of folders.

'Here, take a look at this,' he said, heading for the desk. 'I have a bit of a weird obsession. Don't freak out, but I'm a true-crime nut.' He gestured to the shelves.

I frowned. 'True crime…'

'Yeah, like, massive,' he said. 'I read hundreds of books on it and keep track of live investigations, like serial-killer investigations, you know.' He reached for one of the files. 'So these here are mostly in Europe: there's the Spanish Backpack Killer—he literally kidnapped backpackers in Barcelona and Madrid and cut them up and put them in their own backpacks. Fucking sick, right?' He started taking out neatly ordered folders from the files. They reminded me of school projects I'd had to do back in Year 7 on the Second World War and different monarchies. Printed out newspaper reports, pictures, maps. He seemed to have had fun assembling them. 'This one's a British one. A man found dead by a swimming pool at some wellness hotel; police are baffled; CCTV goes missing; the hotel's guest records are fucking fried in some sudden fire that happens after the murder, but before the police can seize them, one of the hotel staff is arrested then released without charge. A blogger from London I follow wrote about it extensively. When he tried to research it, someone threatened him, to keep away from it. Weird, right? I love crimes like that, where you think there's something else going on. But this one...' He pulled out a dark green folder and started to flick through the plastic sleeves inside, 'This one is fucked up and it's really recent and wondered if you'd heard of it when you were living in England.'

I instantly felt cold, as if the blood had frozen inside me and every organ and muscle had ceased to function. The image on one of the print-outs was immediately recognisable. It was the same image as the one I'd seen on Dad's computer.

The trees.

The sign.

Barret Forrest.

The headline was almost identical. The news story was from *Mail Online* rather than ITV, but I could see the basic facts were the same.

Man arrested.

Multiple murders.

Northumberland, UK.

I felt the same rising panic as I'd felt the first time I'd seen the news. Except this time, I wasn't at home; I was away from Mum and Dad, who would understand the effect this would have on me.

'So this case is really hot, like, in the true-crime blogging world people have theories. It took place in the north of England. Were you from the north or south? Or I suppose there's an east and west, too, of course.'

'I…I…' I stammered.

'Northumberland,' he said, 'Apparently it's, like, not far from Newcastle, or Newcastle's not far from Northumberland. Or maybe they're the same. Anyway, a bunch of bodies were found in this forest and there are *weird* eye witness testimonies. Some people thought they were animal killings at first, but then this guy was arrested. Allegedly he, like, did weird shit to the bodies, but some people claim he had an alibi; others have said evidence was planted to set him up. He claims he just went to the woods to look out for lightning strikes.. It's weird, as they'd been happening across the world throughout that month, causing burnings and damage, and then there were a high concentration of them that night, Halloween. Well, this guy, Owen Beecham, he apparently tracked some of the strikes to this forest not far from Newcastle and was going to have a look to see if more occurred that night. He'd posted about it on Facebook groups. But perhaps he wasn't going there to look at lightning. Perhaps he was going to do terrible things.' He turned the page so I could see a photo. A man's face. He was large, overweight, balding, tiny eyes.

'I don't want to see his face,' I snapped.

Axel paused, his hands on the folder going still.

'What?'

I realised I was breathing very fast. I tried to slow it, tried to keep calm. 'Sorry… I…' I struggled to think of something to say. Something that would explain my weird reaction.

'You OK?' He was frowning, peering at me similar to how Scarlett had minutes earlier.

'Yes,' I said, trying to laugh, 'Yes, I'm fine. I just… You'll think I'm silly, but, I get nightmares about killers so it's … best if I don't see any faces.'

'*Nightmares*? Really?'

'Yeah, I know,' I said, rolling my eyes, trying to act casual but very aware how odd Axel must be finding this. Still, I thought, he was the one showing me his weirdly meticulous files on multiple murders at what should be a fun house party. Surely *that* was slightly odd.

'Ah, well, sorry to hear that, man. I just thought you might have heard of some of these British cases. Thought I might get the inside track, you know.'

'Why?' I said, a little too quickly. I instantly regretted it. After doing my best to keep casual, I couldn't stop the tension returning to my face, feeling heat break out across my forehead.

'No reason,' he said, shrugging, 'Sorry, I realise this probably looks a bit weird. I promise I'm not a killer or anything.' He laughed as he put the folder back in place together with the others.

'Don't worry, I know you're not a psycho,' I said, also laughing but doing it too loud, too eagerly.

'Who's not a psycho?' said someone from the door. We both turned to look and saw Ava sanding there, a drink in her hand.

'Neither of us are,' I said.

'Er ... well, that's good to know,' she said, taking a step inside the room. 'You know, you shouldn't use that word.'

'What word?' Axel asked.

'You shouldn't use the word "psycho" you know?' she said, frowning, 'It's really disrespectful to people with mental-health issues.'

'Oh, yeah ... um ... sure,' I said.

'You don't know what people have gone through,' she said. 'You may have never had any issues, Ethan, but others around you might have their own battles.'

'Don't worry,' I said, nodding, now desperate to get away from this situation, 'I'm aware of that.' I was still feeling panicky after what I'd seen. I needed to leave, to be alone.

'Can I just... I just need to...' I nipped quickly through the gap between where Ava was standing and the sofa in the middle of the room. I saw a whole load of doors across the landing and hazarded a guess, opening one of them and with relief found it was a bathroom. I sat down on the floor. Held my head in my hands. Then pulled out my phone.

Can someone come and get me now

I wanted to leave immediately but didn't want to spend the long walk home alone. I had images of me transforming in the road, scuttling into the darkness, trying to keep out of sight, scared that I might harm anyone who came across me.

Memories of hiding in the bathroom at Kenny's flooded

my mind. Memories of that feeling, that prickling, rushing, fizzing feeling, running down my back.

Images.

Memories.

But none of it was happening now.

Although I felt anxious and stressed and my heart was pounding, I didn't have any of the prickling sensations. My skin wasn't fizzing, vibrating with heat. Nothing was happening to my body. I was having a stress reaction, a borderline panic attack, perhaps, but nothing out of the ordinary. Nothing inhuman.

My phone flooded with messages.

> MUM: Dad's on his way. Stay calm. Breathe.

> DAD: Is it happening? I'm coming now.

> MUM: Remember, control is a choice. Choose control, my love. You can do it. I know you can.

I remembered everything she'd taught me since I'd arrived in Texas. I did the breathing techniques. I calmed myself. Ignored anyone trying the handle of the door. Ignored any noise from outside. Eventually my phone starting to buzz in my lap.

I picked it up.

'Where are you?' Dad said, sounding panicked, 'I'm outside the address you gave us.'

'I'm fine,' I said. 'Don't worry.'

'What's going on?' Dad barked into the phone.

'Nothing,' I said, pulling myself up off the floor, using the sink to hold on to, looking at myself in the mirror as my face came into view. 'I actually think ... I'm fine. But I still want to come home.'

Dad quizzed me on the drive back. I tried to reassure him that I was fine but I think my message must've panicked him. He seemed less angry compared to the time he'd picked me up from the cinema when I'd gone AWOL. This time, he looked more as if he'd come close to having his worst nightmares realised. Or reawakened. And I knew how that felt.

Back at the ranch, Mum brought me a peppermint tea, which I didn't especially like but she told me to drink it as it had calming properties. 'Tell us what happened,' she said.

I took a sip of the tea. 'I just ... had a moment when I thought...'

I looked up at them both. I didn't need to finish the sentence.

'Was there any sort of trigger?' my mum asked.

I thought for a moment, wondering how much to tell them. I didn't want to panic them more than I had done. But I decided to explain. 'Axel... He knows about ... England.'

They were both silent for a moment. Then Dad said 'As in ... what happened ... at home?'

I nodded. I saw the fear in Dad's eyes then and realised what he was thinking.

'He recognised you?' Dad said, 'How? How did—'

'No, no, he didn't,' I said, 'But he'd read about the murders. He's obsessed with true crime. He likes to follow investigations from across the world. I think he said he reads about them on blogs. Well, one of the cases he's been following…'

I trailed off. Dad looked appalled, but I was surprised to see Mum looked totally calm.

'It's a coincidence,' she said, her voice still smooth and untroubled.

'Oh, I know it is,' I said, 'He didn't recognise me. There's nothing to recognise me from. All the stuff he had was about the guy…' *The guy they've pinned my crimes on,* I thought to myself. The guy who may have done awful, dreadful things, but wouldn't have been capable of doing what I had done. Tearing a person apart and spinning their remains in a silken web, tightly winding it around so they couldn't escape. I shivered, remembering their struggles. The moaning. The gurgling sounds they made as I had sunk my fangs into their flesh, squeezing venom down the hollow structures so to paralyse them. I had liquefied their insides, something that still shocked me, so I could drink them from the inside out … sometimes while they were still just on the cusp of life, barely breathing but able to feel everything…

'This is very simple,' Mum said, leaning forwards and taking my hands in hers. 'You don't need to worry about your friend mentioning the situation in England. Because it has nothing to do with Ethan. It was something Hudson remembers. Ethan, however, doesn't remember it, because it didn't happen to him. Remember when I said you had a choice to stay in control or not? This is another of those choices. This is when you choose your new life.'

I looked her in the eyes. 'Isn't that what we've been doing?'

She smiled, kindly. 'You've done a lot of good work, my love, but I think these past weeks, since you've arrived have been a sort-of transition period for you. But now that you've started your new school, now that we're in a new year, you need to see it as a total new beginning. Embrace your new identity as *Ethan*. Leave Hudson behind. Then, as time goes on, maybe we'll be able to avoid any ... any risk of repetition. Because all those things happened to Hudson. They didn't happen to Ethan. So they can't happen again. Do you see?'

I held her gaze. Then looked up at Dad. He still looked worried, doubtful. But there was something about the certainty in Mum's voice that was compelling to me. Soothing, even. A reassurance I needed. Something definitive to clasp on to.

I nodded.

Part III

REAWAKENING

Chapter Thirty-Nine

THE BOY

October 2025

We'd hit reset. *I'd* hit reset. Like a computer finally doing a major software upgrade and when you use it again it's as if it's a whole new device. I felt new.

If someone had told me, when I was going through all that shit back in England that I would soon be having the best year of my life, I wouldn't have believed them. But it was true. I was literally, as the saying goes, living my best life. And it was all down to the reset. Taking on a new identity. Not just answering to the name Ethan, but *being* Ethan. I'd taken on new interests. Random things, like watching foreign films and becoming interested in art other than fan-produced sketches of sci-fi characters. I read books I never would have touched, like heavy historical novels, and found I enjoyed them. I started playing basketball and I wasn't bad at it, even though I'd always avoided competitive sports before, in England. But I found Ethan liked them. Ethan was popular. He wasn't shy, awkward, a pathetic, lonely virgin, a lost little lamb, a monosyllabic invisible member of a homogenous mass of school kids. People liked me. Respected me. Wanted to be my friend. I was the cool British kid. Some of the clichés about having an English accent turned out to be correct. It raised my 'social stock', as Dad put it, considerably from day one, even though I was technically American. I went to parties, hung out, just did regular teenager stuff as if I were a regular teenager. And if non-regular thoughts cropped up, memories from another time, I always remembered how to control my own thoughts. I didn't think of those memories as 'horrific' or 'traumatic' or 'terrifying'. I didn't use words like 'regret' and 'guilt' and 'killing' and 'death'. I just bundled it all together and referred to it in my head as 'all that shit'. All that stuff. All that nonsense. I removed its power. I shrugged. Then I carried on with my day, being Ethan. Being the guy I wanted to be. It was a conscious choice and I knew I was making the right one.

We kept ourselves occupied. Mum had a job at a local library. Dad spent time writing the novel he'd always wanted to write, although I thought he was worried it would become a bestseller and get him lots of attention. I felt bad he was having to limit himself like that—hold back because of me. But I tried not to think about that. I tried not to think about a lot of things. Just carrying on. Moving forward. Making Ethan the best possible version of myself. The version I'd always wanted to be, I just didn't know it.

So I kept practising. Mindfulness, high-concentration exercises, breathing techniques that Mum taught me. I threw myself into tasks and enjoyed the process of getting absorbed in the details. I learnt to drive and took pleasure in holding myself to a near-perfect standard; parallel parking with precision. Perfect, corner turns. Absolute dedication. Focus and commitment within learning helped me remain more relaxed during my downtime. It was a win-win.

Although one thing had been—and remained—missing from my life. It's like I'd created this new layer, a new skin, but underneath it all there was one small grain of doubt. A tiny fragment of concern. I watched as people coupled-up. As people formed friendships that became relationships. And I did nothing. I watched as they made it seem so easy. My new friends talked about dating, the things they got up to, then boasted about it, laughed about it. It was as if I was listening to them talking about exotic skills or foreign languages—things I couldn't be a part of. Things closed off to me. Things I perhaps would never properly experience. For everyone's sake. This was something I wrestled with. The one part of my new identity I didn't allow to flourish. After all, there were other things I did—like being around people my own age in social occasions—that I could argue had close enough parallels to what had happened in England. *All that stuff*. I tried to tell myself that my transformation only happened that first time because of the anger and humiliation that occurred after I had sex the first time. But it still tinged the whole experience for me. That and the fact I was tricked into doing it with a girl I hadn't chosen. I couldn't help worrying. Worrying that if anything happened, no matter what it was, that all that embarrassment would flood back. I occasionally had dreams about it. That I orgasmed too quickly, or not at all, and the girl would laugh at me, the same way Charlene had laughed at me that night, though for different reasons of course. I was probably being over cautious. For months and months, I had practised calming techniques for when I was annoyed or angry. But I'd never felt the strange buzz, that prickle along my skin again. It hadn't returned. I knew I could probably handle it—that I might even have a good time—but the risk was still too large for me. The risk that, if it all went wrong and the worst did happen, I might be putting someone's life in danger just so I could get laid. So I told myself to hold off for a while longer. Not do anything until I'd got past an important milestone, one we've all been waiting for as it approached us on the horizon. Halloween.

The school was hosting a Halloween party for juniors and seniors. It was supposed to be a cute, fancy dress, alcohol-free event, but according to Ava and Scarlett, it was just seen as a warm-up to a number of more outrageous offshoot parties that would apparently take place at various houses nearby.

'You're coming, right?' Elijah had said when he'd caught me looking at the bright orange poster with the words

HALLOWEEN DANCE emblazoned across it in old-fashioned horror-movie font.

'I … don't know,' I paused, feeling uneasy.

But I hadn't felt anything suspicious since arriving in the US, and that was nearly a year ago. *You're fine,* I told myself. *Just treat this a just a regular activity. Downgrade its importance in your mind. Reject negative thoughts. Think positive.*

So I agreed. 'Yeah, sure. Looking forward to it.'

The morning before Halloween, I woke up early, rubbed my eyes and looked at my suit hanging up on my wardrobe door. Some people wore full-on fancy dress to the dance—Elijah said one year he'd gone as a glow-in-the-dark skeleton—but apparently the trend had become to wear a suit as if it were prom but accessorise it with a masquerade-style mask. Ava had insisted that 'the truly creative people decorated their masks', but I hadn't bothered. I quite liked the plain-white effect of it with the black of the suit.

A sound to my right interrupted my thoughts. I rolled over and saw Elijah through the window, standing on the veranda.

I clambered out of bed and went over to open the window doors. 'Morning,' Elijah said brightly as he strolled in, dropping his bag down on my crumpled duvet. 'Wow, this the suit? Very dapper.' He picked up a sleeve of it and gave it a rub, apparently impressed. 'This will get the girls turning their heads.'

'Hmm,' I said, starting to look about for clothes for the day. Even all these months in, I still couldn't get used to not wearing a school uniform, although to be fair, even if I'd stayed in the UK, I would have been allowed to wear normal clothes in the sixth form.

Don't think about England, I told myself. Not today.

'Why do you never make a move?' Elijah asked, looking at me quizzically.

'What?'

'A *move*. With girls. It's clear they fancy you. Ava says she hears people talking about you. Not just Scarlett, although she's still keen to try her luck again, even though she said the other day you've now snubbed her three times.'

'I haven't *snubbed* anyone,' I replied, feeling uncomfortable having this topic brought up just when I'd rather talk about anything else.

No matter how much I'd tried to move on, no matter how much I'd left Hudson behind and embraced this new identity in Ethan, there was one thing I remained frightened of. The one thing practically all guys my age were desperate to do was the one thing I just wouldn't go near.

'Er … Ethan? You there?' Elijah was waving his hands at me playfully.

'Sorry, yes, I … I was just thinking I might shower quickly. You want breakfast? Mum's making pancakes.'

Elijah grinned. 'Yeah, definitely. If she doesn't mind feeding me for the second time this week.'

I told him she wouldn't mind. Both Mum and Dad liked Elijah, saw him as a sign that my life here was a success.

'Great,' he said. 'And you didn't answer my question. You never do.'

'About what?' I asked, playing for time.

'About why you never ... you know. We talk about everything, but never *that*. You've got to lose it someday. So why not with Scarlett, if she's still keen? Just get it over with. Best to before college, right?'

I shrug, feeling my heart rate quicken.

'Ava's going to try to set you up with her again at the dance tomorrow,' Elijah said, flicking his eyebrows in a comic, suggestive way. 'Could be a good chance for you to—'

'No,' I say, turning round to look at him, sounding firmer than I'd meant to.

Elijah's eyes widened in surprise. He held up his hands. 'Sorry, man. I didn't mean to ... upset you...' He looked hurt and it made me feel instantly regretful.

'It's OK, sorry I snapped, I just...' I sighed, 'Maybe you're right. I'll... I'll think about it.'

He nodded, looking at me as if he was aware I hadn't told him the full story.

I went and had a shower, still feeling bad. It wasn't his fault, but I'd had felt a horrible stab of déjà vu when he talked about setting me up with Scarlett—or Ava having a plan to do something like that. It took me back to a dull, cloudy October day in the north of England. A day I never wanted to think about again.

Doing my best to keep my mind clear, I pulled a towel off the rail in the bathroom, tied it round my waist and went back to my room. Elijah was sat on the bed, his phone out, watching something.

'Have you seen this?' he asked, 'It's weird.'

I walked over and sat next to him so I could see the screen. 'What is it?'

'Lightning strikes. There have been an unusual amount of them over the past two weeks. Some of them have struck buildings, but they're mostly hitting trees. They've been happening all over the world. Someone's plotted a map, and there have been some not far from here. Apparently they're getting closer. It's been happening around this time of year for years, going back to the early 2010s, according to people on Reddit—some say it could have been even longer, like back into the twentieth century, but less frequent back then. Nobody had really pieced it together, at least nobody anyone was really listening to. I think it's because some of the people making a deal about it were, like, wackos, saying the strikes were like communications from aliens or other planets, or signs an ice age was coming or shit like that. Stuff that doesn't make much sense, so it's easy to just dismiss them. But other people are starting to notice now that it's more widespread. You must have seen some of the viral videos? People getting shocks from things, even after the lightning has gone?'

I didn't say anything. I just got up and started to get ready for the day.

'It's weird, right?' Elijah prompted, after a few seconds.

I took a few seconds before I responded, waiting for my

heartbeat to settle. Then, trying to keep my voice casual, I said 'Yeah, it sure is. Right, let's get some breakfast or we'll be late.'

Chapter Forty

THE FATHER

October 2025

It'd been nearly a year since our lives changed and we moved to Texas. Nearly a year since my world had shattered. Since I'd lost my husband. Since the way I viewed my son had changed for ever. While Hudson—or *Ethan*—moved on and blossomed in front of us, turning from boy into young man, I couldn't move on. I struggled. More than Adelaide or Hudson could ever possibly know. Sometimes I would look at my son eating his breakfast or hanging out with his friends and wonder if it'd all really happened. Maybe it'd been just a dream I had had. Maybe our time in England had occurred in this strange parallel world. I tried to marvel at how quickly Hudson had managed to put it all behind him. How committed he was to sitting with his mother, practising things like breathing, mindfulness, meditation, a steady programme of exercise, all of it geared to making him more in control of his emotions and feelings. Adelaide took it all in her stride and took to this second chance at motherhood with the flourish and confidence of someone who had excelled in the role all her life. As if there had never been a decade-plus blip in her history.

I knew part of me was being unfair to Adelaide. The truth was, I'd always blamed myself for what had happened between the two of us—the night of foolishness that resulted in Hudson being conceived. We were two drunk best friends who should have known better. I'd told her that night that I couldn't imagine ever having sex with a woman and I'd seen the sparkle in her eyes—the love of a challenge. The next morning, I woke with a lethargy-inducing sense of dread. I wanted to go back to sleep and hoped I would wake up again to find it had all been a dream. Not because we didn't use contraception and I hadn't predicted the consequences of such an error (I wasn't thinking that far ahead), but because I worried I'd forever ruined a friendship that was important to me. Adelaide was my confidante; a presence who had made my time at university a joy. We mended broken hearts, soothed troubled souls, enjoyed life, lived it to the full and discussed everything that happened in between. It was a remarkable time, a time that continued after our graduation. And then we put all that at risk for one sudden, drunken whim. It gave me a feeling of trepidation. One that I carried through Adelaide's pregnancy, through her decision to keep the baby, our plans to co-parent together on her family's ranch in Texas. And when it all started to unravel, when Adelaide herself started to unravel, it felt like the fears had been vindicated. It probably contributed to my decision to take Hudson to England and convince her it was the right thing to do. Not that she had needed much convincing. In the worst of her hallucinations, she would scream to have the child removed from any room she was in, convinced the boy was dangerous. So leaving the country, in some ways, was a simple choice. I thought, by doing so, I'd leave the dread behind. But as it turned out, I was simply paving the way for a whole new nightmare. A nightmare I couldn't stop thinking about.

It was all I'd been doing for nearly a year. Sitting in my 'new study' in the ranch house, trying to write a novel. I didn't for a million years ever think it would be published. I spent most of my time sitting there, staring into space, replaying things I wish I'd never seen.

All this while Hudson bloomed into a happy, confident, handsome young man.

I felt awful admitting it to myself, but I couldn't help it: it didn't seem fair. Didn't seem fair that all this happened to Hudson—not to mention the things he did—and it was me who was left wrestling with the residual demons.

On the day that would have been Mattias's twenty-fourth birthday, I found I couldn't be around either Adelaide or Hudson. Adelaide didn't know when Mattias's birthday was, and Hudson hadn't referred to it. I wasn't sure if he was just being sensitive, thinking I wouldn't want it being brought up. Or perhaps he'd just forgotten. I lied to them both that morning, saying I was going on a research trip to the city. But I didn't. I just drove out into the desert, in the opposite direction. I didn't think either of them noticed. I sat on some rocks in the shade for a few hours until the sun turned round and it got too uncomfortable. So I drove past the ranch towards the town. Sat in a coffee shop for hours, holding a book in front of me, not reading the pages. Some days the horrible things that had happened didn't enter my mind. On this day, I couldn't stop them. No matter how hard I tried, I couldn't build a big enough cerebral dam that would hold back those details. The details of what I'd seen in Hudson's bedroom. Nobody should get to find out what the torn flesh of a loved one looks like. Or the sticky feel of their internal organs when you get them on your hands as you try to sort out the carnage your son is responsible for. As I tried to hold back those memories, my eyes wandered to a diner across the road. I thought my mind was playing tricks on me at first, but it was definitely him. Hudson. *Ethan*. My son, sitting at a table next to the window with friends. Elijah and Ava and another girl I vaguely recognised but didn't know the name of. They were laughing. Elijah holding out a chip to one of the girls who was trying to get it from his hand before he snatched it back. I watched as Hudson tipped his head back as he laughed. He didn't care. Didn't know or care that it was the birthday of the man he had torn apart in his bedroom. Wasn't aware his father was going to pieces less than a hundred yards away across the road.

It was good thing, I told myself in that moment, and continued to tell myself to this day. It was a good thing. He should be able to forget. To live his life. To move on.

I just wish I could, too.

Both Adelaide and I had been watching him closely in the lead up to Halloween. So far, our fears of some kind of annual return hadn't come true. And he hadn't mentioned the anniversary to us. Hadn't said anything at all. Whether this was denial or repression, or a combination of the two, I didn't know.

But something happened this morning; I'd been sitting at my desk chair, the whir of the air-con above me, thinking about it ever since Hudson had gone off to school. His friend Elijah had come over early for breakfast and he made some joke about the approaching school Halloween dance being 'Ethan's lucky night'. He winked at him and I saw in my son something I hadn't seen for a long while. A look of panic and fear. Elijah didn't seem to notice and continued to eat, and Hudson recovered quickly, but I know what I saw.

And the more I thought about it, the more I was able to piece it together. Elijah was referring to him potentially getting friendly—perhaps *very* friendly—with a girl. It didn't take me long to realise why that thought might be upsetting to Hudson. What memories it might bring back. I understood why he was afraid.

I sat at my desk wondering if I should say something when he got home or if bringing it up would make things worse. Maybe I'd got it wrong and it hadn't even crossed his mind. Maybe I'd be the one to disrupt what would be otherwise a carefree, happy week. His last week of school.

I thought maybe the whole thing would feel different if

he was going away to university, but I had to admit I was relieved when I heard he was thinking about the University of Texas in El Paso. It wasn't for a while yet, but the idea still comforted me. He could commute in and out easily. So in a way, his last week of school wasn't quite the 'ending' it would have otherwise been. Adelaide and I hadn't explicitly said it to Hudson, but we were both relieved he was choosing to remain at home for the time being. Just to be on the safe side.

A sound ripped through the night. A shout. A boy's shout.

'Hudson!' I yelled, forgetting in my sleepy state to call him Ethan. I tumbled out of bed and run for the doorway.

The shouts continued, turning into screams. Actual screams. I flew down the hallway and started to run down the stairs to Hudson's room on the ground floor. I flung the door open and rushed in to find him writhing in his bed, the sheets tangled around him, his legs kicking.

In the darkness, disrupted by a ray of moonlight shining through the window, I worried for a moment that there was something unnatural about his shape under the duvet and thought I could see more of him—more limbs, more legs, more arms. But as I took hold of him, trying to keep him still, I knew I'd imagined it. He was still Hudson. Still my boy.

He woke suddenly, the screaming stopping instantly. 'Dad…' he gasped, sitting up. 'Dad … it was…'

'What?' I asked, the feeling of dread starting to peak again.

'I need ... some water...' He got out of bed and walked shakily to his desk, picked up a water bottle and downed its contents.

'What... What were you going to say?'

Hudson didn't speak at first. His breathing was heavy, as if he'd been running for miles, shoulders bent over. 'I don't want to talk about it,' he finally said, shaking his head.

I was about to respond when I heard more shouts. Hudson and I looked at each other, confused as to what we were hearing. 'It must be your mother,' I told him, moving quickly to the door and running back upstairs, with Hudson following close behind me.

Adelaide had the master bedroom with the balcony at the back, but when we burst in all we found was an empty bed, the covers and pillows all tossed about. 'Adelaide?' I called out to her, looking round. I heard a shout again, coming over from the open balcony doors. The curtains swayed gently in the light breeze. I pulled them aside and found Adelaide curled up naked on the floor of the balcony, sobbing uncontrollably.

'What's happening?' Hudson called from the doorway.

'Bring me the sheet from the bed,' I called out. I reached around the curtain to take it from him. I didn't want him seeing his mother like this.

'Come on, up you get,' I said. 'It's just a nightmare.'

It took a few seconds for Adelaide to acknowledge I was there at all. She was clutching at her stomach.

'What is it?' I asked her. 'What's happened?'

'I gave birth,' she whispered, as I helped her up and wrapped the sheet around her.

'What?' I asked, puzzled. 'You had a nightmare. It's OK.'

But Adelaide wouldn't be calmed so easily. She broke free from my grasp and raced to check her bed for something, pulling up the duvet, the pillows, under the bed.

'Mum,' Hudson said, walking forwards towards her. 'I know. And it's OK. I'm here.'

She looked at him. He looked at her. Something passed between them—a look. A clear indication of understanding. She took a few steps towards him. Touched her son on the shoulder. Then raised her hand to his cheek.

Confusion and fear started to stir inside me, as I looked on, feeling like an outsider, not knowing what was going on.

'Come on, Hudson,' I said. 'Let's leave your mother to get back to bed. You should get some more sleep, too. You don't want to be tired for the Halloween dance.'

On the way back downstairs, after we'd guided Adelaide back towards the bed, I asked him, 'What did you dream about?'

Silence greeted this.

'Hudson?' I prompted.

'You don't want to know, Dad. And besides, like I've told you a thousand times, it's *Ethan*. You called me 'Hud' in front of Elijah the other day. You'd think after all this time you'd—'

'You're evading, and you know it,' I said, grabbing his arm.

He pulled it away and went into his room.

'I should be getting some sleep, like you said,' he muttered. 'Just … get off my back.' He sounded harsh, dismissive and more than a little American, which although was only natural, living out here, I couldn't help but find it annoying.

'I want to know,' I said, folding my arms in his doorway as he got into bed and pulled his covers over him.

He was silent for a bit and I thought he was going to blank me, pretend to go to sleep, but then he said, 'Dad, I think, back in the past there were times when I said there were things it was probably best you didn't know. Well … I think this is one of those times.'

I let out a slow breath. 'I'm sure it is, but … just tell me,' I pleaded.

Hudson rolled over in his bed so that he was facing me and I could just about make out his eyes in the darkness. 'In the dream I was being born. I felt like I was coming into this world and was awake for the first time.'

I think about what he'd said. 'Well … that's not so awful, is it? As dreams go?'

'Dad … I was being born as a spider.'

That shut me up. And then I found I knew what he was going to say next.

'You heard what Mum said, didn't you?' Hudson asked.

'Yes,' I replied. 'What do you think it means?'

'I don't know,' Hudson said. 'But I don't think it's good.'

Chapter Forty-One

THE BOY

October 2025

I barely managed to sleep after the nightmare. After an hour of rolling about, unable to get comfortable, I got out of bed and took my phone off charge. Opened the web browser and started to type.

I typed in things I had previously avoided focusing on. Things I never wanted to revisit. Things I had desperately pushed to the back of my mind. But after the dream I had just experienced, I knew I needed to look. Look for things that I'd avoided looking at for so long. Because there must be things out there. Signs. Whispers. Or outright evidence. Evidence that I wasn't the only one.

It took some searching. A lot of things that clearly weren't real; movie scenes and a lot of fantasy-fiction writing. But then I stumbled across something on a forum. A video. A video some people were claiming was fake, others saying it was actual footage that had been taken down from various, more regular social-media websites. A video from a user in Sapporo, Japan.

Fuck this is awful, someone had commented.

I'll never un-see that. The legs… said another.

I clicked play.

The shaky footage showed a dark corridor, juddery footage suggesting someone was walking down towards a light at the end. That light at the end turned out to be a lounge. There was a young man lying on a sofa reading a magazine. A woman in front of a TV watching an exercise video. It all looked very … normal. The woman turned around and said something in Japanese. 'Ah not again, man, give it a rest' the guy on the sofa replied in English with a strong Australian accent. The person filming moved the camera over to the large windows at the end of the room. 'I didn't imagine it,' the camera holder said, another male, also in English. He directed the camera to the window—his indistinct reflection appeared, then the image focused to show a clear view of a square courtyard surrounded by a tall block of apartments.

'I definitely saw it,' he said. He held the camera steady for a few seconds. Part of me was tempted to scroll the video on to see if there was actually anything worth watching. But then I saw something. In the twilight of the courtyard, I could see movement. A … *thing* … coming out of the window of one of the apartments opposite. It was one floor above and at first looked like a dark mass squeezing itself through the window frame. Then the legs became identifiable. So many of them. It was like they were pouring out of the window and spreading around the grey concrete like roots of a particularly horrible plant. 'Holy fuck!' The guy said. 'Hey, come and see this, come and fucking see this! Shit!' Out of sight, the woman said something in Japanese that sounded dismissive. The guy from the sofa called out 'Calm down, Al.'

'Fucking hell!' the camera holder shouted as the spider fully emerged from the window and started to crawl slowly down the side of the building.

'Oh what's all the fuss…' The Australian guy muttered, coming over, his reflection just about visible in the glass. He seemed to jostle against the guy holding the camera and the image moved. 'Hey, watch it. Shit, where's it gone?'

The frame became extremely jerky, the image badly defined as the man scanned the courtyard.

'I'm going to go down and take a look,' the guy said. 'This is fucking insane.'

'There's no spider down there, mate,' the Australian shouted after Al. He didn't listen, just ran, the camera going to his side, half of the frame taken up for a period by the material of his shorts or his legs, but as he got to the bottom of a stairwell, he lifted the phone up so the camera showed a clear view of the courtyard as he walked out into the wide-open space. I could hear him trying to catch his breath, and coughing a little as he turned the camera around, looking up the buildings. 'Come on, you fucker,' he said, 'Come on, come on.'

He walked across the courtyard and directed the lens at

the window from where the spider had emerged. There was no sign of it and no way of seeing inside the flat it had come out of. Al walked the entire perimeter of the courtyard to no avail. Eventually, he got back to the stairwell of his flat and walked inside. Then stopped dead. It was clear he had seen something, even though the camera was pointed to his trainers and the bottom step. Then, very quietly, he whispered, 'Oh… Oh, my god…' Then he lifted the camera. Slowly moving up the wall of the stairwell was the spider. Bigger than a car tire, legs thick with twitching long hairs, the eight-legged creature, was crawling slowly up the wall. Al moved forward, presumably to get a better view, but he stumbled, knocking into the bottom step, jogging the camera. 'Shit,' he said, turning the camera back up to the spider, but only just catching sight of it as it ran fast up the wall and then out of sight, disappearing over the banister of the staircase.

'Jackson!' Al yelled as he climbed the stairs two at a time, 'Himari!' I knew he was panicking. Warning them. And he was right to fear for them. The screams became audible before the image showed what was causing them. Then, when Al had got up the steps to the first floor and had dashed into the apartment, the door left open wide, it became clear what was happening inside the room. The guy on the sofa was no longer on the sofa—he was on the floor. Blood pouring from his neck. The spider upon him. Wrapping him. Turning him with its legs with amazing strength, the man flailing until, remarkably quickly, the webbing had restricted his movement. The woman was screaming. She was holding a kitchen knife in her hand, though apparently too scared to approach the creature. Then the image changed as the camera fell. Things went black for a split second, possibly when the phone hit the floor, but came back, the action of what was playing out in the flat only just about visible at the far-left side of the picture. The woman was still screaming, and another person, Al, I assumed, came into the frame and took the knife off her. He appeared to have an attack in mind, lunging at the spider, but it was no use. The knife clattered to the floor when the animal ran onto him, its fangs clamped onto his side. His shout of alarm became clear screams of pain, suggesting he had been penetrated by its fangs. The woman ran past him, perhaps in a bid to save herself or get help, but she slipped in the pool of blood surrounding the wrapped guy on the floor. Her head collided with the sharp corner of a shoe wrack with a sickening crack, then she was still. Lifeless. Al wasn't, though. He was still thrashing and screaming, until at last he too went quiet, his face a sickly grey colour. He was limp and the spider unclamped itself and began to wrap him. Even though he had no fight left in him, he still occasionally twitched and jerked. Nerve endings and muscles spasming, perhaps. Or some desperate, though ineffective, attempts to still get free. Maybe he knew he was about to be eaten. That his insides were fast turning into a drinkable mixture. That there was no hope left. None.

The screen went black after that, when Al was still only about half-covered in silk. A grey-white coffin. The end of a life after probably only about twenty years. He hadn't looked much older than me.

Or Kenny.

Or Charlene.

I rubbed my eyes. They felt strained and sore after focusing on the harsh light of the phone screen in the darkness of my room. I clicked out of the video and looked through some more of the comments. One said an officer in the Japanese police leaked the video online when the phone was recovered at what they thought was a crime scene. Someone provided a link to a local newspaper article; apparently it pinned the murders on the young woman, saying she was having an affair with two visiting male tourists, and when they found out and confronted her she flew into a rage and stabbed them both. A cover up. Framed, after her death. Comments varied.

The MSM haven't touched this case, or if they have it's wall-to-wall total lies.

It took me a few seconds to clock that MSM meant 'mainstream media'. Another user underneath.

Well, that's because this is obviously some amateur AI-generated bullshit.

Others also doubted how real the footage was. People seemed to swing between angry defenders and scathing sceptics.

I didn't need persuading, though. I knew it was real. And I knew something else, too. Something I think I'd always known, but hadn't dared to confirm: that I wasn't alone in this. Something bigger was happening here. Bigger than me. Bigger than my victims. Bigger than Barret Forrest in Northumberland or a tree stump on a ranch in Texas. So much bigger.

Chapter Forty-Two

THE BOY

October 2025

I needed to get outside. There was no way I was going to be able to go back to sleep, not after seeing that video. I felt an uneasy mixture of nausea and restlessness, as if I needed to both vomit and run miles at the same time. I opened the door to the veranda and went outside. The morning air wasn't exactly cool—noticeably warmer than my air-conditioned room—but the breeze made it bearable.

I stared out at the patches of trees, and then further, looking at the rocky, desert terrain. Rough and primal, like the surface of an untouched planet. And out there, just about in-sight, was the stump where a tree had once stood. The residue of unease and panic both the dream and the video had provoked was strong. But there was something else I wasn't able to shake off. A sense of foreboding—a feeling I'd had ever since Elijah had sat down on my bed and started to play that YouTube clip of lightning strikes. Random bolts of electricity shooting down from the sky across America. Puzzling scientists. Fuelling speculation. Getting closer. Everything that had happened may well be bigger than just me, than this ranch, than my own story. But I couldn't ignore the feeling that there were answers to uncover right on my doorstep.

I went back into my room, pulled on some tracksuit bottoms and sliders, then headed out, going down the little steps and through the back yard. I walked further, as the land around the ranch merged with the desert beyond until I got to my destination.

I knelt down on the floor and touched the dried, charred hunk of wood. There was nothing particularly remarkable about it. I'd come over to it a year ago, just after Mum had told me the story of the storm and how I'd wandered here as a toddler. Just like then, there was no sign of spiders.

Although there was one thing I didn't do back then. I don't know if I was afraid or if I just didn't think of it.

I leaned forwards and looked in the hole in the stump. I'm not sure what I expected to see, considering how dark the whole place was, but unsurprisingly the result was nothing: there was nothing visible, nor could I hear anything. I hesitated for a moment, wondering if I should go back. Then I reached out a hand. My fingers traced the rim of the hole, feeling its gnarled edge. That was when I noticed the heat. How surprisingly warm this part of the wood was. Warmer than it should have been at night. If the sun had been beating down on it, perhaps it would make sense, but, at three in the morning…

I reached past the opening. Put my hand further inside.

The pain.

Pain so forceful and blinding it shattered every sense I had. Shattered every concept, every emotion, every piece of my brain's ability to function.

Then something switched. The pain was there. I could feel it, strongly. But I could also feel something else. Movement around my fingers. In my wrist.

And then I knew things. Really knew things.

Clear pictures filled my head.

Information streamed into me.

It was incredible, dazzling, astonishing.

I knew what was happening to me. The truth was so clear, it took on a feeling itself, a flavour. I could touch words, smell ideas, listen to plans, such incredible, vast, expansive plans, plans that had gone wrong, plans for the future. Things I must do.

When it was over—and somehow I knew it was over—I pulled my hand out and walked back across the desert floor to the house. I went up the veranda steps calmly and quietly. Through the French windows into my room. I got into bed and instantly fell asleep, without trouble or fuss or even properly thinking about it.

The next morning, on Halloween, I went out for a run early. At breakfast I smiled at Mum and Dad as I helped myself to French toast and fruit. Mum still looked shaken and cautious. I gave her a squeeze of my hand to show her things were fine.

I barely thought about what had happened during the night as I went about my day. I did more exercises and caught the bus into town to see a movie with Elijah. I ignored what had happened, sending it to the back of my mind, like a package ready to open later. And as the day continued, I forgot about it completely. Everything was fine. Because it was, surely? Why wouldn't it be?

'He shouldn't go.'

Mum said this while I was in the midst of getting changed for the Halloween dance. I was standing in my white shirt, doing up the buttons, when I heard it. I wandered out into the hallway and to the living room where Mum was standing on the bottom step. Dad was in one of the sofa chairs reading a book.

'What?' Dad said, looking up.

'What are you talking about?' I asked her.

She hadn't got properly dressed today. I'd only just realised it, but she must have been wandering around in her dressing gown all day, her hair untidy.

'You know you shouldn't,' she said, looking straight at me.

I shrugged. 'No, I don't. I don't see why...'

'You saw the same thing I did, last night. I know it,' she said, still staring at me. I couldn't maintain eye contact and looked away.

'You go nearly a year without any dreams like that, and then suddenly we both have one at the same time? That can't be a coincidence.'

'How do you know what I dreamt?' I snapped, getting irritated. 'You're not inside my head.' She was right, though. I hadn't experienced anything like that ever since I left England. But I didn't say this.

'But you see, I think I am, my love,' she replied gently, coming down the last step and over to me. She put a hand on my face, looking deep into my eyes. 'Like I said when you arrived here, when we tried to get things under control, I *knew* things were happening. I knew everything wasn't right. Then when you and your father moved in, we got things under control. But that control is slipping away now. Something has changed. And I think you can feel it, too.' I saw a tear in the corner of her eye slip down the side of her cheek. Then she moved one of her hands onto her wrist. Onto the faint mark, her fingers pressed against it. 'I think something might have happened to us both, that night. That night in the storm. I think you took the brunt of it, but like I said before, I know I was affected. I think we have a link, Hud. A link that goes beyond a normal tie a mother has with her son. You *know* this.'

I brushed her hand off and stepped away. 'No, I don't,' I lied. 'And I'm going to the Halloween dance and to college and I'm going to live a normal life. That's what we've been trying to do, isn't it? Otherwise, what's been the point of this whole experiment?' I glared at them both, furious that Mum was attempting to make this into some serious situation, and at Dad for his silence, staring with his worried eyes, unsure how to contribute. 'So what am I supposed to do now? Because we both had a nightmare, I'm supposed to … what? Just live in isolation for the rest of my life?'

'I'm saying we should just hit pause until we know what's going on here,' Mum said. I could tell she was trying her best to sound calm, reasonable, even though I knew I'd hurt her with my words and stressing her with my defensiveness.

'I'm not going through another "reset" or however you want to dress it up this time,' I told them. 'I know it's because of me we moved here, but surely all the work I've done to move on and stuff matters? Surely it counts for something?'

'Darling, it does,' Mum said softly, her eyes wide and earnest. 'And I understand more than you'll ever know. When I came off the pills and stopped drinking, it was like I was given a whole new life, that I was letting go of a monster. But I knew if I took some more pills, just one single oxy, or had just one drink, I'd be risking everything. Do you see what I'm saying?'

I almost gave in, then, almost softened my expression. But a hardness in me made me continue to push back. 'I'm going tonight. I'll have a good time. Do you know what? I might even get laid. Elijah's going to hook me up with someone.'

I saw Dad shoot a panicked glance at Mum. It wouldn't have surprised me if this had been a topic they'd discussed, wondering if I was seeing anyone, if one day I'd bring a girlfriend home, navigating that risk. But why would it be a risk, I thought, if it was completely different to how it was … back then. I'd been restricting myself for too long. Pushing down a natural urge, throwing away chances of closeness and intimacy, things other people my age would regard as important parts of being young. Before I'd even been aware of my train of thought, I felt myself going back there. Only for a second. To Halloween night. Last year. In Barret Forest. I shivered a little as I thought about it. Both Mum and Dad noticed.

'Something's wrong,' Dad said, speaking up at last. 'We all know it, Hud. And I for one don't think you should be hooking up with anyone. After last night… There's been some kind of … change.'

'That's what I've been *saying,*' Mum said. Hearing her sounding so distressed was making me feel even more aggravated. Her calm, soothing way of life over the past year had been one of the most important things in keeping *me* calm, keeping me on the right path. Seeing her losing composure so quickly in front of me was making me feel ill and shaky, like the ground was moving underneath my feet. 'I need to get ready,' I muttered, turning away. It was true, I did—but my leaving was more about trying to keep my resolve than anything else. I needed to keep it together. I took a deep breath, remembering the breathing tactics Mum had taught me during my first months here.

Mum and Dad didn't follow me into my room, but I heard them continuing to talk. I didn't try to listen, instead I got my suit trousers on and took out my carefully polished shoes. One movement at a time. Precise focus. Controlled breathing.

I was aware that while I continued to prepare, something else was at work within me. The part of me that had been allowed to take a back seat was slowly reaching out its arms and gently guiding me. Making me certain I didn't just want to go to the prom tonight. I had to. It was imperative.

I needed to be around people.

And people needed to see the true me.

Chapter Forty-Three

THE BOY

October 2025

My parents didn't try to stop me leaving. When they saw I was committed, they just started offering advice on drinking and what time they wanted me back—the sort of things they would say normally, just now with a heightened sense of worry and, when it came to my mother, barely concealed panic.

Part of me did feel bad leaving them, especially when I insisted on driving my newish car, snapping at Dad when he reminded me that drink driving is illegal. 'Do you really think I'm likely to do that?' I replied. 'I won't drink. I promise.'

It was true. Ever since what had happened in England, I'd never had any wish to touch alcohol again. Never given into peer pressure, the little that there is at school. But clearly Mum and Dad suspected I occasionally drank on the sly the way 'all teenagers do' (generalisations like that often annoyed me). I waved goodbye to Mum as she stood on the veranda, watching me leave. I felt a pang of guilt. But I didn't stop.

Elijah was standing in a parking space when I arrived at the school. One of the keen 'sports hero guys' I couldn't remember the name of wanted to park his four-by-four in the space, but Elijah was refusing to budge. When he spotted me, he ushered me into it. I got out grinning and slapped him on the back for holding his ground while the other boy scowled at us.

Inside, Elijah didn't waste time trying to set me up with Scarlett. She'd tried to kiss me a couple of times since Axel's party at the start of the year, but each time I'd ducked out or faked some excuse to leave. Today, I wasn't making excuses. I was ready. I chatted with her for a while at the edge of the hall while some old Rihanna song blared out of the below-par speakers. Scarlett started talking about how she liked my mask and how she'd also got hers—which was patterned around the edges with black butterflies—months ago on eBay. She began to talk about some TV show she liked—a comedy on Netflix set in Paris I'd never heard of—and she asked what I watched. I started to mention *Doctor Who* and *Star Trek* but I saw her eyes glaze over and in less than a minute she said, 'I think we're coming to the end of the small talk, Ethan. I'll be back with drinks.' She patted my shoulder and walked away. I couldn't help watching her legs as she went and then allowed my eyes to travel up the rest of her figure. I felt alive. Empowered. Excited.

I talked to Elijah for a bit, and when Ava took him onto the dance floor I returned to one of the corners of the halls with Scarlett. She got very friendly with her hands and I didn't stop her. We talked some more, though it got to the point where it became clear our conversation was second to what she actually wanted to do. Again, I didn't stop her. She nodded at the fire exit and I grinned back in response. We'd probably get thrown out anyway if we carried on the way we were doing.

We left the hall through the fire exit, which had already been propped open by someone, probably by people with the same idea we had. I knew there was a narrow alleyway behind the back of the gymnasium that led up around the science and geography block, and it was there that we found shelter. The shelter was already occupied. I looked over and saw someone standing there—a guy with his arms around a girl, mouths on each other. As they broke apart, I saw it was Elijah and Ava.

'Oh, hi,' I say, laughing, 'Sorry to interrupt.'

Elijah grinned. 'Popular venue, this,' he said. I was about to suggest Scarlett and I found a new location a little more secluded for our private gathering, but she took the lead. She pushed me up against the wall right next to Elijah and Ava, kissing me hard on the lips and then proceeded to kneel down, unbuckling my belt and unzipping my trousers.

I glanced to my left, slightly mortified by Elijah and Ava's presence. Elijah caught my eye and laughed. 'I'll see you back inside, man,' he said, offering me a thumbs-up, 'Come on, Ava.'

Scarlett's determined hands were on me now. 'Oh, god, OK,' I said, feeling my heart pounding.

And then a memory floated into my mind.

A memory of me in a tent.

The first time a girl had ever touched me.

A voice through the thin material of the tent.

Kenny's voice.

Kenny trying to joke with me while Kirsten—no, *Charlene* —began to take my virginity.

And with the memory, something else. The part of my mind I'd kept wrapped up, out of sight, was unfolding. Slowly but surely.

That was when it began to go terribly, terribly wrong.

I heard the voices before I saw them. They were down the end of the alley which opened out onto the car park. Laughing and clapping.

'The boy's got some *action*,' one of the boys called out.

I rushed to zip up my trousers and step back from Scarlett. Then one of the other boys spoke—and this one sounded a lot less friendly. 'Wait a moment… Fuck, that's…'

'Oh, shit,' Scarlett said, straightening up, 'It's my brother.'

The group of lads were getting closer, having to go single file down the alleyway. I took Scarlett's hand. 'Come on, let's go back inside.'

I pulled her towards the door but one of the boys dashed out and pulled me away from the entrance, 'Hold up, you randy fucker, who says you could get off with my sister?'

'Fuck OFF, Chris,' Scarlett shouted, too close to my ear,

making me jump back. My head collided with the door frame, sending a splitting pain across my scalp. I let out a shout, then another as a further bolt of pain hit me, this time across my face. It was one of the boys. Chris, probably, punched me for what I'd done with his sister—or rather what his sister had done to me. I fell to the floor, hoping someone would hear the scuffle, would hear me cry out, that a teacher would come running.

'Get off,' I shouted, trying to scramble up. Panic. Pain. The flood of something, something breaking through barriers that I thought were strong enough.

But they weren't strong.

I wasn't strong.

And then I realised, they didn't need to be strong. Because that just-out-of-reach part of my mind that had stayed wrapped, patiently, waiting, was now stepping forward.

And through all the disorientation and panic, I also felt a warm glow. A comforting warm glow.

Hello, old friend.

I was aware what was happing as soon as the fizzing started to focus in a line down my back.

I can't stop it.

I can't stop it.

And I don't want to.

The boys walked away. I felt Scarlett trying to pull me up, then saying she was going to get some help.

I stood as soon as she was gone. And then I went after them. Down the narrow alleyway. Through the courtyard between the buildings in the direction of where Chris and his mates were going. Out onto the grass near a line of trees which backed onto the sports field. Dusk was close to turning to full darkness, but it was still light enough to make the boys out, illuminated by the orange lighting thrown across the grass from the outside light fixtures fixed to the wall of the sports hall.

I went after them. The pain in my head was ebbing away. My legs carrying me on. They were making their way to the trees. The two others shouted something, said they were going somewhere. I heard Chris call out 'I need to pee.' They walked off in the direction of the swimming pool building, connected to the other side of the sports centre.

Chris was alone.

Pissing up against the trunk of a tree.

His back to me.

It was so simple.

I felt the tension in my body, my arms shifting, starting to change, but my mind remained clear. I could still walk towards him on two legs. The in-between state, that used to be a matter of seconds, now seems stretched-out, extended.

As I approached Chris, I felt something happen in my mouth. A sour taste, and a dull ache and then something sharp.

I came up behind him. Could see the texture of his shirt. Hear the fall of his piss. He was swaying a bit. Probably drunk. He finished. Zipped up. Turned around.

There was still a part of me that thought I was here to speak to him. Tell him what I thought of him, tell him to fuck off, that what his sister got up to with boys was her business, not his.

But I didn't do any of this.

I struck. It was as simple as reaching out and opening a door. The door in my mind had been opened and something else had walked out. As I threw Chris against the trunk of the tree and sank my teeth into him, I realised what had been happening with my mouth. What had been changing in my teeth. The change was much slower than ever before, it gave me time to still think like a human while the spider took hold.

I pulled back, noticing how curious it felt to have a flap of human skin against my top lip, how it stretched and broke as it snagged on my teeth. Warm and soft. Blood. Coating my inner mouth. Liquid, and at the same time, solid. Strange. I struck again as Chris gargled and tried to scream. He said 'Please ... stop...'. But he didn't have the chance to say anything more. Not when I pulled out his vocal cords and trachea—stopping him from being able to make any sound. The blood began to flow thick and fast. I crunched the parts that I'd removed. Used my hands to push the bits into my mouth.

Then I heard the shouts. Maybe it was his friends coming back. Maybe someone had seen me. Saw what I'd done.

And to my surprise, something else blossomed within me. Something cutting through the calm, easy feeling. Something like panic.

Panic at what I'd done. Horror at what I'd been able to

do, what I could taste in my mouth. The grisly crunch. The pieces in between my teeth. Long teeth. Fangs.

The moment those thoughts crowded my mind, I felt a sharp pain cascading down my back, flooding me, taking me over. Gone was the slow, easy transition, the calm in-between state. It was like it knew I was starting to resist, clawing back my own humanity, and it was trying to aggressively take back the ground it had won. Take the part of me it could fully inhabit. Even if it could never fully take my mind, it could take my body.

I ran.

Ran away from the trees and the field. Down the now-empty alley way between the buildings and out into the car park.

I fumbled with my keys in my pocket. Unlocked the car. Pulled open the door and threw myself inside.

I think I heard a shout coming from behind me, from near the entrance to the sports hall, but I didn't look back. Didn't dare to.

Keys. Couldn't get them in.

Inside ignition. Car starting.

I drove. Drove faster than I should have out of the school car park.

Empty road. Go faster.

It's happening.

It's happening.

It's happening.

Changing.

Can't see. No, can see more. Much more. So much, but the lights. Lights from streetlamps.

Bright.

Back arching, going lower, can't see the road can't see the road.

Turning the car, road to home

Faster

Faster

Can see home, not much longer, not much longer

Can't move clothes restricting can't move trying to stop trying to stop clothes tearing ripping sound can't move

House ahead house ahead

The broken truck

Loud noise

Heavy crash

Glass

Trying to get out trying to get out

Crawl through the window

Off the car

Running

Running

Running

Desert at night no lights no buildings no cars just running

Running

Running

Freedom.

Chapter Forty-Four

THE BOY

1 November 2025

Heat. It was warming up, already. The sun had nearly risen. I raised my head, feeling the scratch of stones and the rough, cracked ground.

But there was something else underneath my head. Something between me and the ground. Something soft and sticky, something I knew the feel of only too well. Webbing. I could feel it around me, like a patch of carpet—a sinister blanket laid out on the harsh desert floor.

I knew I was human before I saw myself. And before I thought about how I got there or what it meant, I knew I must get home before the sun properly rose. I couldn't be naked in the desert in Texas for too long. I'd burn.

As if the sun could hear me, fresh, dazzling rays of it sliced out from behind the rocky terrain in the distance. And they were illuminating something in front of me.

Something that made me draw in a dry, shaking breath in astonishment.

A spider.

On its back.

Large and dead-looking.

I was confused at first. Baffled by what I was seeing. Then I felt something else beneath me. Something harder, wiry, intermingled with the web. Hairs. Thick, dark, long hairs, intermingled with the white of the webbing. I looked back at the thing in front of me. Then I realised what it was. It was a shell. A skin. I must have shed it during my transformation. Or perhaps at the end of it.

My mind hurt trying to remember and understand. So I stopped. I pulled myself to my feet, my soles sore, my toes clicking as I put weight on them.

I got myself steady, then looked around. I didn't think I'd ever come out this far. I usually stuck to the road if I went out for a run. I was relieved to see I could still see the house, although it was something of a spec in the distance.

I walked. Legs shaky, shoulders hunched, back to the rising sun.

As I walked, I didn't think. Like before, in England, there was a protective layer across my thoughts of yesterday. Like my brain knew not to let them crowd my present moment, that it wouldn't be good for me.

So I just put one bare foot in front of the other until I reached home.

Movement on the back of the veranda alerted me to the

presence of my parents. They'd brought some chairs round, near the French windows of my room, and had apparently been sat watching the desert. Waiting for my return.

I saw Mum first. She stood and came forward.

I instinctively moved my hands to cover myself, although I expected it was a bit too late for that. If they knew I was in the desert, they must have seen where I went. And if they saw where I went, they must have seen what I had become.

A monster, scurrying off into the darkness. A creature of the wild, fleeing to the harsh, natural world where it belonged.

But do I belong out there? I thought to myself. Perhaps once, when this all started, I might have fought against such an idea. But now I knew more.

That little bundle wrapped up in my mind wasn't so little anymore. And even though I was back to my normal form, it didn't feel as if it was back in its box.

'Hudson, oh my god…' Mum said. I noticed how there was no attempt to call me Ethan. Not today. We'd gone beyond that, now.

Dad stood, too.

'Hud, are you … are you OK?' he asked, stepping forward. He ran over to the right hand side to come down the steps. He put his arms on my shoulders, looked into my eyes. 'Talk to me,' he said. 'Tell me you're OK.'

'I'm sorry Dad,' I said. 'I've…I've ruined everything.' For the first time, in a long while, I found myself crying. He pulled me into a hug and I clutched on to him, the softness of his shirt, his hard shoulders, all of it comforting in a terrible, heart-breaking sort of way.

'We'll sort it,' Dad said, even though I knew he had no idea how. 'Whatever's happened, we'll sort it. Like we did before.'

I nodded, even though I knew this was nothing like before. Things had completely changed. Moved up to a level beyond what we could try to patch up and control. Over Dad's shoulder, I saw Mum standing there, looking at me. And I could tell she knew it, too.

They sat me down in the living room. The TV was on. I wondered if it had been playing since last night. Dad muted it and said he and Mum had heard me crash the car into the truck.

'Well, I saw the car, first,' Mum said. 'I'd gotten up to get a snack and I heard it approaching. Saw the headlights. You were going so fast, I knew something was wrong. Then … it was as if time had slowed down… I could see you were heading for the old truck, that you were going to collide with it. I shouted, but there was nothing we could do. The crash was so loud.'

Dad nodded. 'We ran outside and then we saw…'

They exchanged a look.

They must have seen me. Mid transformation. Struggling to get out. I thought about what that must have looked like.

Their son's body contorted. Then legs. Many dark, thin, wiry legs tapping and scraping at the windows. Then coming out the broken windscreen. Crawling over the bonnet and away into the night.

'It was just like I'd seen in my nightmares … my … visions,' Mum said. 'Except nothing could have prepared me for what it was like to see it in real life. I was terrified. Not for my safety, you understand, but for you and what might happen to you out there. If you ran off and we never saw you again.' A tear rolled down her face. She didn't bother to brush it aside.

'Well, at least that didn't happen,' I said. I was wearing a T-shirt and tracksuit bottoms Dad had grabbed from my room. I noticed I had put them on back to front. The label was irritating the lower part of my stomach, the shape of them uncomfortable at the back, but I didn't get up off the sofa to correct this. I felt like I never wanted to move again.

'It's really important', Dad said, 'that we know what happened to cause … cause your change. Because it hasn't happened for a year and your mother and I had thought you'd turned a corner.'

I looked over at Mum in time to see her switch her eyes to the ground. I wondered how much she'd told him. About the dream. About what it might mean. They must both be regretting their decision not to lock me up in my room yesterday after I insisted on going to the dance. I wanted to apologise to them, especially to Mum, who I must have made feel mad, hysterical, as if she was overreacting.

Underreacting, as it turns out. If only they'd stopped me. If only I'd listened.

But you didn't want to.

The thought slides into my feelings of guilt and regret. Then another, straight after.

You needed to be around people. You knew this would happen. You wanted—

'No!' I shouted. I then felt furious at myself, seeing Mum and Dad's eyes fly open wide at the loud sound.

'What is it?' Dad said as he jumped to his feet, stepping back away from me.

'Nothing,' I say, rubbing my face. 'Just… Nothing. Sit back down.'

He looked worried and embarrassed at the same time. Perhaps he realised how quickly he had moved, flinching away from me. He was scared of me now, I could see it. Witnessing what he had last night had finally done it. Made him realise that no matter what he told himself, no matter how he tried to wrestle with it, there would always now be a feeling of horror and revulsion when he looked at me. I thought maybe it'd been there in his eyes ever since that moment in England, when I'd transformed in front of him in the living room room. It didn't make me feel angry to see it. I understood it. But it made me sad. Sadder than I ever thought it possible to be.

'Did you hurt anyone last night?'

I was surprised it was Mum who asked this question, but she did have a habit of calmly getting to the heart of a problem. And even though she was obviously upset and concerned, she didn't look like she was about to wail and scream. She was doing her best to keep things under control.

I looked at her but didn't say anything.

'You did hurt someone,' she said. 'I can feel it.'

'What do you mean you can feel it?' asked Dad, looking over at her.

'Please don't— Just... Just let me talk to Hudson about this,' Mum said, stepping forward, her eyes focused on me. 'Tell me, Hudson. You might think I could never understand, that it's so terrible that you can't say it, but we need to know what's happened so we can prepare. So we know what to expect.'

I knew she was right. So I allowed the memories of the night before to come forward. And I found they were not as distorted, disrupted, faded and fragmented as they were when it had happened last year. This time, it was easy. It felt like two systems had been hooked up together, sharing data, streamlining the process. I felt a difference in the way I recollected, a noticeable one, but it no longer felt like mining a precious stone out of the darkness. They weren't glimpses or flashes. There was an unspooling rush of complete images and sensations and feelings.

'I killed a boy,' I said, simply. I decided there was no point me obfuscating and evading. 'At least, I'm pretty certain he's dead.' I thought about the moment my fangs sunk into his neck. I remember the fleshy parts of him that came away as I tugged them out. And the sounds he'd made. Followed by no sound at all. 'No, I'm sure. He's dead. I... I injured him in a way he couldn't have recovered from.'

Dad picked up his phone. 'Nothing on the local news yet.'

I shrugged. 'I don't know about that. His body is probably still under the tree where I left him. Near the sports field. I guess nobody's stumbled upon him yet. But they will.'

'Is there anything to connect you to him?' Mum asked. 'Did anyone see … what you did? I presume, if you were able to drive back you were still mostly … human?'

I nodded.

'So…?' Dad prompted. I saw Mum flick a glance at him, as if silently telling him to shut up and let me speak.

'I don't know if anyone saw me. I suppose I wouldn't be surprised if I was picked up speeding, maybe by a camera or someone walking by, but they may not have got my number plate.'

'But nobody saw you … with the boy? The one who…'

'Chris,' I said. 'His name is … was … Chris.'

'Why did…' Dad started to say. He didn't finish the question, but I knew what he was asking.

I thought about what to say. How much to tell them. It reminded me of when I was back in England, choosing my words carefully when deciding how much to tell Dad about what had happened in the forest. What I had done.

'He was being a dick,' I finally said, bluntly.

'And that's what … triggered it?' Dad asked.

'Sort of.'

'Hudson, we need to know,' Dad replied, close to shouting.

'Calm down,' Mum snapped at him.

'Calm down?' Dad yelled back. 'Are you serious? How the fuck can we be calm? Don't you see what this means? This means everything's fucking ruined. Everything we've tried to do, us doing this whole co-fucking-parenting new start that you've loved so much, it's gone.'

He was being needlessly cruel towards Mum in his anger and I wanted to come to her defence, but I just didn't have the energy. Instead, I ended up just saying, 'I'm sorry.'

'I know you're sorry, Hud, but I can't say it's much comfort right now. I don't think either of you know how hard it's been for me—not being able to go back to my old life, not being able to actually fucking mourn my own husband, not properly. I've sacrificed everything and I suspect, Hud, you're not being completely open with us right now. I suspect this has something to do with either alcohol or sex or both.'

I stood up, feeling my anger soar. 'So what? I'm supposed to go through my whole life celibate?'

'Well, that's better than fucking killing people!' Dad shouted. Then he stopped, instantly upset with himself. 'I'm sorry, fuck, I'm sorry. I… I shouldn't have said that. Just … stay calm.'

I felt my eyes flash. 'Don't worry, Dad, I'm not about to do anything. Besides, I think *it's* sleeping now.'

I knew these words would scare my parents further. But I'd reached the point where I was past caring. Why shouldn't they know? Why shouldn't they start to understand what was really going on here—that I was becoming way more in touch with a part of me that was moving closer to the foreground of my psyche. Asleep, perhaps, but now very present.

I walked away from them and went to my room. Pulled the curtains shut. Got into bed. After a few moments, I realised I was still wearing the tracksuit bottoms, so reached down under the duvet to tug them off. And as I did, I felt something strange, something I hadn't felt before. Snagging. Catching on the material. Making them hard to pull off. I pulled back the duvet and looked down. Ran my hand over my legs. A small but clearly visible collection of black hairs intermingled with the lighter ones on the surface of my skin. Harder. Thicker. Wiry to touch. Like the ones I'd seen in the webbing on the desert floor. I pulled the duvet back over me. Lay my head on the pillow. Tried not to think about this. And what it might mean.

It was Mum who ended up coming in to see me. She didn't knock, just quietly opened the door and walked in. She was still in her dressing gown and holding a plate of toast. She put it on my desk and then crouched down in front of me. I didn't pretend to be asleep. I kept my eyes open, watching her.

'We need to discuss what's changed,' she said quietly.

'I know,' I replied, pulling myself up.

'The dream I had. About … you being born again…'

'I know,'

'No, Hudson, there's ... something—'

'I went out that night,' I interrupted. 'To the tree stump. Where it happened, all those years ago.'

She looked at me, waiting.

'Mum, I *understood*. When I touched it, I understood. Everything was explained to me. And it was so ... so terrible, so completely terrible, I kind of ... packaged it up and moved it to the back of my mind. I tried to carry on. But it was no good. It awoke something within me ... that part of me. That part I thought was gone, but it's always been there. And it's my fault for making it come back. Because when it did, I wanted it to. Wanted it to come back.'

She continued to look at me. Blinked. Dabbed at her eyes. Then said, 'What was explained to you?'

I paused, considering what I was about to say, about the simplest way to explain it. A way that wouldn't terrify her. But I knew that was impossible.

'The purpose. The reason. For all this.'

'And what is that?' she said, speaking so quietly she was almost whispering.

I took a deep breath. 'An invasion,' I say. 'This is an invasion.'

She looked at me with disbelief, asked me to explain what I meant. How I knew this.

'It was like energy,' I said. 'As if I'd found an energy source—a power or a force hard to describe. And as I did so, I realised I knew. I knew what was happening. They told me.'

'They?' she said, frowning a little.

I nodded. She watched me, giving me time to choose my words. Think about how to tell her this.

'The blackened tree roots are entry points for other beings to get to earth. The lightning strikes are the source of the energy surge. They've become more frequent and people are starting to notice now. Something huge is happening. Something that our world hasn't seen before. Or at least not on this scale.'

Her eyes widened.

'I know how mad this sounds. I know ... if it weren't for everything that has already happened, you'd think I was ... insane. But I'm not insane. I promise you. I know it's true. I know it.'

'OK,' she said, quietly. 'Carry on.'

I took a deep breath, then continued, 'In our world, they take the form of what we know as spiders. And eventually, they will be the dominant species on earth once their invasion is complete.' I paused and put a hand out to massage my leg. It was aching. All of my joints were aching.

'I think I'm one of the first,' I said. 'But there will be others.'

I thought to the video Alex had shown me in the library quad at school back in England. Of the man touching the site of the lightning strike and going rigid and losing consciousness. I wonder how many others who were foolish enough to get too close might be experiencing what I was, or will do so in the years to come.

I moved my hand onto the mark on my arm. I felt a surge of energy underneath. What began as a prickle or a slight pulse was becoming a constant feeling, like a hum you can't hear—a steady current running within me. And the skin there was no longer soft and smooth. It was getting rougher and beginning to flake. 'I think, everything that happened before, in England, wasn't the main event. Wasn't something we'll ever be able to move on from. That was just the start.'

Chapter Forty-Five

THE FATHER

November 2025

I felt like I'd gone back in time. To say what had happened over the past couple of days had a massive impact on my mental state was a huge understatement. I felt like everything was closing in on me. Even though the wide expanse of the Texan terrain stretched out from every window, it felt like brick walls had shot up, enclosing me in. Enclosing *us* in.

It wasn't just the emotional turmoil that was causing a sense of déjà vu. It was the process, too. The process of trying to get the details of what Hudson had done out of him. Trying to piece together everything. And the police, too.

The Texas State police visited the day after the Halloween party, once the body had been discovered abandoned in the woods. We didn't get much warning. A local news flash had briefly interrupted the daytime news channel but that was it. An officer arriving on our porch came as quite a shock.

We told Hudson to say he knew nothing. He did this, even when the cops stated that his friends had given statements saying he'd slept with the victim's sister the previous night. They mentioned the crashed vehicle outside. The superior officer, a woman in her forties with the surname Colton, said she knew it was Hudson's car and it matched a vehicle seen speeding away from the school. Hudson said he'd had a bit too much to drink. This worried me, wondering if they'd arrest him for that, whether it was true or not, but they didn't. However, they did insist on taking a DNA sample from him. I wondered about refusing, informing them of our rights, start talking about solicitors to delay things. But that might have made us look guilty, as though we had something to hide. What's the point of delaying the inevitable?

Days passed. The police didn't come back. Hudson asked one evening, as we sat in front of the TV, if we should have heard from the police about the DNA sample. I confessed I was surprised, too, but thought if it had been a match to anything on the victim's body, they would have arrested him.

I heard Hudson talking to his mum in his room later that evening, when she went to see him. They'd taken to having these hushed chats without me. It hurt, the fact they had started to leave me out like this. But I knew there was another aspect to this. The feeling that Adelaide had some connection to what was going on that I'd never truly appreciated. But part of me felt like I was being punished. Punished for putting down her visions to either symptoms of substance abuse, or addiction withdrawal, or delusions or nightmares. I knew now I'd been wrong. I had picked the wrong side. And now I was paying the price for that.

'Perhaps it's not the same,' Hudson said. 'When I'm ... transformed. Perhaps my DNA isn't the same. That I truly become ... someone else. Some*thing* else. Do you think that's possible?'

There was a pause before she replied. 'I think it's possible. I think anything's possible now.'

As the days went on, I noticed the changes happening to my son. Unsurprisingly to me, it was Adelaide who realised the truth of what was happening. Or perhaps Hudson confided in her. She didn't want to talk about it at first, but I pressed her about it one morning after I'd walked into the bathroom while Hudson was in the shower. He must have forgotten to lock the door and I called out 'Sorry' and went to close the door, and that's when I saw him. His back and legs. Dotted with something. Little black spots. I froze, then took a step closer towards him. 'Dad, get out!' he yelled at me, but I ignored him. The closer I got, the clearer they became. They were hairs. Small but visible thick black hairs.

Hudson's shouting made his mother come and she pulled me away, closing the door behind us. We went out onto the veranda to talk. She told me this is how she'd imagined it in her visions, many years ago. A gradual transition, one day at a time.

At times I pleaded with Hudson to come with me to the hospital.

I started to have nightmares—not visions of the kind Adelaide describes, but nightmares—where we found Hudson dead in his bed, covered in thick, wiry hairs. Or fully transformed, but dried out, eight legs bunched up around his corpse. I promised him we wouldn't tell the medics everything, that we'd just say it was a skin condition, but he refused, saying they'd consider him a freak. They'd experiment upon him. Adelaide thought it wouldn't make any difference.

Eventually, Hudson stopped demanding privacy. He seemed to give in, allowing us to see everything in detail. Like he was resigned to the full horror of the situation.

So we watched as, slowly but surely, it continued happening.

The weeks soon passed.

Our son grew long, arching legs.

They started to show through lumps out of the sides of his torso and back. Then they'd break through, like a splinter working its way to the surface. The skin around each one started to flake. Then break. Allowing the new limb to extend and take shape.

We watched as the wiry hairs started to grow along his

body. Each morning and each night we'd examine him. He lay there, on the bed. Docile. Barely talking. Allowing whatever was happening to take its course.

Elijah tried to visit. Before his transformation had properly progressed, Hudson told us he'd messaged his friends' WhatsApp group saying he had severe flu and couldn't see anyone. But Elijah tried, all the same. We sent him away. Told him Hudson was too sick to see anyone. He was worried and upset and tried to ask if this had anything to do with the murder at their school. I found I couldn't say anything. No words would come, so I just shook my head and felt sorry for this kind, friendly boy who had welcomed my son into his life. He would have been a fine best friend to have as they both journeyed into adulthood. The sort of guy that might have been his best man at his wedding, who he'd have stayed in touch with forever, even into old age, when they'd have sat on their front porches with whiskys in hand and reminisced about the old days.

None of that could happen now.

It was a future that had been robbed from both of them.

One night, I think it must have been a couple of weeks after Halloween, a gang of boys from the town came to the ranch. They arrived in a large Range Rover. I worried it was the police again at first, but then saw the boys hanging out of it and shouting. One of them yelled through the window about Ethan. They said they knew he was in there and that he was a killer.

'We've come for Chris,' another yelled. 'We've come to get Chris's killer.'

I understood what they had meant, then. By 'for' they mean 'to avenge'. I didn't know what they expected to do to Hudson—or Ethan, as they knew him—but it didn't sound as if inviting them in for a calm chat was going to help. When I heard them going around the back of the house, I went into Hudson's room. Adelaide was already with him. She usually sat there by his bedside for most of the day and some of the night now .

'What do they want?' she asked me when I walked in. She barely sounded concerned, as if the group of potentially-violent, upset youths were a vague distraction rather than an imminent threat to our safety.

'It sounded like they're friends of the boy … the boy who died.'

Movement from the bed. The body … the *thing* … that used to be my son tried to speak. It was painful to watch. It was horrible to hear. 'Tell … them…'

I moved closer, trying to push away my feeling of horror, disgust, revulsion. The feeling that I was a terrible parent. An awful human being.

'Tell … them … I'm … sorry.'

I shook my head. 'There's no way I can do that, Hud,' I

said. That's when I heard a window smash. Not in the bedroom, but in one of the adjacent spare rooms.

'They ... mustn't ... come... If ... they ... come ... in ... I ... won't ... be ... able ... to ... stop.

I knew what he was saying. Even without his final four words, I understood him.

'I'll ... kill ... them ... all.'

Chapter Forty-Six

THE SPIDER

November 2025

I could sense my dad go outside. Felt the vibrations as the door was wrenched open, heard every tremor the action sent across the frame of the building, even though it was many metres away. It was like my sense of hearing was steadily being replaced by another sense, something taking its place and beginning to feel normal. Part of me.

I could still just about interpret and understand words. Pick out things that were being said. Dad shouted at the people outside. Something about 'who broke this window?'

I remembered thinking how much like a teacher he still was. As though he was back in a seminar class at his old university job. Perhaps telling students to settle down. A job he had to give up because of me.

I heard shouts. Someone yelled at him 'We're here for the killer.' Someone else shouted, 'Where is he?'

I heard something else smash against the side of the house. There was movement. They were getting closer to the window.

Mum stepped forward towards me.

'Mum … please … stay away from me.'

'No,' she said, taking hold of my hand. What was left of my hand. The fingers had started to bunch together. Closing into a point, the arm becoming arched and jointed into a leg. The same was happening to the other arm. It had become impossible to use my hands as I once had. I couldn't grasp or grip things. There was no way I could use a phone, no way I could message Elijah, give him some more excuses as to why I was vanishing from his life. No way to say goodbye.

'Please … Mum…'

I heard further shouts, then a scream.

I pulled myself forward. 'Dad!' I shouted as loud as I possibly could.

'Stay still!' Mum cried at me, but I ignored her. I fell to the ground and started to scrabble, trying to find a position I could move in. Over the last few days I'd been able to head to the bathroom by myself, but it was becoming harder and harder. My own limbs—my human limbs—were close to going now. Leaving me.

Is this forever? I thought to myself as I teetered and scuttled and crawled.

You know it is.

All of my body ached, all of it hurt. I started to cry.

I heard another shout outside. Dad yelling. He sounded in pain.

'Stop it, Hudson, get back on the bed. You shouldn't be moving... You can't be seen.'

I wanted to yell at her to call the police, but I knew she couldn't.

I wanted to tell her to go out and help Dad, but I knew that might put her in danger.

I was powerless. I yearned for the strength I had when I was fully human. I yearned for the strength I had when I was fully transformed. But this in-between state seemed to be a vacuum for any energy I had.

I reached the door, standing just about, trying to step through.

'No!' Mum said, taking hold of me.

'Get off ... me!' I half shouted, holding on to the door frame.

'Hudson, I can't let you—'

It happened in a second. A quick movement of my head. I barely even noticed myself doing it, so intent was I to get outside and to stop her restraining me.

'Mum ... I'm sorry...' Part of me started to say, then I stopped. Something about her expression seemed to override my drive to get outside. The part of me that clung on to the things I knew, the things I truly felt, was managing to have its voice. Managing to keep me there, appalled at what I'd done.

'It's nothing,' Mum said, still holding her hand where my teeth must have sunk in.

'I'm ... sorry,' I said. Then inched closer to the door.

Leave.

'Hudson, come on,' Mum said, and put her arms around the hunched, curved, hair-lined hard flesh where my shoulders used to be. 'You don't need to go outside. Not anymore.'

I allowed myself to be guided back to the bed. It was only once I was curled up back on top of the sheets that I realised Dad's shouts had stopped.

'I'm going to find out what's going on,' Mum said. 'Just ... please, stay there.'

'Mum,' I pleaded as she reached the door, 'Don't... Don't ... come ... back ... in ... here ... again.'

She looked at me and her face collapsed, her eyes flooded with tears. 'Oh, Hudson,' she said. 'Surely you know by now that we're in this together. Until the end. Whatever end that may be.'

Then she left, one hand on her wounded hand as she exited the room.

She returned just before dawn. She stopped at my door when she came in. I thought she'd be surprised by the amount of webbing. It had started to come out of me in clumps and strands from a hole that had formed near my chin. Or what used to be my chin. I often didn't notice it coming out. But I knew, after the night's events, I'd let out more than normal. It was everywhere.

'Dad?' I whispered through the gloom.

'Don't worry about that now,' she said.

'Please ... tell ... me,' I whispered.

Mum paused a moment, then said. 'Your dad's been... Well, he's been attacked. The boys outside... They've hurt him. They've gone now, but they left him rather injured. I've been cleaning him up and trying to persuade him to call an ambulance. He won't.'

I couldn't think of anything to say and there was nothing I could do.

It was my fault.

All my fault.

There is something you can do.

'No,' I said. The word came out of me so quietly, I didn't think Mum noticed. She was still at the doorway. I saw her reach down to a strand of web floating in the flow from the air-con. She pulled something out of it.

It was a fly.

'I'm going to go back to your father for a little bit. But I'll be back.'

I nodded.

She looked at me for what felt like an eternity. The face that was full of sadness before had changed, just a little. Her expression was tired, drained, but it was her eyes. Her eyes were burning bright. Alive in a way I hadn't seen in weeks. Or perhaps never before.

When she turned to go, I saw what she did. A small movement, surreptitious, quick, but I saw it. She raised her hand to her mouth. Then moved her jaw.

She'd eaten the fly.

Chapter Forty-Seven

THE FATHER

November 2025

Over the days that followed, I noticed Adelaide was changing, too. She made up a bed on the sofa in the living room for me so I could recover from my wounds with easy access to the downstairs bathroom and the kitchen without having to use the stairs. Those boys really kicked the energy out of me. I thought I was going to die at one point. I thought the whole thing about seeing stars when you hit your head was a cliché, the sort of thing you got in comic books. Turned out it was true.

I was quickly learning that a lot of things that I once thought were a fantasy now had a place in our reality. And I thought, for a moment, when I was lying in the dirt, the boys still kicking me, that once they'd killed me, they'd enter the house and find my son.

I'm ashamed to say that part of me hoped they would.

Then they wouldn't be so tough. Their pumped-up five-against-one adrenalin would quickly turn to ice in their veins. But I didn't know if Hudson was capable of the frenzied attack he may have been before he had started, whatever process he was going through now.

It was when Adelaide was changing the dressings on my leg that I noticed the bite mark on her arm. When I took hold of her, to ask her what had happened, I noticed the feel of the hairs on her arms under my fingertips.

She spent a few days denying it. Then eventually she told me everything. That Hudson had bitten her the night I'd been beaten up. And that once she'd been bitten she'd felt confused and hurt, angered by what her son had done. She wanted fresh air so she'd gone for a walk, out to the furthest part of the ranch, where the fateful tree stump stood. It marked the location between garden and desert, lush grass and dusty sand. She'd felt compelled to put her hand inside the trunk, through the hole that covered one side of the deadened tree.

She could tell I didn't understand what she was saying.

So she told me a story.

A story about a legion of beings from a distant world. Beings who had been watching this land, this planet, this civilisation for over a thousand years. Planning. Waiting. Beings who have made many landings here over the years, using the lightning as their route, their forms made up of pure energy. And now they were coming more often.

They'd chosen the spider as the animal to initially possess. They controlled the energy in the lightning strikes and they had planned that when it struck a nest of such creatures, more spiders would be transformed. But the spiders that flowed from the tree stump didn't survive the harsh Texan landscape for long and were unable to multiply or bite any humans before they died.

But on that particular night, something else had happened. A human child had wandered out onto the desert floor and touched the site of their arrival. That child's mother, too far away to be infected herself, still caught the after-effects of the energy throbbing around that zone. It gave her an insight into what was happening through visions and an extended sense of empathy with her child. A child who would go on to change the world.

Up until now, this had been a failed invasion, Adelaide explained. Or at least one that had faltered. But that time of failure was now over and the monster was awake. It had taken time, but the plan was in motion. The increasing lightning strikes across the world. Ripples and waves of energy sent across continents. The accelerated transformation and now seemingly permanent change of my son. The first, perhaps. Or maybe not the first. Perhaps this had happened before, one at a time, here and there, over the years when the lightning returned each October.

When I thought about this, my mind took me back to that terrible day, just over a year ago, and the words DS Scott had spoken to me shortly before her brutal death.

There are things out there that you wouldn't believe. Things that happen in this world that we're told never to disclose to the public. And when these sorts of things come up, a very specific set of people are brought in to control the narrative. So the truth of the situation is never revealed to the public. To avoid panic. Keep things tidy.

Well, perhaps the cases had been infrequent enough to keep quiet up until now. But if Adelaide was right, things wouldn't be able to be kept 'tidy' for much longer. I mentioned this to her, to see if she had any more to add. Asked her if she thought things would spill over into other families, if there would be more people in our position in the years to come. She looked at me in the eyes and said, quietly and steadily, 'The rest of the world will look on in awe and terror as the chaos spreads to every corner of the globe.'

'But why?' I asked, trying to remember all the stories and films I'd watched about invasions from other worlds and dimensions. 'Is it for our resources? Our land? Do they want our power? Oil? Water?'

Adelaide slowly shook her head. 'The truth is far worse than that.'

I told her I didn't understand how it could be worse.

She took a moment to answer. Then eventually said, 'Why does a child run into a flock of pigeons or kick over an ant hill? Why would that child then reach for a magnifying glass and aim it on the fleeing ants?'

I stared back at her, slowly getting her meaning.

'For fun,' she said at last. 'We are a massive playground. The human race is a fascination to them, nothing more. Our ridiculous ways, our attempts to keep order, the fact that we perceive ourselves to be intelligent. They like to watch us panic. They're entertained by our pathetic attempts to cope.

Why else would they pick the animal that most human beings are frightened of? They've realised that the biggest disrupter is fear. We are the ant hill. The spiders will be the magnifying glass. It will be carnage. They will find callous joy in it. Thrive on it. Thrive on the terror and the killings and the panic as their helpless hosts turn into killers, or are forced to run from their loved ones. There is not one piece of mercy or kindness within them. And they will not stop.'

When I asked Adelaide how she knew all this, she just said 'They showed me.'

She then explained, in great detail that lasted hours. Every single thing she said— even after everything I'd already seen and experienced—astonished me.

'They can see us. They can watch us. Have watched us for centuries. We think terrible things happen by chance, by some accident or quirk of fate. This is a comforting lie, or naïve belief, that we tell ourselves. Instead, they pull our strings like marionettes.'

'Give me an example,' I said.

'They have revealed themselves in various guises to hundreds of people across the years. Some took their own lives, unable to handle what they'd seen. Many ended up on drugs, convinced they were mad. Or were locked away in institutions. But for some, their discovery led to surprising things. In 1874, a seven-year-old boy and a young man had an encounter in a scoring tent on a cricket field in Kent. They saw a being that couldn't possibly exist and it both terrified and entranced them. During their attempt to break free, the creature broke the little boy's tibia. It was a cruel, malicious thing to do. But they both got free, though the younger was confined to bed for weeks. So terrified were the two, they convinced themselves the leg had been broken in an accident —a moment of rough play. They told themselves this again and again until they believed it. But something of the experience stayed with the younger boy. He started to consume literature at a precocious rate. Then started to write his own stories. Stories that would have a magnificent impact on the world. Stories that would suggest impossible things and conjure up images that few had ever imagined. His name was Herbert George Wells.'

It took a moment for it to sink in. Then I nodded when I understood.

'They like to watch the ripples, you see,' Adelaide said. 'And that little boy caused ripples when he grew older. But that was just one of countless instances. Many of the others are more … upsetting. Such as causing an explosion in a precarious part of the world just to see if it leads to all-out war. Seeing how far social unrest can spread. Or introducing a virus to a crowded city and seeing how long it takes before it has touched every part of the world. But now they're tired of watching from afar and want to come here en masse. They want to have some fun and cause as much chaos as they can. Societal, economic, emotional.'

'Emotional?' I said, still unsure of what she was telling me.

Adelaide looked at me as though it were obvious. 'What could be more upsetting than watching your loved one turn into the creature you most fear?'

I knew what she meant. I was experiencing it in real-time. But then I thought about the wider implications of what she was saying. I told her that couldn't all be true. That it was the stuff of science fiction. A nonsense. Not possible. She didn't reply. She knew how foolish those words were, now. And so did I.

I asked why she was changing so fast if she'd only been bitten a few days before. She told me Hudson's energy was strong; he may look like he was weak, but that was just the change. 'There is so much potential inside him, Rex,' she said. 'Bringing him back here was both the best and worst thing you could have done.'

I pressed my hands to my head. Screwed my eyes shut. This was too much. I was learning too much and it hurt my brain to comprehend it all.

'You brought him back to the place where it all began for him. You brought him back to the original source of his new strength. And now it's taking over.'

I let there be silence for a little while. Then I said, 'So what are you saying?'

She paused. Then said, quietly, 'I'm saying it won't be long, now.'

If I'd thought my life until now had taken on a nightmarish quality, I began to be proved wrong. What had happened in the past was nothing compared to this.

The days became a living hell.

Adelaide was changing, faster and faster, until I couldn't stomach looking at her.

Hudson, completely covered in webbing, looked like a sarcophagus. Or a cocoon. Or perhaps a long, grey-white egg. Waiting. Preparing to hatch.

Adelaide wouldn't let me go near him now that he was completely covered.

Wouldn't let me see my son.

Perhaps I didn't want to see him. Not now.

I tried to think of them both as dead.

I tried to mourn them.

There were two web-like eggs, now. I couldn't remember the last words Adelaide had said to me, before curling up on the floor beside her son's bed and not moving from that spot. I just know that she didn't say goodbye. And I didn't have a chance to. Not before she, too, was covered in that thick white coating, the rest of her changes happening out of sight.

I barely slept.

When I did sleep, I wished I hadn't. Each morning when I woke, I checked my body for signs of puncture wounds, signs that they might have bitten me. I was afraid that the change might be starting within me, too.

On one of these mornings, a thought occurred to me. I'd stripped in front of a mirror in the downstairs bathroom during my checking and in the reflection, through the open door, I saw the door of the cellar. That was when I got the thought.

I sat on the sofa, thinking about it for a long while. All day. Morning turned to afternoon, afternoon to evening.

I didn't hear anything.

At night, I crept over to Hudson's room. The parcel of webbing—the enclosure that had contained what was left of my son—had now gone. Broken open. It's silvery flaps float and sway.

And in its midst sat two spiders.

Large, but smaller than Hudson used to be, during the changes. Before, fully transformed, Hudson was the size of a large dog. Now, the size was closer to a cat.

They were almost complete. I knew it was true without anyone telling me. A new being. Evolved. Dangerous. Ready.

They didn't move as I stood there. After an indeterminable amount of time, I quietly closed the door. Then I went down to the cellar.

In there, I took out a rifle Adelaide's father had once owned. I found the ammunition in a drawer.

I watched a video online on how to load and use it.

I loaded the gun successfully. Then I went back upstairs.

Chapter Forty-Eight

THE SPIDER

November 2025

Scraping

Scraping.

Tearing. Tearing through the coating around me.

Vision. Clear vision. So much space around me. The room was so large. First time I'd seen it like this. Fully like this.

First time I'd been in the house like this.

This was the new me. I could feel it now. I could feel it.

Mum was with me.

It was nearly her time too.

She would be out soon.

I sat and waited. I could think clearer, clearer than I could before.

Spider thoughts mixed with human thoughts. Hudson's thoughts.

I wasn't angry. I could think clearer. Not powered by rage. I was still.

Calm.

Hungry.

Ready.

I waited. Waited until Mum emerged.

Her change had been quicker than mine. Less painful. I could tell. It was good to know there would be someone with me.

We would kill the man upstairs first.

We would tie him up. Watch him try to escape.

He would scream and bleed.

It was what we were here for.

Dad.

The word came out of nowhere, but it was strong.

Dad.

Yes. He was more than the man upstairs. He was Dad.

We mustn't hurt him.

Hudson was fading, but I could still sense his thoughts. Old thoughts. Thoughts from another time. Not relevant now. But I could still feel what he would want. He was still there. Just about.

I'm still here.

I still knew it was Mum. Still knew it was her.

I still felt close to her in a way I didn't to the man upstairs.

Dad.

I had to keep reminding myself. Wasn't sure what I felt. Whether I wanted to kill him or keep him safe.

Mum could talk to me without talking. She could tell me things, now she had hatched and stepped out, made new.

She told me to hold on. Hold on to the part that was Hudson. Hold on for as long as I could.

I don't think I can hold on.

Yes, you can, she told me. We are going to do so many things. The bodies will pile high. The terror the people will experience will be extraordinary to witness, but we still have time. We still have time, my love, Mum told me.

The Hudson part knew it was Mum still, just about.

This will be the last good thing we'll ever do, *I told her.*

She knew I understood.

We could sense so much. Knew so much. We could tell the man upstairs was planning to hurt us. Would eventually try to if we gave him enough time.

This way, we'll always be together, *Mum told me.*

I'm so sorry, Dad.

I'm so sorry.

I'm so sorry.

Chapter Forty-Nine

THE FATHER

November 2025

I blinked in the brightness of the sunlight. Morning. It had become morning and I hadn't noticed it. I slept. Or did I sleep? I remembered my thoughts going round and round, but not the moment of going under, the moment everything went black. I was still in my chair at the kitchen table. And the gun was still beside me, leaning up against the chair leg.

I didn't dream it. I did bring it up here. And the weight of my decision to do so still hung over me.

It took me a few more seconds to realise I couldn't move my arm. Or my hand. Or my other arm and hand. Or get out of the chair. I wondered if I'd been rendered incapable of movement through guilt. Guilt at what I'd considered doing. Then eventually movement returned, like a gradual trickle of life coming into my joints. I was able to lift my right arm up, slowly, heavily, like it had been filled with lead. When it was close enough to see, I realised what had happened.

Two small but distinct holes, surrounded by a raised, slightly red area. I wasn't sure whether I was imagining it or if it was really there, but I felt a faint throbbing, stinging sensation coming from the site.

Horror and dread enveloped me. I knew what had happened. I knew what this must mean. And as I was considering this I looked down and saw that the hairs across my bare legs had coarsened. With effort I reached down and ran my hand across the material of my boxer shorts and noticed, unmistakably, that when I got to where my flesh began, I didn't feel the familiar soft sensation of flesh on flesh. It was like flesh on wire. The hairs that had always been there but almost unnoticeable in texture, had become tougher, denser. Less human.

I began to cry.

I cried for everything that had happened.

Everything that could have been and should have been.

For everything that was about to happen.

As the tears ran down, the door from Hudson's bedroom opened. Two shapes moved across the floor.

They were smaller now, smaller than they were last night. They crawled up the table legs and onto the table surface in front of me.

I could still tell them apart. I didn't know how, but I could.

They were making very quiet clicking sounds and I dimly realised I could understand what they were saying, as if the sounds carried vibrations across my skin. Vibrations my brain could unravel and decode.

There was no other way, Adelaide said.

There was another way, Hudson said, *but we didn't want to do that. But if we didn't do this, you wouldn't have been able to join us. And very soon, you would have tried to hurt us.*

My entire body was buzzing and fizzing and prickling. I looked to the side and saw again the rifle propped there, ready. Waiting. I felt ashamed at its presence. There was still time, a little voice said in my head. There was still time to end this.

As if they knew what I was thinking, my son and my best friend crawled off the table and stepped onto me. They clung to my chest and stayed there. Not moving. Not doing anything at all. I didn't find it threatening. I took it as a gesture of comfort. They were here, with me. Right to the end.

I looked at the rifle one last time.

Then I made my choice.

Epilogue

SOME TIME LATER

Time passed. Days. Weeks. Years. The ranch fell into disrepair. And then, noise filled the once-quiet air. Men in boots and hard hats came in. The rooms were cleaned. Walls were painted. The house's occupants had to hide in the rafters and behind wooden beams, trying not to be seen. Then the men went and, after a short while, a family arrived. A man and a woman and a girl. She chose her bedroom at the top of the house. She liked how she could see the landscape from there. The trees. And that strange little stump, where she presumed a tree had once stood. She drew it, that first night in the new house. Filled her sketchbook with pictures of what she thought the tree might have looked like, before it had fallen. Maybe they could plant more trees, she thought, although she didn't know what trees grew here in Texas. They'd come all the way from Connecticut, New England. It was different here, she thought. Less green. More rugged. Like nature was a different beast, one that needed to be tamed.

That night, as she went to sleep, she thought she could hear things. Scratching noises, as if there was something climbing up the walls. Living under the bed. Or walking very slowly across the ceiling. And when she turned the light on, she thought she caught a glimpse of something moving out of sight. She tried to sleep again, but during that hinterland between unconsciousness and wakefulness, she thought she could see three shapes sitting on the windowsill. Three shapes—hard-to-define masses—sitting there. Watching. Waiting.

The next morning, when the girl woke, she barely remembered what she heard and saw. She thought she might have been half-asleep, that it was one of those waking dreams. She got up out of bed, looked at the sunshine streaming in. Opened the window. It was a wonderful, warm day.

'That you, Julia? You awake?' her mother called, 'Ready for breakfast?'

'Yes!' she called back, 'Just coming.'

As she went to grab her slippers from near her bedside table, she felt a pain on her wrist. *Ouch*, she said to herself. She looked down at it. There was a mark there. Two little marks. She must have caught it on something in the night, she thought. Then she went downstairs to be with her parents, all of them pleased to be in their new home. They had an exciting time in store for them.

Acknowledgments

This book came to me as a random idea and I'm immensely grateful to my agent Joanna Swainson for being so enthusiastic about it and encouraging me to write the book. Major thanks to my editor Jennie Rothwell for being open to trying something so different to my normal psychological thriller output. The whole process has been, and continues to be, such an exciting adventure.

Special thanks to my family: Leno, for continued kindness and encouragement through the daunting process of writing in a new genre, my parents, sisters Molly and Amy, granny and uncle, and to Rebecca and Tom and all my close friends. Thanks to Meg for the horror chats and recommendations which have had such a big impact on my love for the genre.

Huge thanks to Charlotte Ledger, Emma Petfield, Lucy Bennett, Arsalan Isa, Chloe Cummings and everyone at One More Chapter, HarperCollins and the whole team at Hardman & Swainson. Thanks to Lizzy Barber, Fiona Cummins, Simon Masters, Lauren North, Marion Todd and Michael Wood for all the wonderful WhatsApp chats during our writing days, along with joyful lunch trips! Massive thanks to the authors who so generously read early proofs of this book.

Last but not least, a massive thank you to all the booksellers who have championed my previous novels and to all the readers who have posted about them on social media and left reviews online.

Love crime? Don't miss B P Walter's brand new thriller…

The perfect family. The perfect celebration.
The perfect day for revenge.

The day of the garden party should've been a celebration of love for Raphael and his fiancée, as they toast their engagement with their families. But for someone, it's an opportunity to unveil the lies that have bound the family together over the years…

Available in paperback, eBook and audio now!

The author and One More Chapter would like to thank everyone who contributed to the publication of this story...

Analytics
James Brackin
Abigail Fryer
Maria Osa

Audio
Fionnuala Barrett
Ciara Briggs

Contracts
Sasha Duszynska Lewis

Design
Lucy Bennett
Fiona Greenway
Liane Payne
Dean Russell

Digital Sales
Lydia Grainge
Hannah Lismore
Emily Scorer

Editorial
Arsalan Isa
Charlotte Ledger
Federica Leonardis
Bonnie Macleod
Ajebowale Roberts
Jennie Rothwell
Emily Thomas

Harper360
Emily Gerbner
Jean Marie Kelly
emma sullivan
Sophia Wilhelm

International Sales
Peter Borcsok
Bethan Moore

Marketing & Publicity
Chloe Cummings
Emma Petfield

Operations
Melissa Okusanya
Hannah Stamp

Production
Denis Manson
Simon Moore
Francesca Tuzzeo

Rights
Vasiliki Machaira
Rachel McCarron
Hany Sheikh
Mohamed
Zoe Shine

The HarperCollins Distribution Team

The HarperCollins Finance & Royalties Team

The HarperCollins Legal Team

The HarperCollins Technology Team

Trade Marketing
Ben Hurd

UK Sales
Laura Carpenter
Isabel Coburn
Jay Cochrane
Sabina Lewis
Holly Martin
Erin White
Harriet Williams
Leah Woods

And every other essential link in the chain from delivery drivers to booksellers to librarians and beyond!

One More Chapter is an
award-winning global
division of HarperCollins.

Subscribe to our newsletter to get our latest eBook deals and stay up to date with all our new releases!

signup.harpercollins.co.uk/join/signup-omc

Meet the team at
www.onemorechapter.com

Follow us!

 @OneMoreChapter_

 @OneMoreChapter

 @onemorechapterhc

Do you write unputdownable fiction?
We love to hear from new voices.
Find out how to submit your novel at
www.onemorechapter.com/submissions